Jog Rummage

JOG RUMMAGE

Grahame Wright

Random House, New York

Library of Congress Cataloging in Publication Data

Wright, Grahame, 1947-
Jog Rummage.

I. Title.
PZ4.W9488Jo3   [PR6073.R49]   823'.9'14   74-9089
ISBN 0-394-49484-9

Manufactured in the United States of America
First American Edition

For
Neil

Jog Rummage

I

Rummage sat lonely by the edge of the gently lapping Altos and to the music of that lapping, recited the following lines:

> 'For the beauty I have found here
> And the quietness in the valleys,
> And the friendship we have shared
> In the days too soon gone by ...
> I believe we'll see a New Age
> Where we put away our follies
> To face the common dangers
> In the pathways through the skies.'

Thus he repeated the verse about six times; sometimes to himself, sometimes to the tide. But, he had to admit, although it said more or less what he felt, the words were written in a special poetic voice, and not at all how he normally spoke. As he fancied (in the idleness of that moment) someday he might have the opportunity of meeting the person to whom the lines were addressed, perhaps he had better go home and re-write them. So he carefully put away his charcoal and scroll into the bag he carried, folded the poetic manuscript in the shape of a boat, and pushed it out to drift on the inky, moonlit sea.

'You are an incurable romantic!' said a merry voice behind him.

'Oh, Geovard! You shouldn't startle me like that. I nearly fell in.' But Geovard placed a reassuring hand on his friend's shoulder, just to let him know everything was all right. His other hand clasped the hilt of a sword, which he drew in an instant, retrieving the escaping verse from the water saying, 'Why throw it away?'

'I always do. I always feel dejected after writing verse ...' and Rummage went into his reasons. But Geovard took pains to ignore his best friend for a while and, after reading the lines, felt curious enough to enquire again: 'Why throw it away—it seems all right to me. I cannot say I understand all of it, but it seems all right.' It was no good, however, Rummage was lost to his own depression.

'I think I will go home and have a bath. Maybe some other thought will occur to me.'

'Yes,' cheered Geovard. 'Besides, it's not safe along the shore, what with Swoops and Rats about.'

As they clambered, arm in arm, over the shore-rocks in the direction of the harbour, they spoke many a long word in the Moonlight; words about Their Times, the politics of which had become so topical it made everyone—especially them—seem important. Rummage felt safe in the company of his friend—safe from Swoops and the like. And Geovard, though bold and adventurous, felt he had much to gain from the company of wise and sensitive Rummage. Their friendship had begun before they could remember and would last longer than they could forget— or so went their favourite toast, usually made at the end of a very long day spent together.

They ambled by the harbour, by the yarning sailors, each with a bottle or a small clay pipe, sitting in threes and fours. They wandered by the anchored fleet, looming over the longer, flatter cargo-barges, through the drift and chat of excited conversation in the streets on that cool evening, up by the moss meadows until the towers of the pitheads could be seen, and the starry twinkle of miners' lamps extinguished one by one as they went down the mine. It was true, and could not be denied: Their Times was saturated with a special sort of excitement.

'Good-sleep, my friend,' said Geovard, grasping Rummage's hand as they reached a small doorway by the side of the road.

'Good-sleep,' returned Rummage, and he waited until Geovard strode out of sight before he unfastened the door and tumbled into his cottage. Minutes later he was up to his neck in a mustard bath, in a sort of dreamy comfort. 'Yes,' he said to himself with a sigh, 'I have much to think about—*much* to think about.' And believe it or not, there he fell asleep.

Somewhere between dreaming of the fabled Marble Halls of Meltamor, and dispatching Minister Rats with orders of procedure, these visions were strangely replaced by one of tiny black islands in a cool mustard sea. To his ears fell urgent cries which shook him from his dreams. The tiny black islands were in fact his toes. But the cries were no dream.

'Put out those lights—we're under attack! Rats! Rats! Do wake up in there!'

His heart filled with fear. Even so, he quickly dried himself and blew out the lights. Taking Courage, a stick he kept in a handy place, he slowly opened the door to the Moonlight and his caller. Behind the silhouetted figure there was much commotion in the street.

'Oh, Mr Rummage, sir,' said the young miner, recognizing the figure with the burly stick, 'I didn't know it was you. You must come. The Rats are on us again. Up there, at the warehouse. And they say the old storeman's been badly shaken.' Without further word, the two joined other Jogs called from their sleep, all making their way up to the road, bristling with rage. Eventually they came to the warehouse.

Nothing could be done. Long before the guard had arrived the Rats had fled across Altos, taking with them most of the store's contents. The storeman related to the gathered throng of miners and engineers—between sips of mossbrew—how he had given one or two of the villains a good pricking, despite his age, before he was overpowered. But their sympathy, though genuine, was clouded by anger and helplessness. The Rats had gone and they had arrived too late. But nobody felt it as deeply as Geovard, who always took these things in a bad way. He stood apart from the rest, staring moodily at nothing. Rummage shuffled on his feet awkwardly, not knowing quite what to say. But before he could say anything, Geovard turned, as if expecting him.

'It's just no good! *Something* has to be done!'

As usual Rummage had risen early, although he had had an uncomfortable sleep, and went to see if anything had been delivered. There had: one oddly shaped parcel, left on the doorstep, which he excitedly dragged through the door, into the middle of the floor. Even by the light of the candles, and the twitching light of the fire, it could be seen that the parcel contained some sort of pitcher. Attached to its neck was a label. 'Good morning, Rummage,' it read. 'We've sent you this Smelly Sticky Black Wet Stuff which we found at the bottom of a new

3

shaft in No. 4 mine. I'm afraid it smells rather strongly. Your friend as always, Snug.' 'P.S. I've just been down to get the wrapping paper, and I can still smell it.' 'P.P.S. I've just finished wrapping it up and I can still smell it. I do hope you find it of no value. We won't have to bother with it then.' 'P.P.P.S. Oh, by the way, I rolled a large stone over the hole to try and stop the smell.' These latter additions to the barest description of the stuff caused Rummage to smile. This habit of Snug's had taken root not because he had a poor memory or muddled brain, but it was his way of recording what he called 'up to the minute facts'. Quickly Rummage took up the wrapping paper for a closer look. When he found what he sought for, the smile gave way to a chuckle. For there was a further P.P.P.P.S. stating simply: 'I can still smell it.' If Snug could have his way, there would have been no label at all and he would have written his 'up to the minute facts' freely all over the wrapping paper—even if it meant him having then to add a label to carry his last final thought. But Snug seldom really wanted his own way, preferring to complain rather than to improve.

Perhaps if Rummage, in his private thoughts, had spent less time chuckling he would have paid more attention to the facts that were on the label. As it was, he hurriedly found a clean empty thimble-pot, and after struggling with the pitcher's stopper began to decant the Smelly Sticky Black Wet Stuff. But oh, the smell! Getting no further than pouring the merest drop, Rummage hastily replaced the stopper, tears already in his eyes, hand clasped to snout. The smell continued to billow out like invisible smoke until, half choking, he staggered to the door, flinging it open in search of fresh air.

Just as it happened, Geovard appeared, and seeing his friend disabled thus, caught him anxiously by the arm.

'Whatever's the matter?'

Rummage tried to recover, telling him nothing was the matter. However, Geovard looked sideways at his inventive pal with an expression of certain disbelief.

'You've discovered something! I know you. You're trying to hide it!' (Rummage had by this time closed the door.)

'No,' said Rummage, it was only that he had a bad cold, hence his red eyes—and he had just poked his head out of the door for a breath or two of fresh air.

Suddenly there was no longer any time for inventiveness, for with the swiftness that is peculiar to the creatures, a Swoop dropped from the Shadow. Without thinking, acting purely on instinct, the two flung themselves through the doorway, tumbling nose over tail, Geovard over Rummage, to land flat on the cottage floor.

Now in times of great stress or confusion, Geovard was prone to strange moods, usually coupled with strange actions. This was such a time. Without so much as an 'excuse me' to his poor friend on whom he had landed, he leapt to his feet, himself choking now on the smell, and charged to the open door. Defiantly, he shouted 'Rats! Rats! Rats!' after the threatening Swoop, adding a further 'Rats!' when he was quite sure the beast had gone. Neither did it end there, for he re-crossed the cottage floor, and taking the offending liquid in its thimble-pot from the table, heaved it bodily into the curling dance of the fire.

Several Jogs, on their way to work or returning from a shift, had been drawn to the cottage by the shouts. Yet before they could approach too closely, dense beams of bright light suddenly burst through window and open door. Eventually Geovard staggered out backwards, shading his eyes and unable to say anything further than 'Ohmygoodness!' followed shortly afterwards by a badly shaken Rummage—far too shocked to say anything at all.

II

Geovard took the incentive to move—it was his nature—and successfully orated at a meeting, leaving Rummage to consume his time in deep thought. The facts could not be argued. Under the increasing pressure from the Rats and their despicable policies (the alliance between Meltamor, Emperor of All Rats, and the marauding pirates being chief among them) every Jog was compelled, for reasons of peace, to vote for Geovard's plan. The vote was cast and the result came out as everybody expected, unanimously in favour of the plan. It was pointed out, however, that the responsibility would fall squarely on the shoulders of Geovard, which was how he preferred it, thus giving him a free hand in its design and control over its authority. Much to Snug's disgust, the stone was removed from the shaft and the engineers built special pumps to extract the liquid. But from that point on

5

—for the layman at least—everything was enveloped in a kind of secrecy.

Rummage set about his task as diligently as he would on any other occasion. During the test, the Smelly Sticky Black Wet Stuff was burnt, boiled, smeared and stirred, mixed, dripped, ladled and poured, until nothing else could be done to it. Of its nature, he measured, noted, timed and temperatured, hypothesized, studied, calculated and recorded, until nothing else could be said of it. Exhausted, he finally took a fireside seat and with weary eyes, stared into the dulling embers. The draught from the chimney snatched the wispy smoke away now and again, and the rounded ends of the fire-rock would grow orange bright, as if lit by some concealed flame within.

'Flame within ...' sighed Rummage, now speaking his thoughts. 'A prisoner moving inside your ember like life itself. Yet if I break your walls, if I release you, you will die out. A secret is a "flame within" and when the mystery that binds it breaks down, the secret dies.'

And so his thoughts meandered, turning new directions as his eyes fell on different objects in his room. Against the walls, by the walls, on the walls, and on most other flat surfaces, were jumbled the collected samples reaching into the history of the Rummage family—as far back, in fact, as the Fourth Rummage, of whom a scanty, solitary diary was the only record to survive time. Then there were the samples of iron, tin, softmetal, wire, fire-rock, and clay. Besides these, in thimble-pots were samples of sweet-rock, sour-rock and mustard; then seawater, ooze, stain and Shadowfall. In addition there were stuffs, fluffs, wood and paper, Shapes, fibre, wax and weapons—all stacked in natural untidiness, breaking the smoothness of the walls like a rocky landscape against a pale sky. These things had been discovered in the mines in days when Jog and Rat joined hands in labour, long before the latter had left to live apart in the land across Altos, to develop their foreign ways; when the mines were worked by Jogs and the sea-traffic by the Rats, and all shared all and thought nothing of it.

Inevitably, Rummage's eyes fell upon the stoppered pitcher, and there they stared, as if entranced. For all his brain, he feared what he had found, for all his wit, he could not raise the slightest smile. It was as if his spirit transformed, whenever called to

6

ponder on this find, to imitate in every detail the contents of the jar—the Smelly Sticky Black Wet Stuff—until hope dissolved like sweet-rock in water and neither rhyme nor reason could save him. He wished, in that moment, in private, that Snug had been born without a sense of smell, and Geovard without his sense of duty. But that would have been a different world with perhaps no one to tell of it.

The next morning found him in the same downcast mood, and, no longer having urgent work to do, Rummage had taken a stroll down to the harbour, to tangle himself in sailors' yarns, and watch them work the barges. For it was a well-known fact that Jogs made poor sailors. There was a saying: 'A Jog in Altos is a Jog lost!' How the Rats knew about this natural fear, and how they used it to their great advantage!

Rummage was well liked among the sailors and their families because of the open admiration he showed for them, his willingness to listen to their stories, and to share in their food and customs. But all knew of his greater passion for the Moonlit valleys and mountains, where the Shadowfall pools, moss-meadows and mushroom groves wooed his poetic heart. After leaving the harbour, accompanied only by Courage, his handy stick for Swoops, he walked along the rocky shore in the direction of the Great Star, and reaching his favourite paths would climb to a plateau which overlooked the valleys. Here began the land of High Mountains, so high their tops disappeared into the Shadow. There were myths which said these mountains supported that vague place where Swoops and other creatures of the Shadow dwell. So here Rummage could sit on the very edge of fear and superstition, and tackle the biggest mystery that imbued Their Times.

Once, upon the shores beneath the Great Star, the body of a monster was washed up by the sea. For weeks neither Rat nor Jog, either by boat or on foot, dared go near it, but stood at a distance, in fear. It was just before the Winter Triple Pause, and many Jogs had already tucked themselves away. Both Rummage and Geovard were among those who remained, and, with Meltamor and Sulk, his cross-eyed companion, they made an expedition to put an end to the fear which had gripped their people. Thought-

7

fully, they had taken candles on long poles, rope and weapons, and paper to sketch what they saw, for they had received so many descriptions from terrified sailors they found it impossible to imagine the beast. Some said it had five legs; some said three. It had no snout but a huge, gaping grin of a mouth with teeth as long as Rats' tails. It had an eye as big and as yellow as the Moon, and claws upon its feet like clusters of bargees' hooks. But of one thing everybody was sure—Rat and Jog alike—it had fallen from the Shadow, and the spirits of drowned sailors had called the black depths of Altos to claim it.

The four had a difficult journey. The terrain grew steeper the further they penetrated this wilderland, the rocks seeming to get bigger and bigger, and the light dimmer and dimmer as they left the Moon behind. Twice they were surprised by Swoops, and having no place to hide, they had to face them in the open, hand over their eyes, waving their cudgels madly about so that it was a wonder they did not strike each other senseless. Finally, when the Swoops had disappeared, they could gather their scattered belongings and continue. The second attack, however, was more serious. For a Swoop brushed so close to Sulk (snatching at his ear) that he lost his balance on the rock he was climbing and toppled headlong into the sea. It gave him such a fright, he never quite got over the experience, and the memory of it was at a later date to prove fatal.

When they reached the bay, no monster, nor trace of a monster was to be found. They searched the area thoroughly. Now, there had been too many eye witnesses, all of whom had stated this same bay in their accounts, for the four to consider themselves misled by superstition. They were left to assume that the wishes of the drowned sailors were now granted, and Altos had indeed claimed the beast into its deep. So dismally the party made a late return home. They had barely reached the outskirts of the familiar territory when the darkness of the Triple Pause overtook them, and they had to continue with the rest of the journey in fearful darkness. This final experience concluded their total disappointment in the results of the expedition. For they had returned with no evidence and knew that, as had happened in the past, this monster too would survive in legend, only in legend, and the mystery of the Shadow would remain unsolved.

Whenever Rummage felt proud, or conceited, or in any way

8

greater than he really was, he would come to this plateau which overlooked the foothills to the land of High Mountains beneath the light of the Great Star, and sit on the edge of fear and superstition, until he felt it necessary to return home.

Working as always in the cosy half-light of candles, and with the inner full light of his own enthusiasm, Rummage drifted almost effortlessly through the hours, unaware of the things outside his room. Before him, on a low table, in a space especially cleared for it, the precious diary of his ancient ancestor, Rummage the Fourth, lay open, staring back into the scrutinizing gaze of its current owner. The pages, though old, seemed fresh, the ink figures sharply scratched on the yellowy parchment. This book was surrounded by discarded jottings and scribblings, piled up like so much waste paper. But on the contrary, they were not waste paper; they were very valuable pieces of paper. The mound represented his entire record of the lunar Pauses which Rummage had recalled living through. But the older, more dignified-looking single manuscript, that his most distant ancestor had spent a life preparing, had given him the key enabling him to produce his own very satisfactory piece of work.

Then creeping, seeping into his private world, like the finest line of the thinnest crack, came an interrupting noise, growing in volume, persistence and meaning until the crack widened out into the recognizable irritated voice of Geovard. He was calling to be let in, so Rummage had to abandon his work to open the door. Wearily Geovard thanked him and made straight for the easy chair by the fire. He looked drawn, worn out and only a shadow of his normal self.

'It's plain to see who's been working too hard,' Rummage said, warming a jar of mossbrew.

'And *you*, good friend, I suppose you haven't!'

'My work is altogether different,' Rummage pointed out. He took down their mugs from the shelf by the fireplace, dusted them and placed them, together with the steaming jar, on a small tray. 'When my brain works, my body rests,' he explained, 'and when my body works, well, then my brain rests. But you work body and soul to the point of collapse, resting neither until forced by persuasion or circumstance.' Geovard grunted through

9

a smile. He then thanked his friend for the concern shown but said he was Geovard, as Rummage was Rummage, and little could be done about it, so it was better they tolerated themselves as they tolerated each other.

The Rats had been giving him a bad time, and that was the whole truth of the matter, changing their tactics almost as soon as they had been conceived. The entire guard, of which Geovard was the natural commander, had been forced to dance to the tune of these new invaders.

Rummage realized in an instant the little he could do for his friend—but however small that 'little', he would do it. For now he had something to give him, something which might help the plan. Had not all his work been to present the Jogs with an indispensable commodity? And was not Geovard about the fittest representative of the Jog nation? And had not he been granted complete authority and control over the current situation? And would not it, therefore, be more than meet to present him with his latest discovery, now—now that his ebb was so low? Why, of course he had, they were, he was, he had, it would.... *of course!* So he did.

'I have something for you.' Rummage handed over a clearly written card. Geovard put down his half-empty mug, and in his own easy time, brought his eyes to focus on the title above the column of figures. It read:

RUMMAGE'S COMPLETE TABLE OF
LUNAR OCCLUSIONS

... and was, in fact, a calendar of the Moon.

III

Far out to sea, beyond the sight of even the keenest-eyed Jog, Meltamor watched the movement of tiny distant torches from his spyship. He stood aside from the excited whisperings of Minister Rats, pondering, hand on chin, sometimes unsure whether to believe what he saw or not. Eventually a Minister Rat disturbed him though bowing courteously.

'Your Excellency, have you reached your decision?' Meltamor

wanted to say no in the same way he had said no before, for that was what his intuition told him. Yet he and the Minister Rats had watched and waited for so long now. Could his intuition be at fault? The Emperor Rat weighed the evidence again.

The lights they were watching were torches moving from various mines to five separate and newly located warehouses. By the number of lights, their distance apart, the speed at which they moved and the direction in which they travelled, much had been learnt of the recent activities of the Jogs on land. This much he had been told by his excellent Spy Rats, who were very experienced and knowledgeable in these matters. The Spy Rats had also said the Jogs had been concentrating their stuffs in these new locations for obvious reasons of security. They and the Ministers had urged, therefore, that a mass-attack ought to be waged, for, as far as they could see, the Jogs had merely made the task of the Rats easier by revealing their plan so openly.

Again a Minister Rat urged Meltamor to make a decision, and by this time, feeling he understood all there was to understand about the situation, the Emperor gathered his Ministers to him and gave his decision. There would be what he called a fragmented mass-attack.

His plan was this. When the lights ceased to move—when he was quite certain the places they had been watching were full of stuffs from the mines—five separate attacks would be launched. First, his toughest and most experienced division of 'pirates' would attack one selected warehouse, and in doing so, create such a scuffle, such a desperate scuffle, the Jogs would be more than curious to know why. This brave division would hold the ground at all costs, creating the impression they were there to stay—to overrun and occupy the warehouse. It was hoped the Jogs would find the idea so repugnant, they would engage their whole army if necessary to repel these brave soldiers into the sea, which they would be allowed to do in a convincing manner. But during the heat of this excitement, the other four divisions would make their individual attacks on the remaining warehouses, cleaning them out if they could so that all the barges could get away in good time for the Pause.

Of course, every Rat thought it an excellent plan, faultless in its strategy and fitting in its Jogology—that is, the behaviour of the Jog mind in times of strife—and everyone was confident of its success. Everyone, that is, except for the most important Rat, the creator of the plan—noble Meltamor. Yet he was able to cover his true feelings, and no one, not even Sulk, his closest companion, could reach his soul where they lay hidden. It was for that reason Meltamor was Emperor of All Rats, and no other. For all his other gifts sprang from this characteristic. The situation had demanded he issue the best plan for the job. But ironically he considered defeat would be a better lesson, for he somehow felt victory had always come about too easily.

Having been approved, the plan was speedily put into action, for by this time the torches had ceased to move on land and the shoreline was again a gleam of Moonlight. The five barges were dispatched, the first containing the toughest of Sea Rats. But they actually met with little opposition, even though they boasted of their bravery afterwards. It was the same story with the others too, exactly the same story. And while all Rats swooned in this, their greatest victory (for they had come away with about nine-tenths of the total hoard), there was one for whom the joy had to be an act. Meltamor knew Geovard, and he was not able to forget it. Geovard would never have allowed this to happen, even if it meant tackling the entire Rat army single-handed (and he was crazy enough to do that). Furthermore, no one, not one single pirate, had seen a trace of him. That was the most disturbing thing of all. Meltamor was left to form his own opinion, which he did with great sadness. He concluded that Geovard must at last be dead.

There was no mystery about the Pause. It simply came and went, affecting the habits of Rat and Jog in a very precise way. Rather, because the Pause was a simple phenomenon it had to be embellished to make it appear mysterious. At least that was the belief of Rummage who, to date, because of his table of lunar occlusions, probably knew more about the Pause than anyone— with apologies and great respect to his long-dead ancestor, Rummage the Fourth, who had certainly known a great deal. Curiously, for all his knowledge, Rummage was sensible enough not to ignore his own fears. Consequently, when the Pause came along, he shut his door to it just like anyone else, staying inside until the Moon came back.

What better thing was there for one to do when confined than to gather up all the events and experiences which had occurred between the Pauses, and to review them nostalgically, with toes toasting by the fire, a mug of warmed mossbrew resting on the tummy and the soul yawning inside, happy and content? And when at last one grew restless, why, what better thing was there to do than stretch the soul, put down the mug, poke the fire, then try to capture a little of those nostalgic experiences in verse, or by a charcoal sketch—or anything else similar? Rummage was in fact at the point of drifting from the first of these phases to the second when his door was suddenly knocked upon. He was frightened as never before. It was said the Spirit of the Shadow roamed the streets during the Pause, and just as Rummage was remembering this, the deliberately solemn knocks fell again.

First he tried to hide. Then he ran to find Courage. Then he lit more candles until he could hardly see for light. Then he shook, after which he shivered. And then he said, 'W-what are y-you?'

'Cold,' said the something behind the door.

'I don't know you then. Don't know anybody by that name.'

'But I'm not anybody!'

Oh no, thought Rummage with the blackest of dread. If it's not any*body*, then it could be any*thing*.

But the something behind the door had no time for Rummage's thoughts, for all it could hear was silence, which made it grow all the more indignant as it grew colder. Again there was a bang on the door, this time accompanied by the something saying: 'Rummage, don't you even recognize the voice of your own best friend?'

'You mean Geovard? But it can't be!'

'But it *is*.'

'*But it's the Pause!*'

'I know. And it's cold.'

'What about the Shadow ...? What about the *Swoops*!'

'*Oh, Rats to the Swoops*!' The voice came thundering through the door in a way that was unmistakably Geovard's—so unmistakably that Rummage's fears were subdued enough for him to unfasten the bolts. Yet, still holding Courage in his hand, he stood back in the brightness of the room and waited. In stumbled Geovard, shading his eyes, momentarily dazzled by the light of

13

the extra candles.

'Geovard! It *is* you!'

'I hope so,' said the old soldier, still squinting. 'But what a welcome!' Then realizing more as Rummage fastened the door-bolts again and hurriedly doused the extra candles, and even more as Courage was returned to its handy place, Geovard decided to let the matter drop because their differences about the custom and superstitions would not create the ideal setting for the talk he was about to deliver.

It *was* Geovard. Even so, Rummage could not help but keep a close watch, just in case, by horrific transformation, his best friend turned into some hideous creature, the shape of which he hardly dared imagine. He was soon to argue himself out of these lingering fears, helped by the serious turn of the conversation, until he found himself discussing the Pause in almost a factual way. From the Pause they drifted to speak of the Rats, then on to Their Times, from Their Times to the plan which was to bring them back to discussing the Pause again. Thereafter, the conversation covered and recovered the territory inside these four boundaries. Finally, when they were both up to date with each other's views, and a little tired of talk, Geovard proposed action.

'How very strange,' was the only thing Rummage could say to himself for comfort, sitting as he was, blindfolded as he had requested, sick as he felt, in the bottom of a damp barge, floating perhaps impossibly lost on the sea. Everything to him now was strange—even his thoughts. He knew he was still a little drunk. He would never have been there had he been sober. But the more sober he became, the stranger he felt. One voice close by said he was glad to be part of the plan, a gesture Rummage tried to transplant into his own beliefs, but it did not quite fit. All he could say was that he was glad to be Geovard's best friend. Then wanting to make sure Geovard was still around to be best friend to, he removed the blindfold, took a deep breath and opened his eyes.

Geovard could be seen by the light of the Great Star, standing just above Rummage on a little platform and silhouetted against the Shadow. Rummage noticed that he and the other sailors he could see were protected by some sort of awning, whereas Geovard had none. He therefore gave out his natural warning. 'Geovard!' he called. 'Beware of Rats and Swoops!' Geovard looked down, a smile of deep contentment on his face, and said to his friend in a voice loud and clear enough for all to hear:

'This is not the time for Rats, neither is it the time for Swoops!' He looked out to sea. 'This is the time for *us* and all Jogs, and here begins a tale of Our Times.' With that he turned to the captain of the huge vessel in tow and with cupped hands, shouted 'Now!'

The time came, as every Jog knew it would, for the Rats to be faced at sea. Most Jogs, under the leadership and by example of Geovard, managed to smother their fears of drowning by filling their hearts and minds with visions of victory. Those that remained followed the example of Rummage, whose honesty was respected, and agreed to be blindfolded. For the Pause had by now passed and the Moonlight made it all the more possible for them to witness the dangers at hand. So, in accordance with Geovard's wishes, all able-bodied Jogs, some blindfolded, some not protected in any way, set forth in the thirty barges which made up the entire fleet.

As soon as a particular spot was reached, Geovard gave the order for the barges to line up stem to stern, and parallel to their home-shore in the distance behind them. The black water stretched in front, the image of the Moon skipping on the waves. They waited and waited, and before very long into their sight came the barges of the Rats.

Now the Rats were very surprised to find their advance blocked by thirty barges, even more to find these barges manned by Jogs, spines at the ready. But the biggest surprise of all was yet to come. For as they reached a certain distance, Geovard drew his sword and waved it menacingly in the air above him shouting to Meltamor: 'Keep your distance—for the sake of your skins!' With all that had just happened, together with the shock of seeing Geovard whom he had considered dead, Meltamor obeyed the command, sensing it would be foolish to do otherwise, bringing his own fleet to rest in a line facing that of the Jog barges, still some distance away.

Snug had hidden himself in the bottom of the barge for fear

of a Swoop grabbing him by his sensitive snout and carrying him off, but now he began to complain to blindfolded Rummage. 'It's that smell,' he groaned. 'It's that Smelly Sticky Black Wet Stuff—I can smell it! Am I dreaming? Oh, what a sleep-fear— the sea, the Swoops and this awful smell!' Because he was blind-folded too, he did not see what happened next. He did not see Geovard snatch up a blazing torch, stand poised for what seemed an endless moment, then fling it with all his force at the reflection of the Moon that rippled halfway between the two fleets.

One moment there was nothing—just the shadowy shapes of barges, the glimmer of tiny torches and the gentle Moonlight. The next moment all the lights they had ever seen, together with all the light they had ever hoped to see, leapt out of Altos into the heaven, so not one dot of darkness remained. Rat and Jog alike reeled away—some into the sea for ever. Some saw so much they would never see again. And everywhere rang the cry: 'The light, the light! Stop the light!' But the light would not stop until it had finished.

2

I

Though it had passed, never to come again, there remained a black ghost of light, no thinner near the ground than in the heaven, which spread over the lands of Rat and Jog and the sea between them. Such was the fear of the people that they hid inside themselves, always afraid of what was to come. For in their innermost fears they believed the Shadow had burst to swallow their Moonlit lands as punishment for their stupidity.

Poor Geovard's life had collapsed in misery. He was now blind, after being fully exposed to the light. And being blind, he hid away in a room which before the plan he had seldom slept in. Even Rummage could not help much. Rummage was afraid too, not only for himself, but for the whole future of his people and the Rats. Whenever he slept, whenever he closed his eyes, the image of those last few terrifying seconds hung before him as a mantle of truth, which he could not ignore. Always it was the same sleep-fear—the blackness of the blindfold, the cries of terror from the throats of Rat and Jog, the weight of Geovard's body crashing down on him—and at last, when he tore off his blindfold, looking up—the vision that almost made him die of fright. He was haunted. How could he find the strength not only to help himself, but also to help others?

By accident, he stumbled on his peace. Though his heart was often filled with doom, removing every purpose for his life continuing, though all hope for the present seemed smothered in this foul black mist, ensuring no one would forget what had happened, Rummage had to admit he was still alive. He, and many others had lived through it all. Troubled by sleep-fears, troubled by visions, the burden of new perceptions undermining the old, threatening the very laws by which he lived, troubled by these things he might be, but he was still alive—still alive and still Rummage. The more he thought of things in this way, the less troubled he became. Every morsel of food, every drop of mossbrew, every candle-flicker meant something more to him now. So gathering himself together, he went to see Geovard, to tell him what he had discovered.

He had hardly stepped out of his house when he was met by a group of stern-faced citizens coming towards him. 'Rummage!' one cried out. 'We must speak with you.'

'What is it?' asked Rummage. But no one seemed eager to speak then, until one, a miner, eased his way through from the back of the crowd. He was blind.

'I will tell you,' he said. 'Not so long ago I had sight. I was useful to myself as I was useful to others. But because of Geovard's plan, because of what he did to demonstrate the power of the Jogs to the Rats, I and many others are useless. We achieved nothing and lost everything.'

'Listen,' replied Rummage. 'I woke up this morning after a bad dream, a sleep-fear in fact. When I am tired I am afraid to sleep because this sleep-fear always comes. I am haunted, and my life, my energy is now only half what it was before the plan. Should I blame Geovard for this too?'

'You are Geovard's best friend. We do not expect you to speak against him, but we hoped you would want to see the will of the people carried out.' Rummage turned to them with an expression they had never seen before.

'So this is how you want to pay back the one you chose to lead you, the one whom you followed of your own free will? And now, in this time of tragedy for all, you want to punish him further. Can't you see that a person with only one-tenth of the imagination needed to conceive of this plan would have suffered enough already. For that imagination does not lie dormant now. In his poor, desperate mind he carries all your burdens.' He turned to the blind miner.

'Whatever you suffer, multiply by the combined populations of Rat and Jog and you will begin to feel one-tenth of what he feels, for his imagination is *ten times* that of yours.'

The miner and the others were ashamed. The Jog who had called to him first spoke again. 'We are *all* blind. Lead us, Rummage, you are wise.'

'I am not wise. I am Rummage, and that is all. If you follow me it is because you see yourselves in me. If you follow me— you follow yourselves.' The crowd dispersed and Rummage continued to Geovard's house, strengthened in his views.

Rummage was at Geovard's house on another visit when the news of Meltamor's return reached them. Rummage had visited Geovard often, which annoyed Geovard because his worst fear was of being treated in a special way. Temperamental old Geovard had grown even more temperamental since his downfall. But Rummage always disguised the purpose of his visits, consulting Geovard on all manner of things as he might an almanac, because his best friend had a good memory for things he wanted to remember which, by chance, were the things Rummage wanted to remember, but so often forgot; things like the best possible conditions for growing mushrooms, the effect of winter on the sea and, when he was feeling in a braver mood, Geovard's vivid descriptions of Swoops and other Shadow creatures. So by this method Rummage fed his friend's lively mind and controlled it like a fire, so that it would neither blaze up nor die away, but would burn on, giving out just enough warmth and light. Yet in this instance, when his control was interrupted by the news of Meltamor's return, Rummage feared he would lose all he had strived to gain. He could not have been more wrong, which taught him a comforting lesson.

For Geovard, who had lived by his senses, was now one sense less. He could smell, taste, hear and feel, but he could not see, not with the eyes he had used before. Yet *inside* he saw, often with disturbing clarity. He called it his mindsight and it was to be his secret for a little while. So when the news of Meltamor's return reached him, he showed himself to be a little surprised, and kept it at that.

Meltamor had truly arrived and, with Sulk and just a handful of sailors, he had come in peace. Jogs thronged the harbour—miners from the mines, workers from their trades, farmers from the meadows and mushroom-groves, and soldiers from their posts—all had come to the quayside to stare at the long, low barge hooked into the lip of the harbour. Candles and torches glimmered in an ever-moving broth of heads, while between, Altos stretched like a smooth black marble table from which the Moon-image was reflected.

Much later, across another table, the distance between Rat and

19

Jog was shortened. This table was in the middle of one of the most splendid chambers in the Marble Halls of Meltamor, with walls of red, green, white and black marble either smooth and shiny or carved with patterns. The floor was a mosaic of clear-rock laid over a foundation of red brick-dust and chalk, and here and there were embedded objects of art or great beauty, so when there were fewer people in the room, a visitor could amble across its surface and never become bored. But now there were many people in the room and much of the splendour was hidden. Not even the fine craftsmanship in the bedrock furniture could be fully appreciated, for every piece was either sat upon, leaned against or covered with notes and drawings.

Around the central table sat Emperor Meltamor himself, his cross-eyed companion Sulk, and a young character called Scratcher, who trained the sailors to be soldiers and the soldiers to be sailors, and who had a secret suspicion of the Jogs so few of whom had been trained for either duty. Opposite them were seated Snug, Geovard and Rummage, whose eyes could not stop wandering among the faces in the room. Then around this smaller circle was a larger one made up of lawyer Rats with their clerks, and lawyer Jogs who were their own clerks, whose combined numbers filled the room. Beyond the chamber were the corridors, and in the corridors were the witnesses and special-ists. The witnesses whispered to each other for fear of missing their names, if they should be called; the specialists talked con-fidently to each other knowing that if they should be required, they would be told.

As he sat there, much at the head of matters, Rummage could not stop thinking about the dream he had had long ago—before Meltamor's return, before the ghost of light and the light itself, before the fragmented mass-attack—even before Snug's dis-covery of the Smelly Sticky Black Wet Stuff. In that dream he had dreamt of being an important figure, who would be listened to and respected in the Marble Halls of Meltamor. And before that dream he had composed a poem which he had not fully understood and so wanted to destroy. Rummage could not forget this because now Geovard, who saw and remembered things more clearly in his blindness, not only reminded him of it, but told the others too.

It embarrassed Rummage to be looked upon as a soothsayer,

because he did not want to be different, and in his heart of hearts hoped so desperately he was not going mad. Certain things had come to pass, that was all. He had dreamt many dreams that did not ultimately come true, had written all his poems with hindsight rather than foresight.... but unfortunately he could not persuade the others to see things this way, all having developed a deep fancy for the curious.

After pondering over what he had just heard from Geovard, Scratcher caught a flash of something strange.

'It's funny ...' said Scratcher, running a finger over a well-chewed ear.

'What's funny?' asked Meltamor.

'I was just thinking.' And he left it at that for effect. But Meltamor knew him.

'Good,' said Meltamor, and he went on to discuss the sketches and compare the testaments. Because of this Scratcher lost his courage, and kept his thoughts silent.

Now Geovard felt he ought to speak. And when he did speak, because he was so definite in his views, everybody listened. With Geovard they could only either agree or disagree, for his words seldom contained room for discussion.

'Before the plan, before the light ...' he began, 'we had an existence that was secure. This squabbling among ourselves over who should have what and for what purpose was the result of us both having nothing better to do. Squabbling was the only insecurity we felt ... you know we both developed a code of behaviour which took into account our natural fears—Swoops and the like—by accepting our lives were influenced by such fears and mysteries that we would never solve. But now we have a key. Before we felt ourselves a part of Nature, and not Nature a part of us. Now we have discovered something else. Our own heaven was created. Each of us individually witnessed, though only for a brief moment, the structure of heaven, and we could understand it because we construct our world in the same way.'

All eyes that could see in that chamber gazed briefly upwards towards its ceiling, all eyes closed, all brains behind those eyes thought. And what was thought was unanimous—Geovard was right. Only one mind obstinately fought against this conclusion, but fearing reprimand from his master, Meltamor, for speaking out of turn, Scratcher ran a finger over the raggy edge of his well-chewed ear and kept his extra thoughts private. However, Melta-mor saw him half turn away and reminded himself to speak to Scratcher later.

The Jogs that had come across Altos for this meeting stayed on through two Pauses. By agreements, Sea Rats were employed to teach some of the finer arts of shipping to the sailor Jogs, and a party of miners organized and led by Snug sank test-shafts into the dusty, arid lands the Rats had chosen to live in. Between the discussions, to work out a frame-work for a New Existence, Rummage was given freedom to wander as and where he pleased. For it was Rummage who had striven to bring Rat and Jog together, and it was Rummage whom the Jogs had chosen to represent them. The more he wandered the more he began to love the land as his own. He was struck by the stark rockiness of the coast, the chasms and cliffs. By Moonlight he would pick his way along the crumbling edges, always in search of adven-ture—always with Courage close by, his handy stick for Swoops.

Whenever and wherever he wandered, a few words accom-panied him. It was true, since the plan, and for as long as it had taken the ghost of light to shrink finally into nothingness, leaving the lands of Rat and Jog much as they had been, Rummage had grown to look on things differently. Now *all* was for the meaning and reason of existence. And the words that shepherded his thoughts were Geovard's: '... we felt ourselves a part of Nature, and not Nature a part of us.'

He picked up a piece of green marble one day in an open quarry, sat down and looked hard and long at it. Snug was sniffing close by in a dusty sneezy way, not much enjoying what he was doing, when he heard these words: 'Tell me, am I a part of you, or are you a part of me?' And because Snug did not hear the piece of marble answer back, he decided to offer his own reply to Rummage's question. 'Does it matter?' he asked. 'In any case the piece of marble cannot hear you, or if it can, it does not under-stand you, or if it does, it cannot tell you.' At this point he ran out of both words and ideas, so returned to the job he was better at. Rummage noticed this, noticed it the more because of the bad-tempered way Snug jostled among the piled stones. It was clear he did not like his stones being talked to.

II

Towards the end of their first stay in the lands of the Rat, the framework for the New Existence needed but one more spar before it could be considered a thoroughly sturdy piece of construction. It was as if they had built an engine, and had not yet given it motion; it was that sort of spar, which was why it was a difficult one to add. And who should start the wheels turning? Scratcher, always plagued by extra thoughts when everyone seemed content with the thoughts they had, felt sure it would be a Jog. It had always been a Jog. He could not help but feel every move a Rat had made was because of a Jog. There was something in a Jog's mind he could not fathom, perhaps the quiet way they always won. Who had foreseen the events that had happened—a Jog. Who had discovered the Smelly Sticky Black Wet Stuff? A Jog. Who had devised the plan? A Jog. Who had brought the Rats and Jogs together? A Jog. Therefore, if his suspicions were right—who should start the wheels turning? No, this time of all times it had to be a Rat. It must be a Rat, and that Rat, of course, must be Scratcher.

What Scratcher suggested to Meltamor was that they should try to reach the Shadow to see exactly what it was. These words were very brave indeed, to suggest they should fly right into the jaws of their greatest fears. But he implied that this was inevitable. Their behaviour in the past had shown that once a threshold had been discovered, it just had to be crossed. Besides had not they agreed that the Shadow they understood now, was not at all the Shadow they had known before the Light. Therefore they no longer knew what they feared. Surely that was a very important thing. In essence then, he suggested, they should, as always, try to establish the true source of their fears. For the first time in his life, Scratcher was cheered by a Jog. That Jog was Geovard, whose hearty cheer was echoed by all, until the noise was deafening. Scratcher wished he could feel proud. Yet again, he could not help but think every move a Rat made was because of a Jog, and therefore did not enjoy much of his glory.

The Moon was under suspicion as was anything too deeply ingrained with mythology. Yet the Great Star was different. It had always been considered an object of beauty. Sometimes it was so bright that it outshone the Moon; sometimes, even in the Pause, it could hardly be seen at all. The Moon could not be trusted, so it was at the Great Star the adventurers would travel. Besides, it was towards the edge of the Shadow and seemed closer to the ground, which they were sure would make the journey safer and quicker. But how? How in history were they, Rat and Jog, going to defy every law understood and raise themselves bodily above their fellow-creatures? Scratcher had provided the engine with motion all right, but who was to give it direction...?

They should build a road; a road to the Great Star. As far as Rummage could see it was the only solution. There had been a few other suggestions. One had been that, as smoke rises, perhaps they ought to try catching some, then they could rise too. And whilst they were in a catching mood, someone else suggested that perhaps if they caught a Swoop or two ... This caused so much laughter, the speaker could not continue. How could they catch something no one had ever seen? What sort of trap should they use, and where should they place it? It was too ridiculous! Catching a Swoop would really be asking for trouble. Yet after the laughter had subsided, the idea appealed to some, because the idea was adventurous, and Their Times had become adventurous.

Rummage offered his own sober solution, pointing out that it was better to use the methods they had, than to speculate on discovering new methods in time. For didn't they know they had already started the adventure?

And so the days of conference and discussion were gradually replaced by days of work and construction. Snug was asked to abandon temporarily his normal duties, and to lead minor expeditions, guided by ill-made charts, to find the best place *to begin the road*. While he was away Scratcher was placed in charge of planning the construction of the road, with Geovard as his adviser on all subjects. Meltamor used his expert knowledge of stuffs and supplies, to ensure everyone got everything they required—and no more—so there would be no waste. Sulk was put in charge of the Combined Navy, and the shipping lines between the lands of Jog and Rat were the busiest they had ever been. There really had begun a New Existence. Pauses, Swoops and old quarrels could all be damned! Both Rat and Jog were too involved with learning to be bothered by such things. The old song of life returned, as the bad memories were smothered beneath renewed friendships.

Because Rummage had thought of building the road, and Rummage had always proved himself in the past to be best at thinking, he was allowed to help wherever he could, and to be at hand in case of problems. This was Meltamor's idea, and, as he had told Scratcher when Scratcher had objected, he knew Rummage's sense of duty would cause him to render all the help he could, whenever he could. Rummage, then, wandered from group to group, and considered nobody could be happier than he.

The time when Snug returned alone earlier than he was due, everyone more than suspected he had brought good news. Rummage, Geovard, Meltamor, and to a lesser extent, Scratcher, all hoped it was because something had been discovered, and therefore found it difficult to be patient. However, they succeeded, generally hanging around the place, pretending this and that issue was suddenly of great importance. Because of this, they fell to discussing the most trivial of matters in such detail they even uncovered some genuine errors! From all this, Snug was about as detached as one could be. He would have found it difficult to believe that two grown and important Jogs and two grown and important Rats should put on such an elaborate and convincing display merely to conceal their impatience. But luckily, he was far too busy with the serious job of cleaning his snout, and when he had done was grateful for a minute or two of their time.

'Our party found itself in the area of your High Mountains just recently. Dingy, drippy place it is too—full of badmoss and ooze, shadowy and shivery. And we had to stay there—to make maps —because *you* have none.'

'We have maps,' cut in Scratcher. 'Military maps! I know the place you refer to well. And so do the soldiers who trained under me.' Had it not been for Meltamor interposing with a rapid explanation, a quarrel would have arisen there and then. For under the New Existence, secrets, plans and information were to be made common knowledge. There were, however, some departments still a little slow in succumbing to the new policy. The explanation the Emperor Rat gave as to why Snug and his party did not receive any maps was that they were in such poor condition—tattered and obscured by marks indicating manoeuvres —he thought new ones ought to be made. To this Snug gave a grunt, signifying himself to be only half-satisfied with the explanation, and continued by saying: 'Anyway, the point is your High Mountains are different from *our* High Mountains.'

'In what way are they different?' asked Rummage, hardly able to control his excitement.

'Much the same in every detail—except one.'

'And what is that?' asked Meltamor.

'A detail so enormous I'm surprised *you* didn't notice it too. A detail I would say bigger than all the others put together. In fact, it's hardly a detail at all—'

'In that case, you can be sure we know what it is!' said Scratcher in annoyance, but he was experiencing a terrible sinking feeling as he realized that he had never seen the Jogs' High Mountains, so he could not possibly know what the difference was.

Scarlet coils of rage began to unwind within Geovard. In his own warm darkness he could see them. The old soldier could not bear the young soldier, Scratcher, in his insinuating moods. But in all fairness, Scratcher could not bear himself. He seemed eternally plagued by a voice which called him to greatness, then withdrew its confidence to leave him alone—quite alone. Geovard imagined Scratcher to be sneering at the Jogs, and in an instant one of the visionary scarlet coils suddenly writhed and dashed about, exploding into verbal flames: 'You insinuating beast— you shadowy, hop-toed creature! I hope a Swoop settles on your smile and carries you off by the tail! If *you* knew something— why didn't you out with it? Why make extra work for us? It can only be that you are still too proud to be taught—by the Jogs.' The rest of what he had to say was clouded in further oaths until the flames died away. He stumbled about an unfamiliar room in an effort to make an exit. Rummage looked at Meltamor and Meltamor looked at Scratcher. Snug felt embarrassed, fidgeting while he waited for Rummage to lead Geovard from the room.

When Rummage returned, Meltamor coughed and Snug continued. 'It's a very tiring place,' he related. 'The land is dry and rocky. Dust collects in all the corners, lying thickly along the pathways. Where the cliffs are high often the whole chasm is in shadow. On the maps we have made I marked the lighted paths and the shaded, and you will see, on almost every occasion one has to go the long way round to meet the nearest objective.

'When the mountain is reached nothing but hardship and discomfort faces the traveller. Here the land becomes damp and chill, and here the feeble Moonlight mingles with the strange light from the Great Star, which seems to hover above this High Mountain. Furthermore, there is a smell—a black smell—a smell of foul ooze and Shadowfall. And all about the moss is dead. Oh, I tell you, it is such a worrying place I might well be afraid to return.'

Meltamor fidgeted. 'You have recalled it through such dismal eyes, my friend, my heart turns from enthusiasm. Yet you trouble yourself with such detail ... I wonder ... what can there be at this mountain for us?' Slowly Snug pondered over the words, wondering if Meltamor had really meant him to answer and indeed whether or not a question was being asked.

Rummage helped him out. 'Oh Snug! *Is* there something for us?'

'Not so much for us—as for the road,' replied Snug at last.

'A *beginnings*?'

'A beginnings. And—as far as I can tell with these dismal eyes —perhaps some *further*.'

III

The military maps proved to be as Meltamor had implied—too tattered and marked to be of any real service. But guided by the provisional map that Snug had produced, the party was able to find its way back to the camp the Rat-guides had dug out while Snug had been away to report the news.

It was a fairly made camp. The guides had worked well, building a shelter whose roof was covered in small rocks but otherwise flush to the ground, and it could accommodate up to seven full-grown Rats or five full-grown Jogs—or four Rats and two Jogs at a squeeze, providing the Jogs did not mind sharing the squeeze between themselves on account of their prickles. However, it was not long before all were comfortably settled in and

Snug figured there was enough time before the Pause to take the newcomers to a nearby vantage-point from where they could see the mountain he had named Understar, to gain some appreciation of what lay before them. They went and saw—and returned in silence.

From when they returned until well into the Pause, Rummage was content to stay in his corner. The others played a game the Rats had invented in the Old Existence, when, because they seldom had cause to work, they had to find some means to occupy their time. The game was called Pebblepocket.

There were many ways Pebblepocket could be played but all relied upon the players' powers of estimation. The simplest of games made use of a clear-rock cone, which was the 'pocket', and three sets of pebbles. In each set the pebbles were the same size, yet one set was a different size from the second, and the second a different size from the third, all sets containing twenty beautifully polished pebbles. The key purpose of the game was to test a player's accuracy of estimation, in either a simple or highly intellectual form. But the difficulty was found in the various combinations that could be attained by the three sets. Rummage would at any other time have enjoyed setting his skill against that of Meltamor and Snug, but since his sight of Understar he had been too preoccupied, adrift in a world of recent wonder.

So Snug, the two guides and Emperor Meltamor began to play the simplest version of Pebblepocket, using just one set. Though as the game progressed and combinations were involved, the two guides made so many mistakes that they were obliged by the rules to drop out. It was ironical that two characters of distinctly different natures found such wonderful alignment through the course of a few games of Pebblepocket. Yet it clearly delighted Snug to find himself dealing in material which before had only occurred to him as work, to handle objects that were the 'jewels' of his trade, and to apply skilfully his natural talent for 'guessing' correctly. And Meltamor took some of his pleasure in appreciating this, and the fact that he had now found a worthy opponent who would give him a good game without having to handicap his acquired talent of 'deduction', as he had had to do with opponents in the old times. And so the two played on, until the Pause had dwindled and the Moon came back.

Rummage had stared continually at the low, flat ceiling, unaware even of the chucklings, gasps and sighs rolling from the others grouped around a makeshift table. His own emotions forever pivoted about the sight he had had of Understar, set amidst the huge, vertical climbs of the High Mountains. There was no more doubt in his mind that Understar was a different kind of mountain—in much the same way as there are different kinds of being, and that Understar was special—just like there are special beings. The more he thought, the stronger his inner feelings grew. From nowhere, there began within him a chant, at first a whispering rhythm seeming to grow from his heart-beat, then words, solid words over and over again, forcing them-selves to be spoken out loud:

You have found me,
You have found me—
In your dreams
I'll always be.
Whether in sleep-fear,
Or in sleep-smile,
You'll always hold
The sight of me.

Travel onwards,
Travel onwards—
Let not the Shadow
Turn you back.
Keep in mind,
You keep in mind
The steps you took
To find this track.

But go carefully,
But go carefully—
For I am old
And I am worn
And if you treat
My words as footsteps,
No Rats nor Jog
Will I do harm.

You have heard me,
You have heard me—
Saying all
I came to say.
Yours to remember
And to puzzle
Slow as you
Make your way.

IV

Soon the area that was once desolate became transformed by clusters of workers' dwelling places, designed after the one the guides had built for themselves and Snug sometime previously. And beside the new dens were even more elaborate constructions built solely for the purpose of housing stuffs and other materials which would be required to keep the community going and to begin the building of the road.

Snug had finished his survey of the foothills. The manufacture of maps was well under way and everything seemed to be in proper order. The rhythm of industry returned among those in charge of producing new tools, and there was generally just about enough work to be done to keep everybody occupied, without feeling oppressed by labour. Rat and Jog worked amicably side by side 'For the road—for the road!'

There were squabbles—there were scuffles too, which were followed by a reshuffling of duties and positions until the best teams of workers were selected. The road would be difficult, difficult to build and difficult to live with. There were fears— shadows, smells, Swoops and maybe ... maybe.... All these things would have to be met along the road, so it was going to take every ounce of wit and wisdom to persuade the workers from feeling dispirited. For the only thing they had to fall back on was the word of a Jog, even if it had been rephrased by the voice of a Rat.

Meltamor more than appreciated the problem he had to face every time he spoke to his fellow-creatures, and had to rely heavily at times on the fact that it was Scratcher who had suggested they should reach the Shadow. Scratcher had long since decided that he would never publicly admit that he had, for he still had his Jog-complex, often hoping that perhaps in time Meltamor himself would forget it. Meltamor though could not afford to forget it. He at least had some faith in Rummage who, more often than not, was convinced they were doing the right thing, or at any rate, was willing to share the consequences.

Perhaps Geovard and Scratcher were the only two who were not happy, and, surprisingly enough, this time both Rummage and Meltamor could not help them. It took a character the court had somewhat forgotten to set things almost right, for Scratcher and Geovard being such awkward customers meant that things could never be completely right.

Sulk had returned after completing his organization of the Combined Navy. Even though he constantly had to fight against a fear of the sea, which had been secretly growing inside since the time a Swoop caused him to fall into Altos when he was on an expedition, he had made a grand success. The Navy (now almost completely merchant) was the essential link between the two lands, but more importantly, between the Rummage mines and the road. Sulk had extended the charts of navigable water, re-established some old ports and opened some new ones, revived the traditions of the sailors, and ensured a regular service between the lands either side of Altos. The Jog tool and weapon makers (in that order) had made for him, on behalf of all the Jogs, a wonderfully worked measuring-stick that could also be used as a ceremonial sword, in gratitude for his kindness and help in teaching the Jogs to be better sailors. So it could be said, although he had been temporarily forgotten at court, there were a great number of common folk who had remembered him.

It did not take long, however, before Sulk had resumed his old position as Meltamor's companion, and being so, it took even less time before he realized his master was being constantly troubled by a problem. Then, when he met Rummage, he too behaved as if he knew of no happiness that was not accompanied by a shadow, which was not at all like the Rummage Sulk had known. Surely Rummage too had a problem.

While he was acquainting himself with the news of the road, and of the discovery of Understar, he had the opportunity to talk to both Geovard and Scratcher, on separate occasions. 'What do you think is the matter with Scratcher these days? He seems so moody—lost all the zest he used to have. Sometimes I really think he ought to have *my* name.'

The reply he at last received from Geovard, who was reluctant to pass any comment at first, Sulk considered very strange indeed. But it was the strangeness that appealed to him—made him believe it was of sufficient importance not to ignore. Geovard had replied that Scratcher was very young and had not begun his career.

When at last he had a chance to talk to Scratcher, he asked him more or less the same question about Geovard.

'I don't know whether you've noticed, Scratcher, but poor old Geovard does look miserable these days, always mooching about the place, unable to speak to anyone ...'

'I know what you mean,' said Scratcher. 'Sometimes I've felt like having a good row with him, but he always comes off best. He uses his blindness to dramatize the situation, taking advantage of the fact we can see him—even if he can't see us. He always has to go one better. Meltamor often seems to side with him rather than with me, especially when it comes to anything said that might upset the Jogs' prestige. It's more than very annoying at times. I take it as a downright insult to *our* endeavours.' After this, Scratcher fell suddenly silent, if not a little troubled. Perhaps he had gone too far, he thought. He wanted friends.

'I suppose,' he began slowly, 'you have the opinion that I still have a lot to learn. You, like the others, may be right. But if impatience is my handicap, make sure complacency is not yours, my friend.'

What Sulk did about this was to ask Rummage to arrange for all Geovard's personal belongings and effects—his chair, his mugs, his table, his rugs, his bed, his bath, his sword, his sticks— all the things he had collected in his long life, to be transported across Altos to furnish a new cottage, the same design as the old, to be built in a suitable spot near the outskirts of the town. He felt that if this was done, Geovard would have at least one place he could 'see', then perhaps he would find peace.

Then Sulk arranged with Meltamor for Scratcher to command an army of workers for the road, because he was young and ought to be given the chance to demonstrate his capabilities. For if he was not allowed to do so this way, he would find some other way, which might not be pleasant for anyone.

Both Meltamor and Rummage agreed to these things, eager to try anything that might solve the problems that had caused them so much concern. So when Sulk's suggestions were carried out, and were eventually successful, they marvelled at his insight as Geovard and Scratcher became once again as amiable and good-natured as their natural characters would allow.

When they asked Sulk how he had arrived at the solutions so quickly, Sulk looked at each of them and grinned, his crossed eyes seeming to concentrate that grin, that warm and friendly expression, until it reached their souls.

'I consider myself to be a natural creature of halves,' he said in reply, 'half-proud, half-humble, half-handsome, half-brave, half-blind ... and half-witted! I therefore consider myself to be halfway in everything—the solution to problems included. And if I am fortunate to be made a present of the other half, then I have the whole solution, which is what often happens.

'My being cross-eyed is sometimes like blindness. I very often have to rely on knowing exactly where things are placed before I can feel comfortable. Geovard, as you know, is totally blind. It is therefore important that he is surrounded by objects he can remember the shape and the colour of, and that they are kept in their familiar places—just for his comfort—for his peace of mind.

'As for Scratcher, well ... he's young and ambitious. There is a certain energy in him which recently has only been allowed to escape as word-power, which is weak, when he should be judged by his capabilities to lead and organize which are strong.' Here he turned to Meltamor. 'You see, I am halfway between your wisdomed age, Excellency, and Scratcher's eager youth,' and then he turned to Rummage, 'and between your good, full sight, and Geovard's total blindness. And though I am by nature always bound to do things by halves, I can rely on others to make them whole.'

But as Rummage and Meltamor pointed out, Sulk had to admit, his wit and his eloquence were certainly more than half-successful, whereupon they concluded their talks with bursts and fits of laughter.

3

I

Understar spread its beckoning slope before them, almost like a solemn finger pointing to the curious source of light that was the Great Star. The workers as yet knew only the base of this finger. Too few of them had eyesight good enough to see far up the Mountain and of those, none wanted to see too far ahead, fearing still that they were making their way to the land of Shadows, that den which fed their grimmest superstitions.

Scratcher lived with the workers, though in separate lodgings. He would have lived in the same lodgings had not Meltamor advised him against it.

'Give them a bit of peace,' he had said to Scratcher, with a laugh one day. 'You work them hard enough as it is.'

He had worked them hard too, for the beginning of the road was now complete, the stores were full, the tools were ready and the torches were lit.

As the road slowly crept upwards, past the pools of bad ooze and Shadowfall, Rat and Jog worker alike dropped out as fear got the better of them. For now there were noises on the Mountain that no one had noticed before. They were low booming noises that seemed to shake the very earth on which they trod. And then there was often a faint squeal, so faint it could hardly be heard, except by those who wanted to hear such noises. Scratcher kept the workers in line the best he could, but he could not ask them to continue against their mortal fear. And in the blackness of the Pauses, when even the Moon would not favour them with its feeble light (for it was lower in the sky now, and some distance away), many were troubled by sleep-fears, and could not rest, so that they gradually became exhausted and had to be relieved of their duties.

As if the creatures knew, as if summoned by some 'spirit' that lived within the mountain, Swoops returned to plague the lives of those who remained to build the road. Work was becoming impossible. It so happened that Sulk was with the workers, trying to list their complaints when a Swoop attacked. The workers scattered for cover but Sulk remained motionless. Then there were two Swoops. Suddenly, Sulk's old fear returned. In that moment he remembered the time a Swoop had knocked him into the sea. Now there were two Swoops after him. In a daze, he began to run, not down the road to the safety of the camp, but to the side, off the road, scrambling and stumbling badly, screeching in torment as the Swoops pursued him until he reached a cliff, a high cliff that seemed to stretch from mountain bottom to top. But poor Sulk did not look in front of him. He looked up as he ran, up at the black beating wings so close to him now. He thought he saw a face. Yes, a face and body between the wings; as he fell, before he met death on the rocks beneath, he thought the face was like his own.

What a great loss Sulk's death had been to the New Existence. Sulk, who had achieved so much, who had gained the respect of so many, no longer lived, except in memory. Upon a large stone by the side of the road was written:

> I died through fear
> of Death,
> Sulk

And although Snug had engraved it upon the common stone, the words were in fact Sulk's, for he knew death was his greatest fear and had thus laid out his own epitaph and had given it to Meltamor.

The shock of Sulk's death showed itself in many ways, despite his self-confessing epitaph. More and more workers dropped out, until the numbers were halved and the road crept slower and slower towards the mountain-crest. And the workers who prepared materials to supply the needs of the road, the sailors in the cargo barges who had been greatly moved by the tragic accident, the miners in the land of the Jogs, and the tool-makers who had wrought the ceremonial sword measuring-stick for Sulk, and many others found reasons which persuaded their interest in the road to slacken. What had once been a common, jovial cry: 'For the road—for the road!' was hardly heard at all now, except perhaps when those with grievances uttered it in contempt.

Meltamor did what he could to restore the people's confidence though he of all had suffered the most by the loss of his companion. And there were many times, when he was alone, he wished he had never heard of the road. But then he remembered a few words of Scratcher's and, perhaps for the first time, appreciated the keenness of his perception: 'Once a threshold has been discovered—it just has to be crossed!' Meltamor knew such events were irreversible. But he also knew that the details of history could never repeat themselves. Inside that, there was hope. The Shadow must be faced; there was no turning back. They must discover exactly what they were afraid of. There must be no old 'mysteries' in the New Existence. These were the things Meltamor repeated the most when he was alone.

By now Understar had come to mean different things to different people. To Rummage, it was the gradual revealing of what 'he' and 'they' and 'it' were, their purpose and reason for existing the way they did, the clues towards their uniqueness. He knew it was the song of his life, and he followed the music like an enchanted dancer.

But for Geovard, Understar was a living sleep-fear, at its worst, full of shapes, smells and noises that were a torment to his imagination. At its best, the fact that the road might lead somewhere gave him hope. He therefore continually urged its progress.

Scratcher could only see the road as his sword—the Shadow his enemy. The workers he governed were there to keep the edge and tip of this sword keen; as he was there to keep it thrusting upwards, towards the Shadow's eye—the Great Star. This was his fight. Every worker lost meant the power of the thrusts lessened. So he endeavoured to make the balance right by working harder himself, to encourage the others.

II

When the road had crept up as far as it could go before the next

36

Pause, a second camp was made. This was a small and compact one which they had planned to enlarge when the road had reached its end, a rough shelter which could accommodate three Rats, or two Jogs at a squeeze. There were not many who wanted to spend a Pause so far away from their comrades enjoying the pleasures of the camp in the foothills, so there were no arguments when Rummage and Scratcher volunteered.

Rummage had spent his time as ever, collecting information from all the sources he could uncover, trying, in his painstaking way, to find a reason for it all. Because Understar had so many mysteries, because the solving of mysteries was what the road stood for, at times he could hardly contain himself. Discovery seemed so near—he had been smelling, listening, feeling and watching all things, for he alone was privileged to do this. But most of all, he had been watching the Great Star.

Just before the tragic news of Sulk's death reached him, Rummage had been piecing together some information he had managed to collect by observing the Great Star. But the news came so unexpectedly that in the ensuing turmoil of emotions he had temporarily laid aside his work, having to attend a Death Council and to persuade its members not to abandon the road. It had been a difficult time.

Now all that had passed. The isolation of the Pause and the discomfort of the living-quarters brought him to resume his work, while Scratcher did his level best to get some sleep. Rummage browsed over the figures and looked again at the markings he had made on his calendar.

The light of the Great Star seemed to oscillate between a bright orange-white and an almost imperceptible inky blue. He was sure the alternate phases of bright and dark light occurred at regular intervals, although the light's intensity varied considerably in either phase.

But the thing that excited him the most was that there appeared to be some connection between the habits of the Moon and the habits of the Great Star. By the time the Summer Triple Pause (the long Pause which would come next, according to Rummage's table) was over, he should have the proof. For he predicted there would be four dull phases and three bright ones in that Moonless time. The Moon would disappear in a dull phase of the Star. Then there would be a bright phase, and a dull phase, a bright, a dull, another bright phase and a final dull phase before the Summer Triple Pause was through.

Not too surprisingly, the Triple Pause had got its name from lasting roughly three times longer than the ordinary Pause. It was quite remarkable that according to Rummage's calculations there should be three bright phases in the Triple Pause. This could open up a whole new concept of time and it humoured him to think their lives might ultimately be measured by the pulsations of a star!

Snug led them to the place, and they all saw, as he had described, how the loose material they had been using to build the road ended in a pile of impossible rocks beneath a confronting cliff-face. They could readily believe what he had seen with his own 'dismal' eyes, that beyond this cliff was a plateau which seeped into shadow. The crowded workers huddled before the rocks, a strange breathlike wind snatching at their torch flames, causing their own shadows to heave and swing. And there they made their decision—they would go no further! The Shadow and the truth were almost upon them. How many more signs did they need? No persuasion hereafter could convince them otherwise. Understar did not want them to continue. For Understar was fast becoming a 'spirit' to them. It had voices, it had breath, and it had an eye which slowly blinked but never closed ... Rummage had proved it.

So the road was open only for those who still believed in it. The sword had been knocked from Scratcher's hand, but he himself was not yet beaten. He would thrust himself forward though determination be his only weapon. He knew there was nothing else for him but to win, or perish on the back of Understar.

For Geovard, the fears ahead could be no greater than the fears he had lived through. So long as there was Rummage— his true friend, who had never deceived him, who had always supported him in his sight as well as his blindness—so long as *he* needed his company, he would remain. Geovard must take care of him now, by faking helplessness. His own secret must remain as such until the very end.

Rummage needed support, feeling as he did that they were poised on the edge of all truth, powerless with the weight of discovering it. The Star had hooked him long ago, and now drew him slowly forward; the Star had wooed him, and he had fallen; the mountain had whispered to him, and he had listened. The Triple Pause had passed. *He had been right!*

Meltamor and Snug returned to their separate lands, for there was other work to be done. Snug had earned great respect and favour for his part in building the road, and many workers—particularly those with troubled consciences—were pleased to see him back. With his added experience he prospected new areas for deep mining and opened up quarries where he put many of the tools made for the road to good (some said better) use. He also did a lot to encourage the game of Pebblepocket when new strata of softrock, in which pebbles are so often found, were discovered. Thus his name grew to be very popular while the names of Geovard and Rummage, his friends, grew as distant as the road itself.

The Marble Halls of Meltamor were soon again noisy with celebrations and parties. With these many of the old customs were revived, to the extent that some of the older Minister Rats started issuing policies in the manner of the Old Existence. Meltamor was often unaware of what was happening in his own chambers. He did not realize that his age had become the foremost topic to be discussed behind his back. Even if he had, he still might have suspected little because, since Rummage's recent Table of Stellar Variations, a new game was in circulation. It pretended that life could be drawn as a line and on that line could be notched at equal distances the phases of the Great Star, and that life could be measured like a piece of wood, with an end for being born and an end for dying, and in that game where you stood along that line was important.

Meltamor missed Scratcher now almost as much as he had missed Sulk, doing, as only he could, his best to retain the people's interest in the road. He talked about it often, delighted at first there were so many young Rats eager to listen, until one asked him if he had ever seen Understar. He was baffled—for had not he been talking about building the road on Understar? But the young Rat said she had meant its face—had he ever seen its face? From there on he was appalled to learn of the new legend that had sprung up among the young. They were quite sure Understar was a monster upon whose shoulders rested the Land of Shadows. It had an eye that never closed and always watched them as punishment for allowing the Jogs to blind the other one with light. And he heard how Sulk had been thrown from the road they were building on Understar's back as a sign that the road should be stopped.

III

Rummage, Scratcher and Geovard checked through the equipment. Actually it was Rummage and Scratcher who did the checking while Geovard thought hard, calling out the names of the tools and provisions he thought they would need. In his mind-sight he imagined them climbing impossible heights, traversing horizonless plains, and having to suffer all other insufferable ills. As each imaginary dilemma was envisaged, he would shout out what equipment was needed to overcome it, and that piece would be added to all the other pieces in the pile. When he had finished, Rummage and Scratcher looked at each other gloomily, then they looked back at the pile. It was enormous. They counted the number of bags they had to put things in, the number of arms they each had, the number of backs and shoulders they had between them, the number of legs they had to distribute the load, and finally they looked at the shadowy unknown path before them. They came to a simple conclusion—there was too much equipment, far too much.

'We ought to select the equipment that will be of greatest use to us,' suggested Scratcher.

Rummage turned to him. 'The difficulty is—do we know what will be of greatest use to us? The road ahead is unknown.'

'Then ...' surmised Geovard, 'we take only those things which are basic to our needs—rope, sticks, candles, weapons and the like. Anything further we will construct from materials found along the way.' This was agreed upon and they set off towards the road's end with Scratcher walking along ahead, torch in hand while, behind, Rummage led blind Geovard.

They journeyed on, meeting many obstacles along the way, but always their combined characters could cope, and in this manner they were able, if at times slowly, to progress. For when there were not physical hardships to overcome, there were still the fears—fears seeming to drag on every footstep, and round every corner. Almost imperceptibly as they climbed, the scenery altered, not so much in kind but in colour and detail. It was the strange trick of the light, the Starlight that was everywhere.

Scratcher led most of the way, which gave him great satisfaction. Geovard could not lead and often surprised Rummage with his patience and endurance as he allowed himself to be guided over the trickiest climbs they had ever experienced. Thus Scratcher developed a mood of independence which was sometimes useful, sometimes frightening. In one of these moods he would undertake to do most of the physical work, like making camp or forcing a way up a crumbling cliff; then in the same mood, he would disappear, to return a short while later with news of the way ahead. Although the others were grateful for his enthusiasm—they wanted nothing to go amiss, and they thought splitting up dangerous. They had not told Scratcher this as yet.

Then suddenly he went away for a very long time.

Rummage was in a predicament. He did not know whether it was better to assume Scratcher was all right and would in time return as he had done before—or to leave Geovard at the camp while he went out in search. They had burned through four torches and Rummage had collected together a few essential things he might need (finally adding Courage, his handy stick for Swoops, to his load) when Scratcher re-entered the encampment. Even without the aid of torchlight Rummage could see his face expressed deep thoughtfulness—if not bewilderment. Eager questions were asked.

'What is it? What have you found?'

But there was no immediate reply. Scratcher simply sat and played with the soil and pebbles before him, as if he were making some comparison. Rummage could not stand the silence any longer.

'Scratcher, what's wrong? Please tell us what you have found.'

'Come on,' added Geovard, who was having to guess at what was happening, 'it *can't* be all that bad.'

After a little while more, Scratcher stopped testing the soil and turned slowly, turned seriously to the two Jogs. In low and measured breath he said:

'I think ... I think I've found Paradise.'

As they sat in the Starlight, they wondered what to do next. Scratcher had done his best to give a coherent account of what had happened. Apparently he had intended only a short excursion, but something he could not quite make out caught his eye. It was a movement in the distance. He began to make his way towards it, yet he soon realized a course of large rocks barred his way. At first he was going to turn back—he was weary and in no condition for rock-climbing—but then he saw how he could get round them, and decided he must know what lay ahead.

The further round the rocks he edged, the brighter grew the light. He became dazzled and again he thought he would have to turn back, but then the light faded away and became bearable, so he continued. He had just managed to clear the rocks and enter the plateau behind them when the light suddenly returned. It fell upon him so strongly that he was dazzled. He staggered about across a thick carpet of moss colliding with stones and softer things. Finally, he stumbled into a shadow.

Then it began, a wild race of sensations oozing from the rocks, the plants, the light—disturbing something ancient within him, yet pleasant ... overwhelmingly pleasant. He could no longer rest where he had fallen but had to be upon his feet and out into that milky, breezy light, running, rolling, jumping and dancing. It was good—so good! His fears, dreams, jealousies, ambitions, schemes, worries and pains, all were gone. He had nothing. He was free, for one precious moment, like an infant with a fresh new life stretching before him. Then ... the light shrank and he dropped, dazzled, upon the moss, yet still in some way deeply satisfied.

Soon, in the half-light, his old senses returned and he looked around. The Star was large and full, suspended just above the soft, green plain. The air was clear and keen, spiced with a thousand fragrances each of which seemed to beckon him forth. But he wanted to share the beauty he had found—beauty that had the strength to liberate his soul, beauty that must be Paradise.

Each step they made now was made with reverence. If it was so, that the road on Understar led to Paradise, then all those who were to follow in these steps would find the liberation they deserved, after their long journey. The rocks were reached and Scratcher showed them the way round the edge. One by one they crept onto the mossy carpet. Within each was roused a curious cry, a yearning. They trembled. Above, the Great Star seemed to draw them, as if it were a gateway. Further and further they sank into the soft, green smells, following the call of the half-light. They felt so good, they hardly dared to speak. But Geovard had to speak. He could go no further until he did.

'There is something I must tell you—a secret I have held for long enough.' The others listened. 'What I have to tell you is strange, but if we are to go on, it must be told, you must believe it and put your faith in me. I do not know what strangely wonderful place we have reached, but I can *see* it—when the light blows from the great star, I can *see* it.'

'But Geovard,' appealed Rummage, 'you are blind.'

'I know ... I know I have been—but since halfway up the road I began to see something bright, brighter than all the spangles in my darkness. At first though, it was so vague it was easily lost, but as we pressed on I grew more and more sure—*I could see the great star!* But as yet, I cannot see by Moonlight, or when the Star is dull. Though when it is bright—too bright for you—then *I* can see!'

'Can you see us now, in this half-light?'

'When you stand before the Great Star I can make out your shapes.' He moved his position slightly. 'There, I know you are on my right side, Scratcher, and you, Rummage, are on my left.'

Rummage stared at him in amazement.

'This is truly wonderful news, but why did you not tell us before?' asked Scratcher.

'Because, my friends, I wanted to be absolutely sure I could be of real service. When the light blows strong again, we will be ready. We will not be blind. Look here, make blindfolds both, to protect your eyes when the light is too strong.'

They rested and made blindfolds in the middle of the green-grow. About their heads the gentle, fragrant breezes blew and they became impatient to follow. Yet still there was only half-light—the Star had yet to blaze. Strange, beautiful moss grew all around, pointing its red, mute flowers to the Star. And the other unknown plants, so wondrously thin and high, bowed towards the gateway above them.

Suddenly the Great Star awoke, gradually spilling its light upon the travellers.

'My sight returns. Quickly, protect your eyes!'

Scratcher and Rummage put on their blindfolds as the golden light touched them. 'I can see—I can see!' shouted Geovard. The breeze swayed round and stirred in them an ancient blood-ache.

'What can you see?' pleaded Rummage. 'Is it Paradise, oh Geovard, *is it*?'

Geovard froze in his tracks. Through the Great Star a flat, moonlike face hovered and juggled....

I

A tawny eye blinked to accustom itself to the dark interior. Even then it could hardly believe what it saw: a flight of crumbling steps leading down to a huge basement whose supporting pillars thrust out of piled rubble and floodwater. The light—that was the most miraculous thing of all! For about two-thirds of the way across, a solitary globe-light hung by its old black chain, and it still burned.

There was a mystery through this hole, but the gap was barely big enough to see through. Fingers pulled at the surrounding charred brick and rubble. From within came the scurrying noise of living things.

'Elizabeth, you know you are afraid, so why do you pretend you are not? You are afraid of the dark, you are afraid of the little noises, you are afraid of slipping on the damp rocks.' Elizabeth paused to think for a moment. 'But you can't be thoroughly afraid, can you? Because if you were, you would have gone somewhere else.' Elizabeth withdrew from the hole, twisting her face up against the glare from the sky. 'Why don't you go away and tell somebody what you have found, all by yourself, with no help from anyone? Why don't you go home and tell your father? It would make him smile—he might even want to see it.' She thought again. 'No, he wouldn't, would he? But he would like to see the light.' A piece of old wall by her side helped her to sit down.

The whole hollow was hers, and the sky above it. It was all hers this afternoon; the sun, the sky, the hollow ... and now the hole, for as long as she wanted it. There she sat quite comfortably —were it not for uncomfortable thoughts. She could not be seen from the road, and the old buildings at either hand had no eyes in their sides; the ones at the back had dead eyes, and across the street the eyes had all been removed. There was a high-arched scorch of an aeroplane, but it was not in her sky, and beneath

45

that, the sound of distant engine groan and a hammer-bang that laughed exactly three times after each knock. Soon the noises would close in. Her sky might have the chance to change its vest perhaps three or four times before the soft-legs came. Then all vests would be dirty with their smoke and their dust, and tattered with their destruction.

It was a perfectly peaceful hollow which every previous child had considered thoroughly explored, from fag-packet to handle-bar, ants' nest to worm cast. Yet no one had mashed their way through the nettles as she had done, so no one, other than she, had ever found the hole. It was perfectly peaceful because she was alone.

'Elizabeth, what are you going to do? Are you going to sit there all day, or will you go to school in the afternoon, like you promised? They will realize what you have been up to, and when they do, it will be the worse for you. I bet they are angry this very minute.' Elizabeth paused to think again. 'If they are angry now, maybe it would be a mistake to go back to school this afternoon. Perhaps it would be better to let them sleep on it. They might think you are really ill then. Yes, take the whole day off and start afresh tomorrow.' She made a mark on the ground to let herself know she fully understood the gravity of the decision, before easing herself back to peep into the hole again.

She could smell a damp, mossy smell welling up from within the hole, but her own shadow made it impossible for her to see what was immediately through the gap. Whenever she put her head too close, she blocked out all the daylight. But she could see many things, outlines mainly, by the old golden glow from the globe-light. She could see the remains of the staircase; she was aware of the flat landing at the top and the one about halfway down. Some pillars were picked out by that deep light which reached up the other side of a black glassy pool, and others near the bottom of the stairs were in silhouette.

Elizabeth looked at those things again, then withdrew her head, squinting across the huge, concrete slab into the nettles beyond, trying to imagine where the tops of the nearest pillars should be. But the ground was uneven, and the growth of nettles and coarse grass seemed to belie the fact that they were really clinging to a roof. It was far too much for a small mind to grasp in one go, so Elizabeth slowly reasoned things out in a series of steps

46

by peeping into the hole, withdrawing, and making a mark in the ground when she had reached a definite conclusion.

She laboured for the rest of the morning into the afternoon, hardly moving from the centre of the nettle-bed, or relaxing from her thinking and marking, until hunger drew her attention to the time. It was by then a quarter past two in the afternoon. Elizabeth considered time as she ate her school lunch of bread and cheese. Soon she would have to leave this sunny eddy-pool that seemed sheltered from time, and step into the mainstream, just as if she had never departed from it, and in such preparations there was no reason to make marks, marks which were for life-time and not for the time of day, for since Christmas, August's ticking bracelet on her wrist had taught her how to measure and fuse her wayward paths to meet her ordained ones. She must meet her father as if she had come straight from school. After Uncle Tony had come to take over the stall, she and her father would walk home together. By the time they had reached home she would be able to guess whether he would be in a likely mood for telling stories. It had been a nice day so far. Her father ought to be in a good mood. She knew that, unless her father was in a good mood, and not too tired, she would not hear those stories about his mysterious past. And that would make so many extra complications.

For a change she looked out of the hollow—the popular name given to the overgrown site—into the blue-white sky. Elizabeth personalized everything. Her sky was not anyone else's; her hollow could only be seen by her; her father was her father, and if anyone else was to say that he was like anyone else, she would earnestly contest it—especially with the softlegs. Her sky wore vests; she had determined that about a year ago when her father said he could not understand why it changed so much. It changed so much because the sun made it sweat—that was why it wore so many vests.

In this new time, the grumbling, distant strain of engines filtered back into her thoughts. But the laughing knocks had stopped. She listened long and deep as she ate, watched the raggy dance of cabbage white butterflies and gave them names before they flopped over the high corrugated fence surrounding the hollow. But these and the spasmodic bursts of sparrows' wings stole her thoughts only for a second or two, otherwise she

47

left everything alone to listen.

Elizabeth's eyes twinkled in the green haze surrounding her. She sucked away at the acrid taste of bread and cheese that had enamelled itself to her palate. 'You've done it again, haven't you? You've looked, and peeped, and you're greedy, you dare not let the workmen have it yet. Later you can leave it to them like they leave you their empty cigarette-packets.' Absent-mindedly, she sucked hard again until the roots of her nose ached. Then she got up and made a very, very big, very deep mark in the ground—once and for all—demolishing most of her other marks. And this she did with her stick.

II

It was her father, who with his gnarled hands took her by the shoulder and led her homewards towards the market. In reality it was only a short distance they had to travel, yet it was long enough for Elizabeth to establish her lie by telling him of her imaginary escapades at school. The lie only became awkward (and only then through conscience) when he asked questions about Crystal, whom he knew to be her best friend. And she had then to lie on Crystal's behalf to keep her own intact. But she got by without arousing any kind of suspicion.

The pink-grey paving slabs passed jerkily beneath them as they plunged through the press of shops and staring eyes.

Behind them now, Uncle Tony stood on his dusty corner, red nose almost central in the encircling hood of his dufflecoat and the ends of long, grey hair poking out around an unshaven chin. The sad, faraway look in his eyes was fixed, as ever, on some unobtainable destiny, always fixed that way beneath the duffle-coat worn summer and winter alike. At any rate, they no longer said goodbye to father and daughter now lost in the mill of late shoppers. He mechanically sold a few newspapers, dropping the coins into a rusty Oxo tin.

They passed the mouth of the market. It was really a cul-de-sac—a large bag. By night this bag would be empty and spacious with lamplight slipping over the cobbles—a silent, paper-blowing desert in the stony townscape—yet by the gradual blessing of daylight on the magical days of the Moon, of Woden, Frig and

Saturn, it became rag bag, vegetable sack, toy sack, lunch pack—a purse for honest merchants and a swag-bag for the robbers. As Elizabeth passed, a large furniture van wedged itself into the mouth of the road like a square cork. Shoppers congested the narrow pavements either side and completed the seal.

'There!' muttered Elizabeth. 'That should hold them.' Her father looked up through his thick glasses but saw nothing strange, neither did he say anything to his only child but assumed her young eyes had seen some small event now passed and hardly worth the value of a question. The huge hulk of the furniture van gradually inched into the cul-de-sac behind their backs as they crossed the road and came to their corner.

They had sat down for their evening meal, and Mrs Trewly was clanking yellow enamelled saucepans together with knives and forks in the kitchen, and there was the chop, chop, chop sound as she dished out the steaming potato, before Elizabeth ever got round to asking her father if he had had a good day. She made it a direct question. Her father pushed his thick goggles back to the bridge of his nose. Behind the misty glass his blue eyes were enormously magnified. He fought over in his mind the best way to answer the question—as he always tried to, for the sake of his daughter's education. He would never deliberately try to mislead her, only when he was joking, and then it was made obvious by him being the first to laugh.

'Well, my dear, it was a sunny day for weather and a breezy day for business.' And that was all she was to hear about it after the laugh. The news crept gradually out of the television speaker and soon the pictures were rolling on the screen.

Mrs Trewly chopped and clinked in the kitchen and doused saucepans in the sink as if she were drowning the landlord's kittens. She was a small, dark knotty string of a woman who lived in the basement flat, coming up once a day to cook 'for the sake of the child'. She was kindly but austere, and her matronly actions were ones of instinct in her stringy, knotty fight for survival against the pressures of living which constantly threatened to smother her. This was the way she often spoke to make others aware of her presence. For if she always remained passive and silent, the world continued without her (and seemed to many

49

none the worse for it). Mrs Trewly had been married to a van-driver whom no one had ever seen when they supposedly lived together in the basement flat. But there was an early separation when her husband had gone to the north of England, leaving her to fend for herself against the pressure of the unasked questions in her friends' and neighbours' eyes, and the pressure of managing without love in an empty flat. Shortly after that she had taken to doing things.

The first thing she had done was to take the landlord to a rent tribunal when he had tried to increase the rent of her gloomy rooms. She did it entirely without aid or support from her friends, thus the victory she achieved was a lonely one. Nobody would have known about it at all if she had kept quiet, but she finally had to speak out to protect the others, in case the landlord tried his hand with them.

Of all the tenants in the house only Mr Morgan was anything like ready to put up a fight. 'Mr Morgan—in *his* condition!' Mrs Trewly had exclaimed to Mr and Mrs DeVann when she called on them with her news. But it was really 'his condition' which, through some hard and bitter years had tempered him. He was a fighting man—a man of steel. Otherwise he might have shut out with apathy the dark, knotty string of a woman he had taken to referring to as 'Yours Trewly', as the others had done

Mrs Trewly scraped the dark and light green cabbage onto three plates; her own, microscopic portion, Mr Morgan's garbage heap, and Elizabeth's pressed out almost flat over the rest of the plate so it could be covered by other food. She had to do this; Elizabeth did not care for cabbage because, the way Mrs Trewly pulped everything, it reminded her of the green stuff that floats on the surface of bottomless ponds—the stuff frogs eat and ducks shovel.

Elizabeth was wise to most of Mrs Trewly's tricks, but acted dumb because she was fond of this strange woman. Even the three plates were different sizes for a reason. Mr Morgan had the only proper-sized dinner plate. It was frilly round the edge and had printed on it, in a rusty colour, a distorted landscape with knobbly bushes, featherlike trees and a river that ran up-hill. The birds' wings were upside down, and the size of the cattle made a mockery of the perspective. The herdsman's hat grew out of his head, his left arm was swollen, his sweetheart had one eye lower than the other and a mere smudge for a mouth. But no matter how bad the artistry, how distorted the image, it was the plate from which Mr Morgan had chosen to eat his food. His daughter had a tea plate from the same set, but it was far too precious to risk among the other household crockery. She kept this piece in her bedroom and looked into that landscape often.

The next-sized plate was Elizabeth's. It was plain and light green. She had asked for this plate because it had a name, not just a meaningless name, but a real name and a girl's name at that. It was called 'Beryl'. It had deeper significance than being just a girl's name; it seemed to Elizabeth to be an old name, a name that sounded and looked Welsh. Her own family was Welsh, she had been told. So this plate, before all others, seemed the most fitting. But Mrs Trewly's plate was even smaller and was pure white. It too had a name, but in no manner did it suit her character or appearance. This plate was called 'Snow White'— a simple virgin of a plate. Now, both Elizabeth and Mr Morgan had at some time or other chosen their plates, and the relationship of their sizes was purely accidental. All three were now set before her in the kitchen, each with mashed potato and stewed cabbage, awaiting the third condition—the pork chop!

Mrs Trewly came in from the kitchen and set down two plates; Elizabeth's and Mr Morgan's. Elizabeth was very hungry, having eaten only two cheese sandwiches since breakfast, and would dearly have liked to set about her dinner straight away. But first there was a task she had to perform for her father. It was one of those personal things which had begun she could not remember when. She cut up the meat on his plate before it was set in his place. She had been doing this service for so long he did not even bother to say thank you, but sat quietly watching the end of the national news and the beginning of the regional magazine programme. Meanwhile Mrs Trewly (now back in the kitchen) assaulted the knife-box drawer, managing to wrench it back into its proper place, saved the saucepans from sliding along the draining board and toppling into the sink, and knocked a milk bottle flying. Finally, her temper subdued, she came in with her own plate and set it down. They all said 'thank you' to each other, more or less at the same time, which was another of those things begun so long ago everyone had forgotten what it was for.

Elizabeth forked through the gravy when no one was looking and found a great sub-oceanic bed of cabbage. She thought a direct, discriminating thought. If cabbage was so good, and potatoes were so good, and meat was so good, and gravy was so good, why did Mrs Trewly always restrict herself to portions that would beggar a fly? She could understand why her father got more than anyone, him being bigger and stronger than herself and Mrs Trewly put together, but not why she got more than the woman who cooked and did a little cleaning for them and got all that she ate free anyway, as the payment for her services.

After the first few silent mouthfuls, talk began to bridge the table, Mr Morgan recalling recent conversations, first with the van-driver who delivered the newspapers to his stall, then with Uncle Tony, then with his customers. He then went on to the daily news in general and the inconsistencies between printed reports in the papers and those on the television, and what programmes were of documentary interest for that evening. Mrs Trewly fretted about the likelihood of losing her job as a stitcher in the small shoe factory where she had been employed for the last few months, hearing a rumour that redundancy was imminent.

Elizabeth was rather grateful for this local tragedy and hid behind its enormity. For Mrs Trewly was a 'do-er' with conversation too. She made people work hard at it, rending the silence between each other, until she was in a lather of words, but as she said, there is no work without sweat. That's why, on the only chance she had in the day, she did the rounds of conversation with the Morgans expecting each person in the room to make a contribution, as if this too were part of the payment for her domestic services. Yet today, the conversation rebounded back and forth between Mr Morgan and Mrs Trewly. Little of it fell on Elizabeth, so she gave little back.

When the dinner had passed away, and Mr Morgan had found his armchair and the television again, Elizabeth thought she might be trapped in the kitchen with Mrs Trewly as they washed the dishes. So, long before she reached that furthermost room which protruded into the washing in the backyard, she evolved a plan that would stop Mrs Trewly asking a lot of awkward questions about what had been done at school that day. Elizabeth would become a Mrs Trewly—the asker of questions. And the questions she would ask, like Mrs Trewly's, would not be random, but specifically to help her extract material for building yet another, bigger plan involving the hole.

As soon as hands were growing pink at the sink, and playing ghosts with the tea-towel, Elizabeth plied her first and most important question. 'Mrs Trewly—what's redundancy?' Her words seemed to touch a nerve-spot in and broke through the lady's corseted reverie.

Eventually Mrs Trewly said, 'It's getting the sack when the firm can't afford to keep you on, and there's nothing you can do about it 'cept to go. And if you're lucky enough to find another job, just like yer old 'un, and you settle in, you could be there a year an' have the same thing happen again. So you'd have to go again.' There she cleaved a grim pause. 'Anyhow, what you want to know for?'

'I heard you say it at the table.' Elizabeth wondered if that would be sufficient. It seemed to hold for a while.

'If only I knowed for sure it was going to happen . . .' ruminated Mrs Trewly, '. . . p'raps I could do something, and prepare for it.'

'Is it going to happen, Mrs Trewly?'

'That's just it. I don't know.'

'Can't you ask?'

'Ask who, pet . . . my boss, my forelady? No, they wouldn't tell me. 'Cause if they said, "Yes, Mrs Trewly, it looks that way," they know I'd be off maybe before it was convenient for them. No, love, they won't tell me until a week before, then give me a week's notice.' Mrs Trewly jingled the cutlery in the bottom of a frothy bowl.

'Is that what happened to my dad, before he sold newspapers?'

'I don't know. You'd better ask him.' But she did know, Elizabeth was sure. She waited for her to continue. 'No. Your Pop got the sack; he wasn't made redundant.'

So now Elizabeth had set things up for asking the most important of all questions.

'What did he do—to get the sack?'

'He tried to do himself and others a bit of good, and got nothing but trouble in return.' Thereafter, Mrs Trewly continued with the washing up in such a determined fashion that Elizabeth knew she would try, probably successfully, to change the subject. At last it came. 'You didn't say much at the table today. You haven't told me what you did at school.'

Nobody had ever told Elizabeth outright, so what had not been told formed itself into a sacred mystery, because those who could tell did not want to. In the last few years she had looked after this mystery, feeding it bits and pieces of information whenever she could pick them up. At first she had thought it had happened a long time before she was born—in the Middle Ages, in fact—when her mother and father had worn those strange clothes she had seen on Christmas cards, and had ridden in horse-drawn coaches. The hollow and the hole belonged to that time; had been built in that time. They had been part of a huge department store that her father had told her was famous throughout the world. It was the place where all the world's rich used to shop, and had a tradition as ancient as a castle's. But then her mother had died, her father got the sack, Mrs Trewly had started coming up and Elizabeth at some time had started school.

These thoughts tumbled over in her mind as she lay in bed. A dim night-light burned by the side of her bed and she was able to see around the room. She saw objects that would help her think herself to sleep, little things like her picture-plate, her fluffy animals and dolls she had been given as presents, and Colpoesne D, whom she snuggled up to in her bed.

Colpoesne D was her favourite doll. He was big and fat with hardly any arms or legs. Some had had the rudeness to call him a Humpty Dumpty (Mrs Trewly had been one) until Elizabeth had shown them his name, printed on a white card in black and red letters, and had got them to pronounce it properly, 'Col-po-es-ne D'. She had been given him shortly after her seventh birthday after she had worked out his riddle.

On her seventh birthday, among other presents, she had been given two pens, one red, one black, and a very curious riddle. Her father told her that Colpoesne D himself had made up the riddle especially for her because he wanted to belong to somebody. If she could solve his riddle, he would be hers for ever.

54

This was the riddle, the riddle of Colpoesne D:

The sea is blue, so it is said,
But you will find this C is red.
The O is fat, just like my head;
Empty, and dirty round the edge.
Some say they know the colour of L
Found deeper than the deepest well.
And look at P—black as a cat.
Burnt by L, I've no doubt of that!
The O is well-red, so he should know
Why E is black, like the first O.
Of S there can be no mistake:
Red for danger—beware the snake!
Here's a hen (to pull your leg)
Black and bent she lays no egg.
That leaves E—and lonely D,
As both as red as red can be.
Now find a word, black letters four,
To take you through a red closed door,
Then you'll have all, and Me, your friend
To say this riddle's at an end.
            Signed   Colpoesne D

It took Elizabeth three days to solve the riddle, and when she
had she felt well-satisfied, for no one helped her. She found that
if she coloured some of the letters of his name in red, and the
others in black, she had discovered his big secret—two words
made up the name of Colpoesne D. 'Now find a word, black
letters four, to take you through a red closed door, then you'll
have all ...' If she could find a word with four black letters, to
take her through a red door that was closed, then the riddle would
be solved. What word could take her through a closed door? She
had heard a story once where Ali Baba had managed it by shouting something magical. But all she could remember was 'Open
...!' and she could not remember the other word because it was
strange.

Then she realized. She could go through any door, if it were
open. And OPEN was in his name, and when she had coloured
all those four letters black (some of which she'd already managed)

she found she was left with a red door—a door that was CLOSED. Thus she solved the whole riddle. So Colpoesne D became hers for ever. Her father took her into his bedroom, unlocked his wardrobe door, and there sat COLPOESNE D. His name was printed in black and red on a piece of card around his neck pillaged from an old shop-door sign. No, Colpoesne D was no Humpty Dumpty—he was far too clever. If anyone could help her, he ought to be able to.

Eventually Elizabeth grew tired and fell asleep.

In the night Colpoesne D spoke to her, led her through her thoughts, arraying all she had come to know about her father's life before he sold newspapers. And she lived for those brief hours in the laps of dwarfs, giants, hunchbacks and the other deformed people he had met, employed in the sub-basement of the department store: Grey Bone the gentle giant, Patch, Whisperer, Bowback, Ironlegs (her father), Blueskin the dwarf and Youngbeard. They had been only names to her in the beginning, but through the years of dreams they had taken on personality and living form—a mention of an item of clothing, a way of talking, the colour of eyes, the type of deformity.

And the sub-basement, too, the rooms, the stores, the lights, the passageways; gradually all came into regular order. She could now even smell the smells; the dull, fruity ferment of wines in their darkened caverns; the cold, wet smell of raw meat in a room constantly rinsed of blood; the hot, decayed smell of greens; the soap smells, perfume smells, the paper smells; the smell of dust on china and fine glassware and the musty air of the Forgotten Room, secret behind the 'Misery' door. Even then the store was dying, but few could read the signs.

Through the concrete passages the wind would gush a cavernous sigh, and stone would seep with winter chill which no scarf or jacket could muffle, and the ancient, winter misery of castle-bound kings would wrap itself about the bones of crooked backs, and crippled hands. While, above the ground, the air was sharp and bright as Christmas, crisp hoar settling on the ginger towers, spires and domes, making the store like an enormous sugared cake for the softlegged rich to share between themselves. They did not hear the groans from the foundations, beneath their courtly laughter.

Elizabeth could hear the surge of trick-tongued Polish, the impossible slide of Greek, frenzied Chinese, the chuckle of the African, stiff German and the acrobatic French, sloven Arabic and delicate Hindi, then all the dialects of the races, colours and creeds that shared the English tongue. Yet she knew most of these belonged to the yearly vacationing ranks from whence Youngbeard had sprung, the nomads who sought simple work and shelter in the undercaves. For that reason, Elizabeth despised them. Colpoesne D would talk to her in riddles up to the days of Youngbeard, when he came among her kind and stole their deepest secrets—and their living. She could hear the rumble and see the mighty power of Silverblade, or the sad bell of the green train, dragging behind the iron-chained baskets with a midget for a driver.

The noise of the street was deafening if one really listened, and the motion random—almost pointless. There was a glaze in Uncle Tony's eyes. Mr Morgan had learnt to respect his serenity, and amused himself by shouting: 'H'chanoos!' And later, 'Aipereer!' as a detached, almost separate chant, to the bobbing, streaming, strolling, wheeling individuals who ventured across his panoramic vision. For Mr Morgan there was no randomness here.

Uncle Tony was entranced by a trick verbal phrase which kept skeetering up his brain, standing briefly on top in self-admiration, then tumbling down again, simply to repeat the exercise. Again and again this would occur, while somehow he sat aside, mesmerized. He marvelled, as a father marvels at his child's most recent accomplishment. For this was his child, this phrase, and it had by now accomplished a sense of balance, a dignity, a poise. Up, up it skeetered, up to the summit of his expectations —a little poetic nymph who, with graceful hands, silenced the world with the words: 'Long live, and happy, the people I love!'

Uncle Tony Lemon's glazed eyes sought the crowd before him, for someone to bless, some incidental human occasion to emblazon with his words. He searched along this tidemark of time in the morning, a vagrant on the pebble beach searching for the yellow pecten, looking for beauty in the slate-grey mussel beds ... 'Long live and happy, the people I love!'

An old man, with stained waistcoat and sagging, ruptured eyes, was caught, confused in a tangle of his own thought. He tottered in the vacuum before his legs stirred again and bore him away, uncertainly, down the street. Tony saw the old man's grave, following him, with a clean, simple headstone. Thinly chiselled on it, with neat, crisp ceriphs, he saw the words: LONG LIVE AND HAPPY THE PEOPLE I LEAVE.

He saw the Queen, pressed into a silver coin, and then in red and white at the end of a red carpet; the blood of mighty England.

He saw her turn her attention from the blood-red line to the wigs and the black-white gowns on right and left, polished brows, bulging golden wine-skins. He heard the murmur effervesce until it was silence, and the Queen, in her high, roundly muted voice, so tiny in that great chamber say: 'Long live and happy, the country I lead!'—the whole phrase splendidly rolling down to the keepers by the door, isolated then by a moat of silence, before the uproarious response:

'Long live the Queen!'

'Are you sure that is right?' said a Pecksniffian man, unfolding his white bamboo fingers in front of Uncle Tony's face so that he could examine the change.

'Eh?'

'I said,' recalled the man, now with some impatience, 'are you sure that is right?'

Over the years Tony had found there was no need for concern about giving the correct change—the law of averages was very accommodating, ensuring that he never lost more than he gained. The Pecksniffian man was obviously not one of his breed and, judging by the tightening eyes and protruded head, was probably used to gaining more than he lost.

'I gave you ten new pence—you gave me two new pence in return.' Even before the man's sentence had been delivered, Tony had finally taken full control of his senses.

'Thought you said two papers.'

'Very likely.'

'Eh?'

'It's very likely I would be buying two papers, isn't it?' Tony was ready to make up the difference, his hand warm with loose change. The Pecksniffian man moved fractionally away, just far enough to indicate that he would not accept the difference without fuss.

A certain feeling of embarrassment began to circulate in Tony's mind. He genuinely had not noticed the man—that is, really noticed him—until he had made his first remark. There was, however, no doubt in his mind that he had sold a newspaper. The ghost of the physical deed was still in him, and the hand seemed to fit the vague shape that accompanied the memory. Embarrassment blossomed profusely when he realized that it was quite possible he had made a mistake. He had told a lie, of course,

59

a cover-up lie for the sake of good business, which the man should have accepted. Apparently, the man did not.

'I think you were trying to swindle me!' said the man, in a tone uncomfortably loud. The man was taller than Tony, pale and grainy, like ivory recently discoloured in the sun. He had a peculiar ancient look about him, though for all that he seemed to be a youngish man. Above a spotless brow his hair was ginger, coarse strands parted carelessly down the middle so that some ends overhung the tops of his small ears, and the droop of his gaucho moustache matched the droop of his eyes. He wore a tie and a dark suit jacket, black-brown and slim-cut, whereas his trousers were very wide and broadly striped in two tones of grey. Furthermore, his shoes were a cheap modern reproduction of an old patent leather style, with a grey spat fused onto the uppers, disappearing up the mouth of each trouser leg. Tony was faintly amused by his appearance and couldn't help showing it on his face.

'I think you deliberately gave me false change!'

'Now come on ... 'Course I didn't.' Tony was not at all sure of the man in front of him.

'I work for the Ministry,' said the man. 'And in the Ministry there are many offices.' That seemed very feasible to Tony, though he did not grasp the relevance. The Pecksniffian man developed his theme. 'In the Ministry there are many offices, and I know them all. I know all the people in the offices and they know me. There is an unwritten code in business called *bona fide*. The expression is Latin. It means "good faith". All businessmen—even if they are only tradesmen—must subscribe to this, otherwise they break the law. Good faith means trust. When I buy something from you, a tradesman, the purchase is made in all good faith and mutual trust. You trust me, and I, foolish though it now seems, trust you not to swindle me.'

'But,' offered Tony, rather blankly, 'you should always check your change.'

'There should be no earthly need.'

'Except when a mistake has been made.'

A fat, cardiganed arm suddenly snaked between the two. At the end of the arm was a dumpy little body. ''Ello Tony, love. *News*, please. Ta.' She could see he was busy.

'Oh, hello, Rose. 'Elp yourself.'

60

'Money in the tin?' But she knew that was right, so there was the noise of money being placed in the tin. Tony didn't even look.

' 'Bye, love.'

' 'Bye.' She waddled off in the direction of Mr Morgan, some yards away from the swirl of the corner. The man looked a little put off; the atmosphere of tension had somehow been broken.

'Look, mate,' started Tony afresh, 'I wasn't tryin' to swindle you. Here's your right change.'

The Pecksniffian man looked at him again, cautiously, then slowly pushed out his hand, coins grasped firmly, having made red creases in the white of his palm. Tony, confident now, said no more but simply dropped the change into the man's hand, and the man turned and sniffed, rather like a mechanical toy, and strutted off towards Mr Morgan. When he reached the second stand he began talking to Tony's partner, pointing, but not looking, in the direction of Uncle Tony. Tony began to feel annoyed, being left out of his own business. Mr Morgan looked his way then, his mouth slightly agape as if in lack of comprehension. The man spoke some words more. Mr Morgan shouted something very short to him. The man tried again, whereupon Mr Morgan dispensed with all politeness, and reached for his stick. The man quickly disappeared among the midday shoppers. Mr Morgan was red with rage, still holding his stick. Tony couldn't leave his stand, not just at that moment—two young girls were sorting among the magazines. He looked hard at Mr Morgan, but Mr Morgan would not look back. So he shouted: 'You all right?' Still not looking back, Mr Morgan waved his hand and dismissed the situation. Tony suddenly noticed the girls staring at him.

'My mate,' he said, briefly. And rubbed his hands together in a businesslike fashion. 'Now, ladies ...'

'Two *Ravers* please,' said the smaller. The other had another magazine in her hand, waiting.

'Two?' said Tony. 'You're lashing out a bit, aren't you?'

'One's for me mate, at work,' said the first girl in a coquettish way. The other giggled.

'Too lazy to come out and get it herself, is she?' He took her money.

'No. She's getting it indoors today,' said the first. 'I hope!'

It was obviously a private joke, and they both left, giggling as they rounded the corner.

There was a green-yellow shimmer, a twitching sea of light, over the floor of the hollow. In what better environment could earth-magic survive? Elizabeth's brown eyes were of the earth, and she was a child of the city—it was to the magic of the city-earth that she must reach, there in the hollow, beneath the shimmer.

She found her place for sliding down to where the air was still and warm. With her stick to help, she sought a firm path where the rubble, tangled with weeds, gave way to the ground that had been hardened by summer months of scuffling feet. Here had raged the trespass of children, the feet of the free. Now it was a lonely place. The neighbourhood was a rattling empty shell. Deep down inside herself, Elizabeth felt suddenly afraid. Up and beyond the rim of the hollow, the hammer-bangs and echoes, the rumble of engines, the destruction of things once built, were growing closer. How long would this last private place be hers?

Her fingers nibbled at the edge of the hole, and with her stick she managed to prise away some bricks. It was a desecration that could not be helped, driven on as she was to find the Forgotten Room. It was down beneath the daylight, in the slumber of the golden globe-light; down beyond the foot of the stairs and the scampering shadows there; it was down among the darkness and the noises she feared—but she could not stop.

In front of the hole she had found the long and deep mark made the day before, and in her blue canvas satchel she had brought a tiny, plastic torch. 'Elizabeth, you cannot go back now. You have made the mark, and taken another day off school, and you have sworn never to return to the outside world until you have found the Forgotten Room, and have solved the mystery of your father's past.' Now the hole was just big enough for her to squeeze through. So she squeezed, legs first, lying on her back, slowly inching forward until only her head and shoulders remained in the sunlight. She looked up at the sky. It wore its best blue vest for her. 'Goodbye,' she said softly. Then she was gone.

She remembered, conjuring visions to blanket her fears, how she had sometimes walked out into a street fog, for no other purpose than to imagine all that could not be seen, then prove their existence by reaching out and touching them. Surely the cold, black air of this cave was such a fog, for she knew brick and moss, the coarseness of the wind-blown grass, growing inside the hole —she knew them! And the dim light of the globe, far beneath, was only like the distant lemon light squeezing along the ever-darkened hallway at home; the great pillars of iron and stone pushing into this inner night were the iron bridges of the fog-bound sleeping city!

Reach out! Reach out! We are yours to find, little one. You are of us, growing out of iron, cold as the earth. You are of us, lost in your own darkness, with one light for hope. The world of day, outside, was where you were abandoned; it is here that you belong.

Coldness seeping through her dress reached her and the visions broke away. Only then she realized—she did not know this place. She groped for her bag and her stick. Without looking away from the crumbled stair in front of her, she pulled out something big and round from her satchel.

Though he had never had real life, even if she almost believed he had, now Colpoesne D's time had come. She quickly showed him the stair, the shadows and the thin shine from the light beneath. Everything was almost as he had so often spoken in her dreams. She knew now she sat in the entrance to the under-caves where the crippled and deformed had once toiled and hidden: Whisperer, Bowback, Patch, Blueskin, Ironlegs and all —even the hated Youngbeard had come here to learn the secrets of the vaults. Though they had all gone—all of them gone—Elizabeth knew she would find their trace.

Somewhere in the vastness beneath her, if she remembered now all that her friend Colpoesne D had ever taught her, perhaps she would find Silverblade, or the green train. And, perhaps if she searched and searched, braving all fear, exhaustion and pain—perhaps she would at last find the Forgotten Room. Only then, as she had sworn, would she return to daylight.

She made a mark in the dust with her stick after thinking this and noticed as she did so her ticking bracelet. Then, without ceremony, she placed it outside the mouth of the hole, where the dusty sunlight buzzed. It was for the time of day, not for the special time trapped here in the undercave. It would only remind her of the world that was now beyond her. But, if in due course she returned, it would be hers again. Slowly, Elizabeth wound up the watch, trying not to notice the time, though afterwards as she inched away from the light she knew it was almost half-past ten. And half-past ten spread out into the undercave, to the very furthermost cracks, and there set solid, to grow no older—like all things seen and unseen in the undercave; no older and no younger, but to remain as they were.

All things that have ever been leave some kind of trace. Some traces are so small they are easy to overlook, or so large that they seem to be the only thing in existence. To a child born to be lonely such a long time is spent in searching for friendly things, that many traces might be discovered, many memories might be revisited.

Man leaves traces everywhere; the housebrick, built by man for man, is now cast onto waste ground. Walls cry out for their secrets to be heard; bridges scream hourly of their strain in voices dirt and darkness can barely conceal. Time has perched upon the rocks, unchecked by man—crouched upon the fallen brick and with the same power that changes young flesh to old, has picked and pressed with his thousand toes until brick crumbs fall away. Time sits purring in the shadows—with his chilly subterranean breath licking the words scribbled on the walls, so that some have faded or been washed away—yet traces remain. Everywhere there are traces.

Elizabeth slipped from the thin draught of day-air which blew in with the sunshine, into the dull, thicker air of the basement, and, as she moved, left a trace of her own carved into the dust with great effort. For at first, where this passage was so small, her legs were useless. Only by clawing with her fingers and pushing with her palms was she able to drag herself through a small tunnel of fallen masonry to the broad open landing at the head of the old staircase.

There she sat, her whole body shaking with the effort, her hands already dry with dust and the colours of her dress spoiled by grime. Her mind was full of childish adventure, an equal mixture of hope and fear. The noises she had made in her struggle seemed to radiate outwards, setting off other smaller noises at a distance. The blackness overhead fluttered, then was still. And down beyond the stair in the world of the globe-light, invisible creatures of that golden dusk scuttled along the shadows. The first difficult part was now behind her. Here, at the top of a crumbling stairway she could sit, rest and think for a moment. She looked down upon the stairs. They did not seem too inviting. Perhaps it was intended that she should go no further. She clutched Colpoesne D tighter. The stair was broad. To such a small girl on unsteady legs, five or six feet was a space wide enough to make her feel helpless. And there were obstacles all the way down the stairs. Their rough and raggy shapes were picked out by the soft light of the globe beneath; obstacles that could easily slip from beneath a foot which had no life, no sense of touch, and send her crashing to disaster.

She groped each side of her with both hands, bringing into her lap the things she had brought with her—her satchel, which rattled hollowly, her stick and her doll, Colpoesne. It was such a simple act but it brought her much comfort. She thought then of all she had done, why she had come even this far. It was for her father, so that he would not have to be alone with the truth, so that he would be able to tell her about when she was a small girl and had a real mother, about the days when he must have been happy but of which he hardly ever spoke. When he knew that she had found his lost kingdom, he was bound to see she was old enough to be told the truth. She had always longed after the tales of the undercaves, of her people. In those long moments of anticipation the stairs seemed less angular and man-made, seemed almost like a hillside or a mountain slope descending into vague sceneries—an eternal dusk of lemon-light, quiet to the eye.

At the foot of the slope was a black pool and beyond that, another land of heaped rubble. The large, full, miraculous globe-light hung alone above the water and all distant horizons were lost in shadow. Fear began to leave the child now. Match the magic of her soul to this earth-magic, and surely, all truth must reveal itself to her. She began to descend the stair, into an enchanted moonlight.

7

The door to August's Eat was still open, with the sunlight smouldering on the red linoleum. Mr Morgan paused by the door, leaning on his stick. The room was empty and he heard no motion from the back kitchen.

'August—you in?'

He waited for a while for his ears to subside after his own shout and heard nothing. He shuffled a little closer into the doorway.

'Are you there, August?' He heard a distant noise from beyond the kitchen, then a closer sound as the back door opened. The kitchen then filled with a busy deep hum and Mr Morgan saw a shadow on a wall. Unmistakably, August was at home. 'August! I been calling you. Didn't you hear me?' August appeared through the door looking surprised.

'Oh—so sorry, so sorry! I been out the back to pat the dog.' He beamed a smile to Mr Morgan as he rounded the counter end and strode up to the doorway. 'You be pleased to know he is in good health—and,' he added with sudden new humour, 'in good hands!'

'What a bloody thing to tell me right now,' said Mr Morgan who was waiting for his customary tug over the doorstep. August looked at his vacant outstretched hands.

'Ah—I washed them just now. I am a clean man, you know....'

'Come on, come on. What are you waiting for? Been out here half my dinner break just waiting to come in.'

'My friend, you do me great honour with your compliments; such patience should be rewarded.' August grabbed hold of Mr Morgan's deformed hands to support him while he leaned back. First one stiff leg, then the other was lifted to the edge of the doorstep and the great strength of the Latvian eased him upright as if he had been a child playing games. Mr Morgan had dispensed with thanking him a long time ago. August was a tried and proven friend.

There was a table by the big window where he usually sat, up against the far corner where he could rest his back, but this day he chose the gloomier of the corners. August noticed this and was about to say something when he changed his mind and decided that food was more important. He respected the fact that this man had not the freedom of most and appreciated that all his little peculiarities made life just that bit less of a trial, but he was perturbed that the routine had been altered.

'I put your cushion over the other side. I will get it for you.'

'You fuss too much. No one asked you to give me a cushion in the first place. You'll be expecting to be tipped next.' August was away in the corner after the cushion, but he heard. What could he do but laugh? Even though there were two laughs: the one Mr Morgan got for a reply was the laugh of a good-natured clown, who could take any amount of abuse, the other August kept to himself and it hurt a little.

'I just try to help you—but, if you don't want no help ...' August held up his sentence as he held up his cushion. Mr Morgan frowned, caught in an awkward moment, and said the only thing he could.

'Well, give it here, then.' August handed it over triumphantly, laughing as he did so.

'I think I go get myself a sandwich and tea. I want to talk with you.'

Mr Morgan allowed himself half-an-hour for lunch which he took about half-past two in the afternoon. That was the time the stalls were least busy. It was also the time when the cafe was least busy, save for the occasional customer calling for a packet of cigarettes, or a sandwich to take away. Though recently things had been altered by the gangs of workers from the demolition sites. There were a few prostitutes in the locality and some of the men took an extended lunch-break. August didn't really like their kind, didn't like their dirty clothes and coarse minds in his shop, but he couldn't do without their custom. He had lost a lot of money when nearby shops and factories had been moved and the buildings pulled down. But things were bound to get better now if only by degrees. After the demolition would come the re-building, and after the re-building of the factory estate would come the rehousing. The people would return, and some of them would find August's Eat.

Mr Morgan, on the other hand, dreaded the whole idea whenever he was forced to think about it. He liked to be alone—
especially when he was eating his dinner.

After a minute or two in the back-room, August emerged with
a plate of bread in one hand and a cup in the other, and steered
himself round the edge of the counter up to where Mr Morgan sat.
He moved a chair across with his foot and sat down. Mr Morgan
ignored him. He would have done anything to prevent having
his dinner-break disturbed, but he knew August knew this too,
better than anyone. He must therefore have something important
to say. He still ignored him. He had not anything particularly
important to discuss with August, so it was not up to him to
make the first move. The Latvian took a sip of hot tea, pursed
his lips, then put down the cup. He looked straight and seriously
at Mr Morgan.

'It's about Tony.' Mr Morgan did not respond. 'I think he
is ill.' Mr Morgan stopped chewing for a moment and looked up
briefly.

'What makes you say that?'

'It is something I have wanted to say for a long time. Many
things make me say it. I don't mean sick poorly so much but—
up here—you know—in his head.' Mr Morgan continued eating
for some time, looking at the table in front of his plate. When he
had emptied his mouth he looked at August.

'And?'

'Well, don't you think we ought to help him?'

'How?'

'Maybe a doctor—or just us talking to him . . .'

Mr Morgan looked at him with anger in his eyes, saying slowly
and simply: 'He ain't mad.' He eased off and went back to eating. There was a sullen silence which lasted until August had
finished a beef sandwich.

'I don't say that he is mad,' he started again, 'but if he keeps
on he soon will be.'

'What do you mean—keeps on?' asked Mr Morgan. 'Keeps on
what?' August was annoyed that the old cripple was making
things awkward for him. He loved Tony as much as anyone. He
had certain things to say which must be heard. That's how he had
managed in the past; that's how he was going to manage now.

68

'This drugs—keep on with this drugs thing.'

'Who?' asked Mr Morgan suspiciously.

'Uncle Tony Lemon—that's who!'

Mr Morgan gave a scornful laugh. 'What—Tony? So what?' August could hardly believe his ears. 'What if he is on drugs—don't mean to say he's mad. I'm on drugs. Would you say I was mad? Been on drugs all my life—does that make me doubly mad?'

'No—you don't understand. Not medicine, not for aches and pains that you can buy in the shops. These special ones, the ones that make you see things. I seen him buy some from a darkie.'

Mr Morgan pondered. It was going to be difficult to explain to a well-intentioned block-head that he knew all about Tony's habits and had done so long before August had ever laid eyes on him. Anyway he just wouldn't get himself involved trying to save someone else's soul. He wasn't strong enough to see it through; he didn't believe in it. But he supposed he had to do something now, for the sake of a peaceful dinner. He would, at any rate, consider it until the end of his break.

August had had his eye on Tony for some time. A few months back Tony had met up with a West Indian in the cafe. The coloured man had made all the moves, bought him a coffee and by the end of ten minutes acted as if he had known him all his life. This man laughed and grinned a lot and generally irritated August to the core, and he paid August too much heed for a man with nothing to hide. Before long Tony had left his dinner and the pair of them had gone out into Thorn Street. August watched them from the door. They walked down towards the deserted end and he saw the man give Tony a small screw of silver foil and Tony hand him a pound note. They talked a little longer then the man went down a side turning and Tony walked back to the cafe. August knew he had been seen by the West Indian. He never came back to the cafe. To him that was proof that the man had been up to no good. But he had never thought of drugs until much later.

By chance a policeman had come by one Sunday when August had been washing out the cafe. August had made him a cup of tea and they had got to talking about crime in the district. Really, the policeman was pumping him to see if he could throw any light on a few petty incidents that had occurred since the beginning of the demolition work three or four streets away from the end of Thorn Street. August got to know about the prostitutes and their connection with the demolition gang, the pimps and international smuggling, which was the thing now—especially drugs. The amount of illicit stuff in the area was on the increase. The policeman used a lot of jargon as he described a few of the basic kinds of drugs and August found it all very illuminating, even funny, until the policeman went on to describe the physical effects of the various drugs.

But he said nothing, and the policeman left with a condescending air, as if he had been talking to an ignorant, north European immigrant.

However, August was far from ignorant. With this strange and wonderful education he had just received, he began to formulate his own conclusions: the West Indian must have been a 'pusher' selling Tony a 'quid deal' of something or other, most likely 'acid' or 'shit'. Everything—even the words seemed very amateurish, but he guessed that it was more than likely true because of the way the policeman had described things.

For a time after that, he kept his eye on Tony. To begin with he despised his weakness. August wanted nothing to do with the police so he avoided anything that might lead to trouble. He could not prevent Tony from spending his dinner-break at his cafe until he had conclusive evidence of his involvement with the illicit drug world. But things never got that far. All he was able to witness was what he considered to be the slow deterioration of a one-time healthy mind.

If ever he saw him with a pale face and red eyes he would jump to the conclusion that he had just 'scored some charge' and had had a quick blast somewhere quiet. It wouldn't occur to him that he might have had a bad night's sleep. If ever he saw him excessively happy he would immediately consider him stoned, likewise if he was depressed it was because he wasn't. If he displayed any kind of imaginative thought, it was because he was hallucinating.

Tony ceased to become a real person with real ideas and emotions to August, but was reduced to a pathetic puppet, one to take pity on, one to try and help, to restore. August never thought he would have any difficulty in convincing the sane world of his conclusions.

He told Mr Morgan his story, drawing on information obtained at the cost of reading a few articles in newspapers and magazines —he had no television. To him it sounded very colourful, very real. He could not understand why Mr Morgan sat throughout, apparently unimpressed, unmoved.

'We know he is no genius,' said August, 'yet he lets himself run free like one, gets himself to believing things that have nothing to do with living. It's a very dangerous thing to do. He will go crazy unless he stops. Look, I will show you something what he give to me ...'

August fished around in his apron pocket then produced the card given to him by Tony earlier. He read the words briefly then pushed it over to Mr Morgan.

'There...!'

Through the thickness of his glasses Mr Morgan angled his face so that he could read the words written in black pencil:

LONG LIVE AND HAPPY THE PEOPLE
I LOVE

'Hmm,' he said and returned the card to August. 'What's he want you to do with it?'

'Wants me to paint it up for him, on a piece of card, I think. But it is not right, is it—for a man nearly thirty. He is like a child. It is the fault of this drug, robbing him of his manhood. He believes in these things, you know. And the shame is that the world will let him down too, least he will think it has let him down, and it will be too late for him to see where he has gone wrong. He will expect too much from the ordinary man. He will not understand him nor will he be understood.' He left things at that for no other reason than that Mr Morgan began to puff himself up as if he was about to speak.

'Look, I've known Tony a damn sight longer than you have. I knew him years ago—yes, years ago, long before we ever got caught up selling newspapers. He don't seem any different now to me than what he was then. He's always had ideas, and he's always had notions for doing things with them. I don't suppose he'd mind me telling you, seeing how you are so concerned with his welfare, but he's been working on a book that he wants to call *News* for years now. I've listened to his theories about news—and they make sense. Could be any time now that book's finished. There's more to that lad than you'd think. He went to university, you know. There, you didn't know that, did you? And I bet you can't guess why he left. He left because he wanted to learn things by himself, the hard way. Why, I shouldn't wonder if I'm not in that book of his, an' you and the whole blinking neighbourhood, drugs and all. Why not?'

The idea of August, his cafe, being bungled together with the pimps, prostitutes, dope-peddlers and every other facet of a seedy back-street life appealed to Mr Morgan. It was not strictly true though. Tony's writings did not include personalities, from what he had gathered. It was a purely theoretical piece of work which revolved around one principle and bred a whole litter of conclusions. 'Any day now that lad is going to take the world by surprise. When he does, that will be it. He is far—very, very far—from being mad, let me tell you! And as for drugs—why, you're worse than an old mother hen. We might as well expect you to give up drinking that old rot-gut you swill. Why don't you grant him some of the common-sense you grant yourself? I don't expect you to become a drunkard just because you have a taste for the spirits, so why do you expect him to become an addict just because he takes a little medicine now and again? I might myself some day, just to see what the fuss is all about. There! What do you say to that! I suppose you'll be putting me on your short list for the strait-jacket next.'

II

The people passed. Some thought and cared, he could tell by their expressions, but more had given up worrying about anything outside their experiences. It would not be true to say they did not care completely—just cared less. They cared less about the complexity of the architecture around them, the technology buried beneath their feet or skimming the upper levels of their own sky. Life had become far too involved, and they had given up trying to keep abreast a long time ago. So long as there were the documentaries on the television, in the papers and the magazines, they knew that somebody along the line must care.

Uncle Tony was baffled, disciple of the street though he was;

72

a demon seemed to perch on either shoulder, whispering: 'It's happened all before, hundreds, thousands of years ago. Great men gave their lives to leave you their worthy knowledge to inherit. Yes, you read the accounts, yet it means nothing to you. It might never have happened. Could it, frail human, be a lesson to teach of your end, and could it be the only one you fail to understand. Civilization, that of working together for the common good is like a ceiling with many cracks; one good shake and it will all fall down ...' And so the demon would chatter in the absence of real conversation, until something in the street would catch his outer eye.

A man had passed, some time ago now, on the other side of the street. He had been a rare sight, a pavement-prophet telling the people of Christ's second coming. Some listened to him, probably hoping that if Jesus did come again He might remember it. Some ignored him just like they ignore everything in the street; some gazed for a while, smiled for a while, then fell back into their own worlds again. The man was an Asian. He looked like Gandhi in a brown coat. He shuffled along between the leaves of a sandwich board, and rocked a little unsteadily.

Perhaps most of them had seen it all before; the end of the world—Christ's second coming—a new skirmish in the war against sin. They saw the word 'Jesus' and fled. But Tony had never noticed a sandwich-man outside of a cartoon page. To him it was like seeing a ghost, or a fairy. He looked towards Mr Morgan. Mr Morgan was reading the paper and would stir for no one. Customers served themselves. Tony felt like shouting something at him. But he didn't for two reasons: he didn't want to upset him, and he didn't want to upset the prophet on the other side of the street.

The man had been a strange sight. He looked Indian, yet he was talking about Christ. Strange, he thought, that the first Indo-Christian he should ever see had been also the first pavement prophet he had ever seen. He thought about and elaborated on that point for some time after the man had disappeared under the railway bridge. It was a beautiful day, not just the weather, but the mood, the prospects—everything seemed to want to lend him a hand. Even his thinking mind, which was usually listening to the deep echo of what might have been, ceased to pirouette about any one particular point and began to unfold like a bud in springtime. Trains of thought had never before left, circuited and returned as they did now. Before they had always set out on lonely, one-way journeys, and he would lose sight of them in the distance.

He sat in his chair, his eyes set in their deepest glaze. Gradually, by an association of ideas springing directly from the Indian prophet, he came to see precisely how the human race would fail and how the earth would fall to destruction. Struggling up to the summit of this horrific realization, he drove in statements like iron seeking the cracks in the rocks, and from such statements he hung suspended until he found the courage to continue.

The earth was shrinking. The earth was smaller, weighing less now than it did at the creation. This was so because if man lived and died and left no heir, he returned the mineral mass he had taken from earth in the form of food by giving his body back to the soil. But man did leave heirs and the numbers of mankind multiplied so that at any one time there were always more alive than there were dead, therefore the amount of mineral mass taken from the earth was always in excess of that given back. In this way, as the overall population of the earth increased, so the real mass of the earth shrank. A statement formed itself. 'The increase in the overall population of the earth is directly proportional to a decrease in its mass.'

A thin, brown-skinned boy brought a comic magazine from Uncle Tony, then ran off at top speed, singing. It created a break like the sight of the valley beneath from the edge of a very high mountain. And Uncle Tony Lemon became filled with new wonder and fear. He gazed across the street. The darkened shop-window opposite served as a mirror and in its reflection a silhouette of rooftops could be seen. In the bright patch which was the cloudless sky a silver disc with a dark miniscus burned. It was the sun.

The breeze caught the ladies' dresses, and light shone in the children's hair. The green paint on the shop door peeled before his eyes. Every once intangible thought now found a point of contact, every haughty complication now bowed in humble simplicity. It was as if he, Uncle Tony Lemon, of doubtful origin, failed existence and random destination, as if this man, who had so few of the games ever invented upon his side, this same glazed-eyed, tousled-haired, besmothered man, had gained the confidence of the universe. The dogs in the street knew, the cats around the corners knew, the sparrows knew, the air, the clouds and the earth, like a good mother, knew. The people in the street saw him but they did not know.

On the other side, shuffling through the drift of shoppers, tiny children, the air feeding life to the street, the pavement prophet returned. The board above his head moved rhythmically to his weary pace. It bore a red cross, red on dingy yellow, like the colours of Christendom, and above and below, the words 'Jesus Saves'. This man, whose kind Tony had never seen before, had come at a time when salvation was needed as never before. As he drew nearer, Uncle Tony called to him, and waved as he stepped off the curb.

The Indian turned very pale, into a kind of grey, and melted away from the street. For some reason he felt he was to blame and that if the crowd decided it were true, they might kill him. That was what was on his mind. So he disappeared. Some people got out of the bus, but when they saw got back in again. Others could see it was going to be a long and complicated job. They got off the bus and walked away feeling very sorry for the driver who was shaking and trying to hide it by talking to the conductor. A middle-aged gentleman with serious, intent devotion took off his coat and laid it over the leaking wreckage of a young man. There was a statue looking over his shoulder, a statue half of iron, half flesh. Mr Morgan's brain was jammed. Trapped inside was one thought that pounded on the walls: 'Again I have lost. Again!' The capable man helped him into Uncle Tony's chair, saying only the necessary things to him, as if he only knew the right things to say: 'I am afraid your friend is dead.'

It had happened in a way which the living would never understand. Uncle Tony Lemon had been so affected by the sight of the prophet, and the natural evolution of his thought that had followed, that he had stepped off the kerb, calling to the Indian who was walking on the opposite side. Tony walked straight into a car. He bounced off the vehicle and was flung onto a lamp-post which broke his neck. His body fell into the gutter and a following bus ran over his legs. The busload of horrified passengers pulled up several yards away. A woman screamed, hearing the bang and seeing the doll-like body go through its spasms. Others, men and women, stood with mouths agape, throats aching. It had happened. They had seen it. Mr Morgan had seen it too, and knew instantly he had lost again, but wouldn't believe it and damned it, and cursed it and cried in his bones with the pathetic moan of a man who had no luck. He jerked across the pavement. The people in the street who saw his crazy staggering, didn't know him, did not connect him to his loss, broken, bleeding in the gutter. A dog came up, before the people had drawn too close, with his eye on the crowd and began to sniff the body and the warm liquid oozing through the rags behind it. 'Get off. Leave him, you bastard!' Mr Morgan cried. The peculiar tone of the man got through to the dog instantly and the animal shot away with Mr Morgan's stick springing after it to come to rest on the other side of the street. It was at this point that the prophet fled. A very well-dressed gentleman prevented Mr Morgan falling over. He had no need to ask if he knew the unfortunate in the gutter. 'Tony ... Tony ... Tony....' cried Mr Morgan and tears tried to force their way through his skin. Another man from the street saw he had metal legs and helped the gentleman to support him.

'Here, take a good hold of him,' instructed the gentleman. Soon he was able to let go of Mr Morgan. He walked over to the body. There was a woman bending over it. She backed off slightly when he approached and tried to say something.

'I've killed him ...' said the car driver to the bus conductor. He waited for someone to say he had not, that the man was unconscious. No one did. The gentleman gently placed his thumb and forefinger either side of Uncle Tony's neck, just underneath the ear. He moved the position of his hand slightly. He looked up very softly to the driver but found he could not speak, so he shook his head. The conductor took the driver away.

There was the faintest smear of blood on the gentleman's thumb. The sight upset him so he quickly took his mac, which he had carried over his arm, and covered the body. Somebody told him that the ambulance was on its way.

III

It seemed a long time before anything happened and the gentle-man wondered just how much longer he could remain gentle. He had been on his way up the road to a bargain shop. He now doubted if he would ever get there. The hideous hee-haw of an ambulance could be heard in the distance. It would stop, then start up again, but seemed as if it were lost.

Then, with no warning at all, a police car pulled up. Two policemen casually got out, but, on seeing the body, stiffened a little as they walked towards it. They were both quite young. They went to the body and saw the mashed legs. 'Is he alive?' asked the stout driver. The other paused as he looked at the dead man's head. He did not really want to touch him but he had to. He felt for the pulse of his hand but couldn't find it. 'Stone dead.' He looked up at the various people. 'Anybody'd think it was a bloody circus, to see this crowd.' He got up still looking at the people almost savagely, then he let it drop. 'Come on Charley, let's sort it out.'

Very slowly, the gentleman eased his way out of his own, controlled state of shock, into the warmer land of the living and life. Eventually he came to realize he had lost a perfectly good raincoat.

I

The green crust on the bricks told Elizabeth there had once been life in the undercave as well as water; minuscule life depicting the revolving cycle of the chloroplast but restrained in these dungeon depths. Leaving nothing but the stained trace, the spark had gone. Now the walls were hoary with crystal growths of rock-salt. Where dust had embraced dust, attracted by tiny forces of static, now moisture had bonded atom to atom and a fragile comb collapsed into cement. It was a knowledge, built not of words that might be spoken, but a recognition of things being as they are.

The journey so far, though short in yards, already seemed to Elizabeth one of immeasurable distance. The vast darkness had added a new dimension to every downward step. Imagination flourished in tones of twilight and an underlying carpet of tiny sounds. Elements and functions present in the hole resounded like instruments, as if being struck or plucked by stone-slip and crumble, softly echoing from the walls and smothering all harshness. Small drops of moisture fell from the shadow above to explode in a series of high-pitched notes back towards the ceiling. Underneath all this, low voices of the tomb spoke out in words that so few of the living are ever permitted to hear.

Through denseness of bonelike shale the lower tympanies of the progress of destruction above still permeated as intermittent drones, rumbles and deepened sighs. Was the earth laughing? Was she the subject of some tormenting prank? She flattened Colpoesne D to her chest. He had been a true friend from the start—even in her dreams—long before she could test his fidelity, before the hollow had revealed its secret. Then, throughout the era of destruction of buildings once held dear to her, Colpoesne's images had rung true in kind and form, though never exact in location or dimension. Yet this was to be the time of real test, and if he should desert her now what star was left to guide her?

She hugged him close now with one hand.

She had reached a place as she descended which was smothered in shadows and where the going underfoot was uncertain. The light was too poor to see exactly the route of the firmest path, but she used her stick both as a probe and as a support as she stepped downwards. Now she was filling the undercave with soft echoes of her own.

As she probed forward once more with her stick, she knocked something over the edge of a step in front. The object felt oddly soft in a landscape of concrete and rubble. Again when her senseless leg followed to the step beyond she felt a lump squeeze flat beneath her full weight. Elizabeth was convinced that she had first struck and then stepped upon a knot of rags—convinced, that was, until a curious sound gurgled up from beneath her foot. For a moment she froze in fear and fatigue, but then moved on to reach the foot of the staircase. Soon she was surveying a much lighter, if equally desolate landscape, where the almost level terrain was pierced only occasionally by spires and mounds of rubbish. She accidentally demolished a few of these as she stumbled her way across the floor to where a large pool of black water spread beneath the globe-light. It was a pool she had to cross, for it barred her way.

Elizabeth was quickly reminded of the virtue of her insensible legs as she began to wade through the ominous pool. Not one drop of the foul water or sediment reached her living flesh, though at times the water level rose almost to her knees. Then, having at last crossed the pool, the final gleaming ripple stilled upon its surface, Elizabeth staggered up the furthest shore into another region of curious sounds.

She had reached at last the place where pillars rose majestically from the rubble at their bases. Yet this was a place, too, where even darker shadows than before began. She decided to rest, giving herself time to collect her thoughts. She leaned, with little comfort, against the deathly coldness of a damp pillar, and turned to face the stairway where the uppermost steps were still illuminated with thinnest silver, the ghost of daylight. A shiver ran through her body. Something moved close by; a single life-sound followed, it seemed, by shadows of similar sounds. She froze. She could feel her eyes growing wider as they searched the gloom about her feet. The sound had stopped. But Colpoesne gave no clues. For a terrible moment she was completely alone again. She called out to him for guidance. Then both noise and motion leapt at her together. Something hit and fought desperately at her left knee. Elizabeth screamed, yet no noise escaped at first. Then she screamed again, as the creature scratched and tore at leather and metal. Down swept her stick as Colpoesne fell helpless to the ground. Elizabeth's terror filled her with a powerful frenzy and she beat and beat. But the creature would not let go. Her screams gave way to cries. Instinctively, she wanted to run, but a lifetime of crawling and walking confused this panic, making desperation even more difficult to withhold. The terrible scratching, scratching sensation ran through her lifeless limbs, passing through her groin into her own body. It was then that a second wave of panic took hold. With two hands now grasping the stick she beat it against herself, hitting the unprotected back and head of the animal, until all the creature's frenzied motion had ceased and its broken body hung as a dead weight from her knee.

Exhausted and nauseated, she leaned against the pillar again, this time to regain her breath. Her head was spinning and her throat was dry from screaming. Yet she was still petrified, all the time praying the body would fall away and she could be free. But the creature, whatever it was, remained as stubborn in death as it had proved in life. Somehow it had become entangled in the straps at the kneejoint. It was only after Elizabeth had regained her senses enough to prise it away with her stick did the body make its final fall to roll into some private darkness. Although she felt hot, she began to shiver as if a cold draught was passing over. Were there more of them out there in the darkness, she wondered? Or had this been only the beginning of some dreadful, living nightmare?

She recalled with fresh horror the sensation of treading on something soft and raglike on the stair and remembered the faint, muffled sound. Had that too been a creature? She had never really considered that things might live down here, that she might be invading their lands and territories—that she was a trespasser. Elizabeth paused for a long moment, peering out ahead into the darkness. A tragic thought came to her; it was possible she had already caused the death of two inhabitants, the creatures that would not reveal themselves to her. More than ever, she needed good counsel, needed the wisdom of Colpoesne D. Yet she had allowed him to fall and be borne away by shapeless things. That must surely be what had happened, for now he was nowhere to be found.

A search began behind the pillars, among the shadows, where the light from the globe was dim, the fear Elizabeth had of the creatures being overcome by the fear of having lost her only friend. She remembered the tiny torch she had placed earlier in her bag. Hastily she fumbled to find it, then having done so, spread its thin beam around her. The weak, flickering haze of light was almost a comfort to her, until it revealed signs of the struggle. There was a little blood smeared on the metal of her leg. Elizabeth hastily turned the torch away and as she did so a thousand grey shapes seemed to scatter into the darkness. Even then, there came a tide of fresh scamperings from all around and for a moment the very stones seemed to twitch with life. For no reason, Elizabeth found herself shouting, firmly and loudly into the false night: 'Go away! Go away! ... I didn't do it on purpose!' As she called out these things, her eyes and ears strained for sight or sounds beyond her own booming voice. But there were none. The movement and tiny noises seemed to have stopped. She knew at last that she must move away from the security of the pillar she had been leaning against. But whether or not to go on, Elizabeth just could not make up her mind. The weak light of the torch picked out the shape of bricks and general rubble lying around, but not the soft, round shape of Colpoesne. Before any decision could be reached, she knew he must be found. Only Colpoesne could direct her.

Suddenly a fresh spirit was kindled in Elizabeth's breast. Her confidence gradually being restored, she pushed herself away from the support and, with the aid of her stick, forged a way across broken, uneven ground further into the shadows, pausing every other step to examine what was at her feet. At a distance of six steps, she drew a line in the soft ground at right angles to her passage, then proceeded on this new course as evenly as she could. Half in comfort to herself, and half extended to the lost doll, she called out Colpoesne's name. This time it was not a loud noise she was making, but one which melted into the local shadows. As the search progressed, so the light of the torch grew dimmer and dimmer. Elizabeth looked sadly down into the beam.

Even so, light from any source was a power to be reckoned with in the gloom of the hole.

II

Drifting from the infinite gloom of the shadows behind the pillars back into the broad spaces illuminated by the globe-light, was like passing from night into day. Not only was Elizabeth's vision clearer, but her dark and cobwebbed thoughts faded like morning mist in the first light. Not all things were clear, though. The undercave, which at one time had seemed boundless, now had definite boundaries. The pale, solid structure of a wall was not far away.

As Elizabeth carefully trod over the accumulated dust and rubble, the wall's surface became more and more detailed, its overall paleness first giving way to various whitish tones and these in their turn becoming recognizable as tiny etchings and drawings. Conduits, too, clung to the vertical surfaces like thick ivy stems from which tendrils of wire sprouted. The wall was a message to Elizabeth—as clear as a chapter of history. And she knew that within such a wall must be the door. The message was not written; it was a physical message, like a star for guidance or a road for travelling.

Lives that had washed against the wall had had the effect of sea against rock. For clearly, Elizabeth had seen the places where force had met an end. Grime had impinged upon the concrete in the manner of salt spray, collecting in microscopic pores and clinging to a film of moisture that was ever present in the atmosphere. So where the wooden shelving had been swept away by some raging tide of change there were marks to show just that.

Her lifeless feet pressed into a soft patch of moss. At once she staggered back. The fear of tiny animals returned. The stick struck out forward on the brick rubble with a crack, echoing to the far corners of the subterranean world. She struck again as a warning.

'Yah!' she half shouted, half screamed. The meaningless word hit the wall and broke in two. Elizabeth's eyes seemed to follow, and in doing so, collected other words. 'Shit! Fuck off!'

They were gone, their message released in a burst of tension before their meaning registered.

The moment seemed doubled up on itself; the fear of the one thing overwhelmed by the fear of the other, Elizabeth's hands clasped to her mouth. Had she really said those words? But, she knew she had. Her eyes were still focused on them—faint but unmistakable comments in dark crayon. Yet there would be no retribution. In the undercave they had some special, unworldly meaning. And they seemed good, powerful words to shout— words she had heard strong men use to allay all fears, as they had done her fear of danger from small creatures. But what anger or frustration had caused them to be written?

Perhaps, thought Elizabeth, in time the wall could teach her everything she needed to know before moving on. Thinking that brought back the acuteness of losing Colpoesne and a little knot of anxiety began to tangle. In the gloom, close to where she stood there was something almost boxlike. The strain of walking was beginning to tell; her thighs were starting to ache. She moved in the direction of the flat object and as she drew closer to it, took her torch from the satchel. At first it seemed to give out no light at all. Then gradually, as she moved the faltering beam over the object's uppermost surface, Elizabeth found it to be some sort of covered seat.

She stared back into the undercave while her blind fingers examined the throne. It had once been a complete wooden chair with both back and arms. Like the shelving from the walls, this too had fallen victim to destructive tides. Then along had come mending fingers and, using materials close at hand and nails from packing cases, the splintered wood had been re-united and the legs braced with wire. To restore a little character to what had perhaps once been a noble piece of furniture, a decorative cushion had been added. Though dingy and damp now, the torchlight still revealed a pattern of flowers.

The seat was relaxing. By the dim light of the single, hanging lamp, Elizabeth stared back along the path she had taken from the stairs. The floodwater offered a shimmer of reflected light in her direction. It seemed very distant. Low hills of rubble and waste out of which grew huge supporting pillars divided the distance between her and the water, and a great arching shadow hid everything above. Elizabeth felt calmed by the sight—almost

83

regal. There was something exquisitely peaceful in the landscape, and the mellow old light glowed like a full moon. For a few precious moments Elizabeth came to know the meaning of perfect peace.

I

At noon the sun came out and smacked the ground with the enormous flat of its palm. All living creatures on the face of the demolition site simply sat around stunned. Even breathing was a major task. A man sat sweltering over ill-kept notes and records in the depths of an office hut, like a mongrel in a kennel. Two others martyred themselves in their thick woollen clothes in this latest blast of heat.

One would not remove his jacket because, so far as he knew, he would certainly die if he did, his polished suit being almost a second skin. The second's better-kept wardrobe lagged his limbs with a thin covering of pride, and considered his shame would be worse than death were he to cast the remnants away.

The larger and prouder of the two men stared moodily into the dust of a world which had come to an end. His eyes did not see tiny fragments of stone, brick and plaster, but projected their own images into the heat-hazed surface. Like the walls, once he had been strong. Now he had been levelled. Fate had made him a murderer.

The smaller man clutched at himself like a monkey. An impulse very ancient, very powerful, had been staunched by the thump from the sky—his capacity to talk. Now he drowned in his own words and he gave out a little muted choking cry. He passed it off for a cough and it disturbed no one.

Sunlight continued to pour down, seemingly in an attempt to melt away the ragged sore of the site where houses had been snapped off or pulled up by their roots. It was a well-smashed, well-trodden piece of devastation with hardly a whole housebrick or unbent rod of conduit to bless it. And on this site, the two men, with their black West Indian foreman, closeted away out of their immediate sight in his hut, were the last of the demolishers— casual labourers with one simple task still to perform: to sweep up the droppings of destruction.

The heat suddenly slackened as if a fuse had blown. Samuel Packet moved his toughened head towards the perimeter wall and the open gateway. Holly, who had been watching him apprehensively, saw this movement. Should he chance disturbing the man again? His body craved a cigarette.

Yet opportunity evaporated before his eyes. For a tiny motion, witnessed in the corner of his eye, warned him. His ears pricked, and at the sound of approaching footfalls, he pounced upon a rusting piece of piping, examining it with passionate interest. A puzzled look crossed his face and he turned aside and began a slow, preoccupied walk to the nearest scrap-heap. A flat, mouthy voice froze him in his tracks. 'Mr Holly. Don't walk off so soon. I got a little job for you two gentlemen, now you've rested.'

Holly faltered on a smile, then threw the pipe backwards across his shoulder in the general direction of the heap. Samuel Packet, however, barely moved. 'Everyone likes a little rest in the sun.'

The huge West Indian, called Winston, crushed his whitened boots through the drifts and furrows of dust as he strolled towards them, his body rolling slightly from side to side as he walked. Before he actually reached the spot, Sam had gently, almost majestically, risen to his feet, knocking the dust from his trousers. Holly had returned on slow wheels.

The foreman looked at his two remaining labourers for almost too long. 'I got some rubbish for the tip—when you folks is ready.'

That message having been delivered, Winston turned and walked back to the black heat of the hut.

Holly saw a rim of anger harden in Sam's eyes.

'The black bastard!'

Holly dismissed the foreman with a wave of his hand. 'Ah—don't worry yourself. But for Jesus' sake—keep your voice down. He might hear you, and then what? You'll only make it worse—for the pair of us.' Sam simply stood by unheeding and rooted to the spot. 'Will you look at all this filth,' implored Holly, eyeing the sea of rubble and then a couple of shovels. 'And are those all we have to work with? You need a bulldozer to shift this lot. And what have we got? Shovels!'

The heat pressed mercilessly down. Holly's need for a cigarette was becoming urgent. It was not in his nature to ask for one straight out. He had to cadge. On the other hand he could not stand being unsuccessful—particularly when he had hinted for so long. Everywhere he had worked, he had received cigarettes as regularly as a stray dog gets scraps. And now, at a time when he needed one more than ever, his sole working companion ignored him as if he were scum.

In Sam's mind the thin, whining Irishman was a constant reminder of a part of his recent past. He looked and behaved and smelt exactly like an old lag, so Sam saw no reason why he should not treat him as he had treated them—with contempt. Although it was fairly common knowledge around the site that Sam had served time, somehow it had escaped Holly's attention. If he had known, he would have been the first to plead for a transfer. So when Holly in his ignorance made his casts for sympathy by incessant chattering and unreal mateyness, searching out character weaknesses to exploit—he really did not know with whom he was playing.

Two things and two things only constantly occupied Sam's mind, the memory of his prison days and the fact that he was being pressurized by a black man. They were two forces of equal strength which, when coupled, unleashed a vile and turgid temper. It was his temper which had landed him in prison in the first place.

He had once owned and run single-handed a moderately successful haulage company. But he had quarrelled with one of his employees and accidentally killed him in a rage. He was eventually tried and found guilty of manslaughter, receiving a three-year sentence. His business folded—there was nothing he could do about it; his life's work swept aside with one stroke. Prison, and prison life incubated his temper. It was just unfortunate that the man he had killed had been black.

'I could do with a fag right now to steady myself,' Holly brightened. 'And I bet you could, too, by the looks of you.' Still the Irishman was ignored. Holly reached into his jacket pocket and pulled out a much-used stage prop. He opened the flap of a dingy cigarette packet, tilted and flicked the outside of the empty container with his fingernails. In pure amazement he said, 'Now will you look at that! Just when I was going to offer you one.' Sam did not bother to look. 'Well, that's my luck finished. That's me out!' Holly waited patiently for the desired response. When none followed he almost forgot himself and asked Sam outright for a cigarette. But he would have been too late anyway. Sam had walked straight by him in the direction of the hut.

II

The hut door was closed. Sam was sure it was just another little insult thrown his way—like the way the foreman called him 'mister' and referred to his labourers as 'gentlemen'. He placed his boot near the bottom of the door and pushed hard. The door scraped open. Sam framed himself in the space he had created just as Holly came up behind him, licking his wounds. A flat velvet voice lifted itself out of the gloom like a tired spectre.

'There is a door handle, Mr Packet.'

'I know,' said Sam, solemnly, 'but you see, I always use my boot.'

Winston was very proud of his door-knob. It was the pick of the site, beautifully fashioned in brass and copper, an orb for his vanity.

'Step inside, please, gentlemen.' Holly tumbled forward and squeezed past Sam.

Before the two labourers in the oil-smelling shade, sat the big foreman. He leaned with heavy elbows on a desk made from an old door resting across two fuel drums. His chair, like the door-knob, had been plucked from abandoned houses. The inside of the office was a minor chaos of ledgers, files, plans, clipboards, notes impaled on nails, telephone numbers scribbled on walls, pencil-ends, cigarette ash, beer bottles and unwashed cups. A single, naked lamp illuminated the far end of the room, shedding light on stacks of valuable lead and copper piping and other potentially saleable materials. A pale ghost of daylight filtered through one small, reinforced and unwashed window and fell upon Winston's desk. A dead light hung over his head. The dark air shimmered in the nostrils while outside butterflies fried on the wing.

'I see you blokes restin' and I think you must be wantin' somethin' to do.'

'We've just finished stacking a whole load of pipes,' protested

88

Holly. 'It's a bloody back-breaking job—you want to try it some-time.'

Winston laughed aloud like a bellows. 'I've done it all, my boys—twice as much for half as much.' Then he paused, altering his tack. 'I have a little job for you.' He picked up a piece of paper and began to study it, sucking and biting his index finger. 'It says on this record that you can drive, Mr Packet.' He paused.

'Then it looks like you'll have to do the drivin'. I've got a load of rubbish I want deliverin' to Morton Street. One of you will load, the other will drive.' Holly's brain was racing madly, and after very little time had elapsed, he came to a stunning conclusion.

'Pardon me, Mr Winston, but that don't seem right. It's damn heavy going, shovelling at brick-ends and all that other muck in the sun, when all he has to do is drive half a mile and dump the stuff.' Sam flashed him a bullying look which Winston caught and considered. What a pair to wind up with, the foreman thought —a whiner and a moper.

'You may have a point,' he said eventually. 'All right, on second thoughts you'd both better load.'

Then Sam started. 'Look, if I'm supposed to be loading, driving and dumping—what's he doing while I'm gone?'

'You'll only be away a few minutes.'

'What? Morton Street is a good fifteen minutes away from here! Then there's the return journey and the traffic ...'

'Oh, so you know where it is, then. That's good. That'll save me havin' to explain.'

'That's how long it takes. It's bloody miles away by road— you ask any of the drivers.'

'He's right, Mr Winston. Half an hour—at least!'

'Then we can't have you hanging around that long. So you'll be shiftin' the rubbish into piles for the next load.'

'But—that means I don't get a break.'

'You'll get your tea-break. That's in the conditions. You gentlemen get paid to work. And work you will, my friends.'

Outside, in the full glare of a midday sun, shifting the first small mountain of broken bricks had become an exhausting and filthy chore. Both men hated every second of what they were doing, for very valid reasons. It was an abominable fatigue. Under normal circumstances a bulldozer and a mechanical grab would make short work of the piles. But the site had been recently robbed of all mechanical units to help tighten up a slack schedule elsewhere.

Sam had driven himself into a sullen temper before the truck had been half-filled. His anger was made even more vitriolic by cursing, under his breath, every living fold of the black man's skin, plotting ways by which he could even the score. Sam could respect a black with a genuine axe to grind—in fact, he preferred them that way. But he hated the one who lived in a white man's world and abused all its codes.

Looking at the surrounding landscape, Holly came to accept the fact that he had lost out. He had decided to harden off all friendly attitudes towards his unfriendly and uncharitable neighbour. The sooner he saw the back of him, the better. Strangely enough, this induced him to work even harder and continue his flourish of spadefuls into the back of the truck.

Even the sparrows began to choke in the spreading dust. It crept out slowly from the region of greatest activity like an atomic cloud, engulfing all and stinking of decay. It was the breath of a century, a breath which had hung clammily to the walls of a thousand back-street cells.

Dust mixed with the workers' sweat had spread a glistening fur over their faces and hands. Their throats grew parched, their noses blocked and their clothes became sour on their backs.

About a half-second after the very last particle of dust had settled in the back of the truck, Winston appeared on the scene as if he had been timing them. He smiled broadly at the two men.

'You done a good job there, gentlemen. It's a pity there weren't no machines to help you. Still ...' he shrugged his broad shoulders, 'that's life!' Sam could not wait any longer in his presence. He slung his shovel aggressively into the back of the truck and started to move towards its cab.

'You sure you know where you're goin', Mr Packet?'

'You've told me once. That's enough for me.'

'You got your delivery note for the rubbish you're carryin'?'

'A delivery note—for this muck?'

'They ain't to know what it is, unless you tell them. They've got an old boy on the gate—and he's dead keen. You've got to have a bit of paper to get anythin' past his nose. You'd better have a note.'

Sam just stared incredulously at him. 'You do know, I suppose, in the first place I wasn't employed to work here as a driver?'

'Yes, Mr Packet. I know exactly what you are. You're a labourer.'

'To be more specific, Mr Foreman, I came here as a casual labourer. I ain't getting paid to drive.'

'Oh, don't worry about that. I won't tell anyone, if you don't. You'll get paid the right rates.'

'And what are the right rates?'

'The right rates for you, Mr Packet, is labourin' rates. You and Holly here get this job done this afternoon and there's an added bonus in it—for both of you. That's all.'

Sam managed to stem the rising tide of anger. It was something of a minor miracle. Winston hung around for a moment expecting something further to be said, but Sam simply held out one opened hand while he scratched his nose with the fingers of the other.

'You got the papers then, 'cause I want to be off.'

'Sure,' said Winston. 'I got them here—somewhere.' While he went slowly through first one pocket, then another, he turned his attention to Holly.

'Now, mister, while your friend here is away, perhaps you'd shovel another little pile together, ready for when he returns. I've been lookin' around. There's enough here for three or four good loads. If you both put your backs into it, my friends, the job should be done this evenin'. And if it isn't, well there's always tomorrow.' As he finished speaking, he found the flimsy note in his top pocket and handed it to Sam. Except for one large pencilled word and an unreadable signature, the crumpled paper was completely blank. Sam could well see it was not a proper docket. There was not even a date on it. He doubted in the back of his mind whether the note would satisfy even the most casual of gatemen.

'What about the date?'

'Oh yes. Got a pencil, Mr Packet?'

'Of course I haven't!'

Sam wanted to be away. He grunted. 'It don't matter. I'd

sooner be off—without the date.'

'Just don't come back with that load, that's all.'

The cab door opened with a squeal which terminated in a long creak. Sam clambered up into the worn driver's seat, and he remembered. But the bubble was immediately pricked.

'You want the keys, Mr Packet?' Winston tossed them up and Sam started the engine. 'And don't dent the wagon, or I'll take it out of your hide!'

III

Sam found the driver's seat hard. Still, he considered, it felt good to be sitting. Driving was no problem for him, even after all this time. In his earlier days he had driven plenty of trucks this size, jobbing around the country. He felt relaxed. Things seemed to be going in his favour at last. This job was going to be easy. He laughed aloud when he thought of Holly, still shovelling muck back at Cowerly Road and he was still smiling about it when, fifteen minutes later, he arrived at the opened gates at Morton Street. A straggly old man came lurching forward to meet him. Looking down into the cigarette-smoking face, Sam condescended to hand him the delivery note. The man looked at it briefly.

'What's this?'

'What's it look like? Look, come on. Stamp it, or take it, or do something with it, will you. I'm on a time bonus.'

'I don't care what you're on. I ain't accepting this—anyone could have wrote it.'

'What about the signature, then?'

'That don't mean a thing, do it, when you can't even read it. And what's this say? RUBBISH. What's that supposed to mean? That can't come in here. What do we want rubbish for? We've got enough of our own. You'll just have to hang on till I've checked this.'

'Till you've—? Bloody 'ell!' But Sam began to see the futility of arguing. 'Well, all right then. Go away and check it. But get a move on, will you!'

The surrounding noise was deafening as brickwork exploded under sledge-hammers. Whole walls slapped the earth, pushed, almost effortlessly, by the pneumatic strength of an excavator, and here and there orange fires raged through the cages of waste woodwork. A rust-pocked machine lifted its greased silver neck above a corrugated high wall, as if to leer at him.

Sam's arrival had attracted a bit of attention, primarily because his vehicle was an obstruction in the gateway. A five-ton Ford, laden with broken bricks, thundered up to him and stopped a few feet off, snorting like an angry bull.

'Shift your wagon, then!' the driver yelled at him. Sam cursed an acknowledgement. He became flustered. The gears crunched under his hands. The uneasy handling brought more attention his way. Out of the corner of his eye, he could see the Ford's driver mumbling things to his mate. As Sam eventually crawled a few yards forward, the driver called out as he passed: 'You want to learn to bloody drive before you do a driver's job!'

A cold patch of anger spread through Sam. He swore, violently. Nobody could teach him about driving—nobody!

The old man came lurching out of his hut again. 'No one here knows anything about this lot. I told you, we don't want your rubbish here. You'll have to take it all back.'

'What—? Don't you piss me about!'

'I'm only telling you what I've just been told myself. You can't dump it here—that's what he said.'

'That's what who said?'

'The boss, Mr Simmonds.' Seeing Sam climb down from his cab, the old man became nervous. 'It's no use you taking it out on me. I've got my job, just like anyone.'

'Give it a rest, Pop. And give me the note. I want a word with Mr Simmonds.'

'You can't. He ain't here. I spoke on the phone to him.'

'Look, if you think for one minute I'm taking that rubbish all the way back and playing a nigger's fool, you're crazier than he is. Now, tell me who I can see!'

'If you really want to see someone, you'd better see Figgs. He's in charge of the site this afternoon. But he'll only say what I've said. We don't want anybody else's rubbish over here.' He began to move off.

'Where is he, then?'

The old man looked about him casually. At last he pointed. 'That fat man over there,' he said and lurched back to the hut.

Sam carried enough bottled anger in him now to blast his

way through any hassles he might get involved in. But when he eventually met Figgs, he found the man something of an anti-climax to the moment.

'Are you Mr Figgs?'

'No, not "mister", mate. Just fat ol' Figgs.' He stood among a pile of charred bricks in a sweat-stained vest. His skin had a rich dull glow about it, like oiled teak, and he was himself a perfect picture of over-indulgence. His voice was fully rounded with humour and perfectly friendly.

'What can I do for you, old son?'

'I've a delivery here nobody seems to want.'

'Seems like a complete bastard to me!' he chuckled, but the incidental humour was lost on Sam. Figgs climbed out of the pile, bringing his huge proportions closer to the stranger. 'You work for us?' he enquired.

'At Cowerly Road.'

Figgs nodded. 'Still much on there?'

'Just the sweepings. That's the point. I've been sent with a truckload of it—rubbish to dump here, and now I've just been told I can't.'

'Oh,' Figgs began to pull at his lip. 'Well, you've been told the truth, if rubbish is what you've brought. We've got enough with our own.'

'A bloody fool's errand!' uttered Sam murderously.

'Oh, I wouldn't say that. Never condemn yourself when there's plenty to do it for you.'

Sam looked around the site. 'Well, where do you shift yours then?'

'Nowhere, for the moment. It's always someone's headache to know where to dump the rubbish. Are you sure you weren't told the city dump?' Sam handed him the note which he looked at very closely. 'It ain't got nothing on here saying where it's to go. Who sent you, mate? Can't read his scribble.' Sam felt like saying something abusive, but he couldn't tell how well Figgs might know his foreman. He decided to tell him straight.

'What—?' exploded Figgs. 'Churchill? Ol' Winnie? He's having you on, old son. He's pulling your pisser! A right ol' joker, our Winston is. Oh yes! He'll have you running all over, give him half a chance!'

'Well, it seems a bloody stupid waste of a man's time to me!'

'You should worry. What's it to you? You're getting paid for it, aren't you?'

'That's not the point. I'm not going to be taken for a ride.'

'Well, you'll just have to learn to live with it, specially with a bloke like ol' Winnie-the-Pooh. You let him see you're put out by it all and he'll do it all the more. Look, my advice to you is to take this load right on back—won't take you long. Say you got a right ol' bollocking this end and you felt a fool and all the rest and he'll drop the whole thing. There's something else—and maybe you ain't thought of this one. He could be doing you a favour. He may be inventing something for you to do rather than laying you off, old son. The company's cutting back, you know. Three got the chop from here last week.'

Sam could not get over the fact of how simply some men see life, completely oblivious to its pitfalls. He saw Figgs to be such a man. Behind him, in the back of the truck, was a few hundred-weight of rubbish. Of one thing he was sure; he was not taking it back. He would find somewhere else to dump it.

I

Elizabeth was asleep, her head bent against a tiny wall-fold of dull, glossed wood. So soft the panels seemed, as if they had been made of foam. Textures in the dark pretended not to be themselves. The very air seemed to lie in visible thicknesses; darkness slept in the corners and nothing was sharp in the purring, lightless air.

Elizabeth slept, drugged by a potion of great weariness served in the chilled breath of the undercave. Dampness had seeped into her bones. Before, only excitement had kept it at bay but now, body relaxed, it fed its slow, invisible breath up through the ground. It was the chill of night locked into the earth; the balm of a land without sun.

On the verge of sleep, as her energies had ebbed, the wall became a pillow—a cool, refreshing expanse to quench the fever of her whole body. Her father came in and then was gone, leaving her staring at the moon, longing for bedtime stories. So Colpoesne sat on the edge of her pillow and whispered one to her. He could imitate any voice, human or otherwise, and with a crescendo of flutes and the barking of dogs, he lifted her onto his back. He was like a balloon with tiny legs.

With Elizabeth holding onto his ears, they floated through the wall. The whole house was asleep; her father grunting at dreams in his big bed and Mrs Trewly in the basement flat beneath, curled herself up like a cat in the bedclothes. The child and the doll glided along the pavement as if they were on wheels—yet they were flying, but very close to the ground.

Colpoesne spoke to her in street riddles and had all the workmen scurrying here and there with their street jobs. He made her count the paving slabs and see how they were laid. He showed her the weeds growing in the gutter, giving each a different name, then pointed out the beauty in the polished iron of a drain. There were all the words to be read on cast-iron coal holes and patterns to trace on paper with a crayon. There were pieces of grit to pick out of the treads of tyres and a neighbourhood of cats to stroke.

On and on they travelled in the light of neither day nor night. Where were they going? To find her father's life!

Where the stars were pierced one by one through the black bottom of an upturned bucket, Elizabeth and Colpoesne came to a news corner. Sitting on a box and lost in the hooded greyness of his coat, Uncle Tony Lemon smiled across the street at a mongrel dog watering a lamppost. When Elizabeth asked if Tony knew where they could find her father's life, he simply turned a pointed finger to a distant dome. It soon became obvious that nobody would buy newspapers from him. A policeman came and moved him on.

Streetlamps glowed like coals of orange sulphur, or the flare of matchheads, or white like polished grains of rice, but most of all the dome was infused with the colour of terracotta. There were scrolls sculpted over each window and black-edged oak-leaves, fluted columns, fruits and sashes were moulded into each layer. It was both cathedral and castle, a building so vast that one's head had to turn completely round three times to see it all.

Colpoesne took Elizabeth into the courtyard where plucked chickens hung by their feet in racks. He showed her the meats and fishes and the men with raw hands and red-stained aprons. Everything was sprayed with water so that it glistened even in darkness. And then, among bales of new cloths, a friend came forward to greet them. It was Polish Patch. He picked them up like a carpet, and with his timeless gait, threaded them through a doorway, as cotton through a needle's eye.

The corridor was round, ribbed with beams and pipes, and the light before them sank deeper the further they progressed. Patch spoke in Polish, each word slipping through his half-mouth like water through a fissure.

Colpoesne had gone, drifted away on a cold draught with the freedom of a balloon. But Patch gently laid Elizabeth in a basket, telling her in English not to be concerned but to sleep. Elizabeth could not close her eyes. The harder she tried, the more she saw.

She saw a tiny 'L' chiselled neatly into the red brickwork then scuffs and scars of abuse. She saw the coarse weave of her wicker basket, edged with pig's hide and strengthened with iron. She saw black links of chain connecting her to another basket, then, turning her head, the neon grin of Blueskin as he sat on top of his train. Three sad clangs of a bell later, iron wheels rolled them across a green-tiled floor. Elizabeth was now a parcel.

In a whirring of electric motors, the green train ran in a slow arc around the edge of a large circular room. All the world's cripples dipped their hands into the baskets. They were secluded here, locked away in their own dark hall for three-quarters of their lives. They had made tables and chairs from packing cases or renovated pieces of broken furniture. And the women had knitted table-cloths and cushions and filled chipped vases with damaged plastic flowers. The train brought them work to do—parcels for sorting, checking and repairing. When the work was complete, conveyor belts swept the parcels away and the train brought refilled baskets.

Lucy Shoe sat alone writing labels to places far off across the seas. Her pretty face was wearing away in the shadows, but when she saw Elizabeth, she smiled and her hair grew longer and prettier. Taking Elizabeth out of the basket she sat her up like a doll. Lucy was seated at a polished desk out of which grew a violin and a bow. Lucy frowned as she looked at a list and wrote 'school' on a label. Elizabeth told her that she had come only to find her father's life and she had lost her way. Lucy said that no one knew the way because the rooms were so big and so many. But she crossed out the word 'school' and wrote the word 'father' on it instead, tying the label to the girl's wrist.

Elizabeth left Lucy, secretly tucking flowers inside parcels, and drifted down this passage and that until she came to four enormous lifts in a row. They each had great metal jaws which sighed each time they opened for loading freight. As Elizabeth stared the lifts formed into four mouths, and each spoke one word at a time from left to right. Seeing the label still attached to her wrist, they said to **her**:

'We—'

'Know—'

'Your—'

'Father—' Then they all sighed, respectively.

'Please,' implored Elizabeth, 'if that's true, will one of you take me to him?'

'Fine!' said the first.

'Surely!' said the second.

'Directly!' said the third.

'Yes!' said the fourth.

Elizabeth was so confused. Only one lift could take her and she wished she had Colpoesne with her to help her. 'I cannot go with you all,' she said. 'Which one is it to be?'

'Only—'

'You—'

'Can—'

'Decide—' said the lifts in turn.

Elizabeth thought, and thought hard. In the end she decided that perhaps only one of them really did know her father and the others were telling tales. Who knew where she might end up if she took the wrong lift. She tried to look as stern as she could and said in a firm, even voice, 'I think only one of you is telling the truth!' All the mouths sighed as if they had been caught out.

'You—'

'Are—'

'Quite—'

'Correct!'

'Which one—which one?' Elizabeth shouted more to herself than to anyone. As she looked up again, an arc of familiar faces surrounded her. They belonged to her father's friends: Lucy Shoe, Patch, Bowback and Blueskin, and they were urging her to answer and to answer quickly, otherwise the mouths would close and would never open to her again and she would not be able to go on.

'But if you should choose the wrong one,' whispered Bowback, 'you will be caught!'

So Elizabeth thought and thought hard. Presently, she decided that the best way to choose the lift which told the truth was to ask a riddle to which there was only one correct answer which would be one word in length. Soon, she had thought up a suitable rhyme. She turned to the impatient lifts and gave them her riddle:

> 'If you know my father,
> If he's stood on your floor,
> How many legs has he—
> Two, three or four?'

'That's—'
'Not—'
'Fair!' cried three of the lifts. The fourth said nothing.
'And why isn't it?' asked Elizabeth.
'Only—'
'Three—'
'Guesses!' protested the three.
'We—'
'Are—'
'Four!' Again, the fourth lift remained silent, but this time smiled.

'In that case,' said Elizabeth, 'I would hurry if I were you, in case you miss your chance. I will give you the riddle again, just to show that I am not afraid to help you.'

> 'If you know my father,
> If he's stood on your floor,
> How many legs has he—
> Two, three or four?'

'Four!' cried the first lift. Elizabeth knew why he chose this number; he had counted two artificial legs and two walking sticks.

'Three!' roared the second lift. This number had been chosen because as Elizabeth had two legs and a walking stick, then her father must have the same.

'Two!' cried the third lift, louder than the others. Even though no real choice remained for him, he felt certain his answer was correct. The others had been silly counting sticks as legs. Her father, like any person, must have two legs.

The fourth lift could not answer, the chances having been used up. But even so, the lift smiled a broader smile. Elizabeth turned to the first three. 'Thank you all,' she said, 'but the answers you gave me were quite wrong and the lift which remained silent is the one I choose.' The first three scowled.

'Why—'
'Choose—'
'Him!' they protested.
'He—'
'Said—'
'Nothing!'
'And that is the answer. If you really knew my father, then you would know that he hasn't any real legs at all. No more than I!'

Lucy Shoe, Patch, Bowback and Blueskin all applauded her, and the three mouths who had given the wrong answers in their haste to catch her hissed, booed and cursed her. As she approached the fourth, smiling mouth Elizabeth said, 'Please help me to find my father's life which is trapped somewhere in this place.' The mouth turned back into the steel jaws of a freight lift and opened up to accept her.

The inside of the lift was like a wood-panelled room and from the ceiling hung a single small lamp which changed immediately into the moon of the undercave. Dark shadows seemed to flutter across her eyes, trying to steal away the sketch of the lift's interior. There were noises, too, which did not seem to fit in—scratchings and scufflings. She turned around and saw a miniature man scratching away at the lift's controls. He looked at her and smiled. Soon the lift's controls were bright brass, like pictures of ship's instruments she had once seen. And with that thought she would have easily been at sea—had she not woken up with a start.

II

For a few moments, Elizabeth could not remember where, or even who she was. Then the memory returned all too clearly in that awful stillness. She remembered leaving the sunlight behind as she had made her pledge to find the Forgotten Room. She remembered making the marks of decision with her stick and all she had met and suffered on the long journey since that time. Now she was as cold as cold—a part of the undercave and everything in it. Elizabeth shivered, uncontrollably. The damp throne had taken her over, turning every fibre of her dress to mildew and every strand of her hair to autumn cobwebs while she had been asleep. No matter how hard she rubbed the numbed flesh of her arms, even in the poor light they appeared to grow bluer and bluer.

She clutched her satchel for comfort, but when she felt around for her stick she found it had fallen. Her hands searched the insides of the bag and, having found the battery torch at last, her slow fingers fought to locate and operate the small button. As before, unless directed into her eyes, the torch gave out almost no light at all. But what little light there was slipped like a phantom over the rubble around her feet. Very soon, the beam heaved itself over a dark, globular mass lying motionless a couple of feet from where she sat.

Elizabeth's heart all but stopped beating. Panic, fear and anger swooped over her again. She let out a piercing scream which seemed to shatter the darkness into tiny fragments, waving her arms and stamping her feet at the same time. Pressing hard back against the wall, she was able to raise herself to full height.

'Go away!' she yelled, several times. But nothing happened. Nothing leapt out from the dark at her and in the end, she was left perspiring and breathless. Whimpering, but with ears cocked to catch the slightest sound, she began to slide back to her former position. Torch and satchel had tumbled to the floor. Now she needed to find all her belongings. Strangely enough, the first thing she recovered was her stick. Once grasped in her hand again, she struck it against the ground with unmistakable firmness. Any creature of the dark near by would certainly know the power such a staff could wield from the noise it made, and be sent scampering back from whence it came. Confidence and courage rapidly returned once her satchel and torch were back in her hands.

With her stick held towards the area where the threatening shape had first been sighted, Elizabeth concentrated every speck of torchlight in that region. The shape was still there; the noise had not frightened it away. The fresh sight of the bulky creature (for she now considered every unexplained shape in animal terms) so close to her feet startled her anew. This time, though, she did not panic, but hissed dark, ominous words after it. Still, the creature did not respond.

Suddenly, Elizabeth laughed. All at once, the shape had become unmistakable. Her eyes saw with true perspective, and all else faded to become part of the shadowed background. She felt both exuberant and triumphant as she welcomed to her heart the sight of Colpoesne D again. She could almost feel his magic, comforting glow radiating towards her as she shortened the small distance between them. Leaning heavily on her stick Elizabeth was able to snatch him up from his cruel bed and cradle him in her arms. Though she still shivered in fits, happiness burned like a brazier inside her with invisible light that filled every corner of the undercave.

Colpoesne had suffered during his mysterious disappearance. His fat, soft body was covered in scuff marks as if he had been dragged, and there was a tear near to the shoulder of his left arm. Elizabeth knew her champion doll must have put up quite a fight against the shadow creatures. And he had won in the end, for how else could he have found his way back to her side? Clasping his cuddly mass to her breast, Elizabeth felt entirely renewed in spirit, but her whole body now began to shake as the chills returned and crept upwards from the steel of her legs. Yet the air about her neck and face seemed to grow thick and humid.

Elizabeth carefully looped the satchel strap over her shoulder. The torch had been placed safely inside, along with most of Colpoesne whose eyes now peered over the brim. She began a journey to take her deeper into the dark recesses of the undercave.

The smoky gloom surrounding her seemed to thicken. Elizabeth threaded an arm around a thick metal pillar for support. It rose from the ground like a tree spreading overhead into a dense canopy of blackness. She seemed to be swaying. Sickness and tiredness surged through her head. Through her eyes vagaries of shade and colour disappeared; all light polarized into white and black, like good and evil. With one movement of her reeling head she saw a band of light hanging vertically upon a black wall. Hypnotized, she stared at the narrow band and, through staring, she came to see a fragile line of islets connecting one dark region to the other. They gradually took shape until they became recognizable letters of the alphabet.

Elizabeth's cold lips stumbled over the sounds. She tried and tried again to break through the numbness. When the word became airborne at last, it was not until long seconds afterwards that the significance blossomed within her. She laughed aloud.

Excitement brought a sudden wave of warmth surging back as she repeated the word over and over again with so much joy that its literal sense grew meaningless.

'Misery!'

At last, she had found the Misery Door which had figured so constantly in her dreams.

I

Somehow, in his anger, Sam had taken a wrong turning and got himself lost in a maze of half-dead streets. Suddenly he found himself driving past the edge of an area of earthworks. It was like a breath of air in the cramped neighbourhood. He studied the barrenness of the scene; earthmovers had once roamed the site like ponderous dinosaurs. Their feet had smashed the ancient paving slabs while their bellies had fed on the minor hills.

Dusty relics of forgotten dwellings looked like decaying, hollow teeth. All that remained of them were flaps of someone's choice in wallpaper which had withstood the weather for years. Step and broken gutter alike had mouldered into a delicacy of neglect; weeds had burrowed into window-sill and where glass panes still existed, they stared out across the street with their dull dead eyes. How long destruction had hovered over the area could be gauged by the utter bleakness—a couple of acres caught in the limbo of a planning decision, where every measure had been halted and every new plan shelved.

The lorry came to a halt—as slowly a smile spread over Sam's face. An idea was on the verge of finality. He noticed a perimeter fence half masking an old, deep excavation in a corner, and in that he saw a dumping ground for the rubbish he had been lumbered with. The site spread beneath him like a green hollow.

Within this lush cavity, time had really taken hold. Clawing into a thin carpet of wind-blown dust, natural flora had fought desperate battles to cover over the nakedness of man-made stone. Weeds like purple-flowered Christmas trees grew atop the stubs of walls, or speckled the sad grey concrete with promises of gold and silver. Plots of tall, flowerless nettles swathed the hollow for its whole length as an unchecked forest. Around its well-worn edges spikes of old prams, cycles and washing machines lay half-submerged in green.

The sparrows, drab from the city's fumes, sped in spectacular freedom to this green paradise. In little clouds of dusty grey they frothed around the taller shrubs, chirping as noisily as gangs of children.

An odd twinge of nostalgia caught Sam as he gazed across the space. In a series of clipped memories, he thought of places he had seen on his travels; of wild flowers overthrowing all traces of civilization. It was a second of time caught in a second—an involuntary emotion. Sam threw it all aside by simply turning his head.

The truck backed up easily to the fence. Sam had kicked away a rotting post and a panel of rusty, corrugated iron which slid noisily down the bank, scarring the soil as it fell. A few seconds later, fluid was pumped into the lorry's hydraulics and the contents of the back spilled down into the hollow. Sam offended no one with the noise he made; murder could have been committed and no one would have been any the wiser. The spot was so miraculously desolate.

Sam went to the edge of the bank and looked down upon his mess with the curiosity of a child. A pinkish dust had arisen from the brick and plaster heap, and laths protruded like broken bones. Sam felt well satisfied, looking out again over the vastness of the site. A final thought dominated his mind: for as long as Winston wanted to play, Sam could now take it.

II

Two hours had gone by. Winston stood with Holly at the edge of the bank. Beneath them, smothering nettles and bindweed, loomed a small dirty mountain.

'He ought to be made to come back,' began Holly. A different kind of anger pumped through the West Indian's veins. The whole childish act had been completely unnecessary. Holly tried again. 'Why didn't you hang on to him when he returned? He should have been made to come back here himself, instead of him telling us to.'

'You'd better get used to the fact that he's gone, Mr Holly.'

The place seemed deserted. A faint hum of traffic could just be heard from a road a couple of blocks away. All appeared to be reasonably fit for a clandestine operation.

Winston removed the two chain cotter pins from the truck's tailboard and allowed it to swing down freely. The bare interior of the truck gleamed like the scraped bowl of a beggar. It also seemed to wear a sickly smile. Holly hated it from the start, for the first thing to meet his eyes was the sight of a shovel. The foreman seized it with controlled malice, but his temper had cooled by the time he turned to Holly.

'Mr Holly, would you be so kind as to climb down into that pit and remove the rubbish?'

Holly stared at him in a daze, even though he had known what was coming. He had seen it all and protested every inch of its progress. There was nothing he could do. As if he had not already worked out the answer, he asked, 'What am I to do with it, after I have climbed down into that choking filth?'

'You are to shovel it into the back of the lorry.'

'But it will take me hours! It must be late by now; I'll never get it finished on time by myself.'

Winston looked at his chrome-plated wristwatch. He pondered for a while over certain calculations. 'I'll pick you up at half past five,' he said eventually. 'That should give you time enough.' He handed the shovel firmly to Holly. The Irishman hesitated and cowered a little. To one side of him stood a hard, black mountain; beneath him, a soft alabaster one. Holly's mind reached its conclusion and he slid down into the thick, dusty pile of rubbish.

'Hey!' Holly called out in annoyance, looking up. 'I can't reach the truck from here!'

After deciding the complaint was a reasonable one, the truck's yawning hod being a few feet from the edge of the bank, Winston disappeared. Holly mouthed many obscenities after him. It was always the little, thin men who suffered the most in his world, who always acted as the butt for life's tiresome pranks. These men were squashed like mosquitoes in the chapters of every event, immobilized, robbed of further purpose in the world. As Holly had often remarked it was a wonder they ever survived to draw breath. But survive they did. What Holly longed to see was a world turned upside down, where he would be on top, and those people like Samuel Packet could no longer leave their rubbish lying about for the Hollys of this world to clean up. It was a sober wish, yet it had been hatched between visions of

cramming the supercilious Packet's mouth with shovels of cal-
careous filth.

Long after the foreman had left, his words still buzzed in
Holly's head: 'And if a policeman asks, tell him you dumped it
by mistake.' For the man whose whole life had been a lie, this
one was particularly bitter. Why should he use his polished
skills for the sake of a deserter—and a miserable, tight-fisted one
at that? Holly snatched up the shovel for the fourth time and bit
it deep into the mountain's peak. Embedded rocks rang on the
blade. Holly flung the small load upwards and a fine, acrid
powder enveloped him. The acute disadvantages of the job became
apparent immediately. Apart from the gentle rain of putrid dust
smothering every pore in his flesh, the heavier lumps of plaster
and brick fell short of their target. Soon, the pavement became
littered with wood, stone and paper and the horizontal lines of
the tailboard grew drifts of dingy snow.

All proceedings came to an abrupt halt with a tremendous
shout of frustration. Holly did not care how much he ranted and
raved; nobody could hear him. He was in a desert in the heart of
the city. He could drop dead with heat or exhaustion and no one
would ever know, let alone care. All they would find of him
would be a pile of rags and bones, lying on a dust heap. The
thought shocked him so much that he just had to sit down and
think.

The sight of his surroundings became hypnotic in the strong
warmth of the afternoon sun. Holly settled back on a soft soil
carpet and allowed himself to be taken. It was one of those timeless yawns which fused each gurgle of the human organism with
the vibrations of earth itself. Holly's eyes were almost closed.
A bright, spangled light squeezed between blood-red eyelids and
a sneeze began a jig in the roots of his nose. Life was so peaceful
down here, he thought.

His eyelids relaxed and had almost fluttered to a close when,
suddenly, a sharp, urgent message crashed onto his retina.

He sat bolt upright, as if stung, then sprang to his feet, his
whole being focused on some tiny point in the swathes of nettle-
green. It had been unmistakable. He had seen the glint of something precious; something incongruous in this landscape of
worthless waste. He had seen something made of gold.

In a moment Holly scaled the furrowed bank and stood in the

gap of the fence. But the gilded fairy disappeared. Holly slithered down again, placing his head in as near the same position as he could remember. His efforts were at once rewarded by the sight of a fiery pinpoint of golden liquid forcing its beams through a forest of nettle stems. Very slowly, he raised his head, and very slowly, the gleam dulled as if a growing thickness of cloud obscured it, until it disappeared altogether.

Holly had the instinctive eyes of a scavenger magpie. He could detect in one blink any type of metal or shiny object by the way it reflected sunlight. Glass-dazzle could not shake off its rainbow corona, chrome was a white mirror, copper was brown; brass soon dulled to the most sombre of yellows—only gold moved with the heat of the sun. Excitement shook his ragged frame. What precious object could it be, he wondered, a locket or a ring? Treasures of far greater value had been found in less likely places.

The labourer began to dream of wealth in an uncontrollable manner. Visions of retrieving a crock of gold solidified into newspaper pictures, and he grinned in them all with his dog-toothed leer. He could almost read the headlines.

The area in which the golden object had been sighted was directly in line with a crooked chimney belonging to a house on the far horizon. It was along this sighting that Holly crashed his way over the loose, tangled ground, through a perimeter sea of rosebay willowherb. The gossamer down of the tall flowers swirled in a dance in his wake. Bees and silver moths tumbled out of his way. Sparrows, too, dancing on the heads of wild parsley escaped to the corrugated fencing where they seized the metal in their claws with anger. Although the traps which nature sets for trespassers could not hold him, those of mankind did a better job. Wire and old bedsprings caught round his ankles, frames and buckets bit into his shins and water-logged paint pots drenched his shoes. And Holly cursed the whole breed of wastemakers with every smash of his shovel.

He soon reached a small mound and stood on its crest like an explorer. Tiny overgrown footpaths ran hither and thither, either side and back in the direction from whence he had come, but none ventured forward through the unkempt nettle forest facing him. This only filled him with greater delight. Whatever treasure lay in the interior must have remained undisturbed for ages. Bubbling with excitement he set about smashing his way towards his goal and in no time at all he had reached the centre and stood on the edge of a small clearing. As naked as if it had been dropped from the sky only seconds before, there rested a small circlet of gold —a wristwatch. A fire of excitement burned in Holly's blood.

12

August considered what he should do next. He closed the glass door of the sandwich display with a thick forefinger. Everything had been higgledy-piggledy even before the telephone call, and now.... Two youths were sitting at a table by a wall, eating spaghetti. They wore green school blazers and open-necked shirts and they had only just started the meals they had paid for.

The lazy part of the afternoon would soon be over. It was well after four o'clock. There would be more school-children, a scattering of workers finishing their shifts and the oddbods from the demolition sites. They would all bustle into his cafe and want serving. How could he escape, with no wife or children to look after things for him?

The sudden sight of the crudely inscribed piece of paper which Tony had given him just a few hours before almost brought tears to the Latvian's eyes. He then remembered the conversation which had taken place between himself and Mr Morgan. It was almost as if the words he had spoken had been the harbingers of disaster—as if by uttering them he had been responsible for the whole bloody tragedy.

August had barely taken in the news of Tony's death, when a telephone call brought him other alarming tidings: Elizabeth had been missing from school all day. The call came from the local police station. They were sending someone round to see him. Someone had to break the news to Mr Morgan and they thought it might be better coming from a friend. The thought of him having to wait for a policeman just to answer a lot of stupid questions annoyed him. They seemed to know everything, anyway. Elizabeth had waited for the school bus that morning with another child of the district. She had then told the girl that she had to visit a special friend and that she would not be able to go to school. She had also asked the girl not to tell anyone, but eventually the truth had come out. Elizabeth had played truant before.

August thought of the cripple already suffering through the sudden loss of a very special comrade, he then thought of having to inflict on him the news of his missing daughter. He thought how Mr Morgan would be, at that very moment, crouched silently in his parlour with an old grey stare in his eyes while a nervous policeman tried to console him with tea. What the man really needed was the solid comfort of his friends.

The two youths laughed after a schoolboy joke in a very lewd manner. The exact words had not reached August but the noise brought him to his senses. He had started to ease his girth through the counter's small hatch with the full intention of asking the boys to leave, even if it meant giving them their money back, when a small bandy-legged creature fashioned itself in the doorway. It drew immediate attention.

'I'm about to close!' August roared. The two youths looked at him astonished and began making noises of protest.

'Oh, that's all right,' said the newcomer, hopping in. 'It's just fags I want.' He trotted right past the spaghetti-eaters. August frowned at this scruffy heap of rags approaching him with a clumping of oversized shoes.

'Ten Woodies, please,' requested a thin, whiny voice. 'Oh yes, and a box of matches.' While August slowly and silently reached onto the shelves behind he never took his eyes off him for a second. He really could not stand, let alone trust, smelly, filthy gang-men. Normally he would not let them into his shop, but over the recent months he had had to lower his standards. He was going through a bad patch financially.

'What a scorcher—eh, friend? What an absolute day it's been!' As Holly's fingers fretted over the only money he had, they also came into contact with his treasure. It was wrapped in the gritty folds of an ancient nose-rag. As he put his money on the counter, his face lit up suddenly.

''Er, any chance of a cup of tea?'

'I told you. I'm closing.'

Holly shot a foxy glance at the two seated customers and then returned, relieved that the lads still had a long way to go.

'I know that. Just a quicky is all I want—to clear me throat. It's blocked with dust and dry as grass. Shan't stay any longer than these others, now—I promise.'

August thought for a brief moment. Realizing that there was at least a shred of reasoning in what the thin Irishman had said, he granted his wish. For the second time Holly was relieved. He hastily lit one of his cigarettes and let out a long sigh of smoke.

Something in the way the labourer took his slopping cup of tea into the remotest corner made August even more suspicious of him. The cafe-owner had a strong intuition about strangers which he often acted upon. The spaghetti youths also took stock of the nut-brown figure in the corner and used him as material for their continued amusement, as they crammed more boiling pasta into their mouths.

Holly ignored them all and behaved himself for at least a quarter cupful of tea. Soon the proprietor was busying himself wrapping sandwiches in foil and putting small bottled drinks into a cool cabinet. The youths raced each other at sucking-up spaghetti.

When Holly had stumbled into the small clearing in the centre of the over-grown excavation, he had seized upon the small bracelet with febrile relish. The tiny, sun-warmed wristwatch still ticked away its minute hours. Although he had been disappointed at first, finding it to be the only treasure casually lying around, he soon became overjoyed as he caught sight of hallmarks hammered into the wristband. It was a worthy find. He then noticed a few scuff marks around what appeared to be an opening in the ground. Instinctively, he stopped everything he was doing and checked to see if he was still alone. Finding the skyline to be clear, he dropped to his knees and peered cautiously into the fissure. Long before his eyes had time to adjust to the gloom, he heard the definite, though distant, sound of something within. It was a noise like the sharp crack of brick meeting brick. The sound registered well.

Not bothering to wonder how, why or what, Holly slipped his prize into a pocket and hastily made his way from the noise, the hole and the clearing. From the sanctuary of the bank by the small, dingy mountain, a half-idea formed in Holly's mind. The noise that had frightened him had probably been caused by falling masonry. Holly looked carefully at the half-submerged lines of the hollow with its broken walls and buttresses. It suddenly occurred to him that rooms might exist beneath his very feet; that a whole sub-basement existed beneath him. What if he had been prancing about on a thin shell covering a honeycomb of chambers? The thought sent shivers down his spine. He focused his attention on the child's wristwatch, then he scrambled up the bank with it.

'This place is bloody dangerous,' he whispered, 'even for kids!'

As quickly as the idea of the sub-basement had formed, it disappeared to be replaced by a much more basic logic pattern. The watch told the time: the time said that he had less than an hour in which to dispose of the find and to make it look to Winston as though some work at least had been attempted.

To find a back-street, cash exchange shop was what had brought Holly into Thorn Street. As yet, he had not even given himself time off to celebrate his good fortune. Furthermore, he had gone for several hours since smoking the last clipping he possessed. So, when he stumbled across August's Eat, he went in.

With acrid cigarette smoke trailing over his moist brow, Holly finally gave way to an urge to see the watch again. His brain was working fast, spinning the first skeins to fabricate a sales story. He flicked the cafe's other occupants a darting glance from the tops of his eyes and decided that things looked safe enough. Holly hauled the filthy rag from his jacket pocket and shook the contents out onto the seat beside him. He quickly looked up again. The thick-set proprietor had left his counter and was making his way across the red linoleum to the open door. August changed the sign to read 'closed' and trapped a hastily scrawled note behind the curtain.

It read: 'Business as usual—tomorrow.'

When he closed the door the room grew a fraction darker. Returning, August cleared away the winner's plate in the spaghetti competition. By the time he had taken it to the counter the second youth had finished. The lads belched and slowly got to their feet with much chair-scraping and sniggering then made for the exit. The loser in the competition turned to August when he reached the door.

'Thanks for the grub—you miserable old sod!' he yelled and in a flash both he and his mate were halfway down the street. August said nothing in return, neither did he move—he just stood blinking, like a great ponderous bear. Slowly then, he walked to the table to collect the other crocks and was about to go back

114

to the counter once more when he remembered Holly, wedged almost unseen in the furthest corner.

Holly could not tell whether the cafe-owner was intending to come his way or not because as August reached each table in his path, he swatted crumbs and picked up pieces of paper from the top and upturned the chairs. The big man was only a table away when Holly decided he had better leave. He clipped the remainder of his second cigarette and dropped it into his sagging top-pocket then, as the left hand felt for the handkerchief and watch, the right brought the dregs of his tea to his lips. He took a sip and replaced the cup.

'Nice drop of tea, that. Very refreshing!'

Suddenly, disaster broke. The watch tumbled out of its dirty hammock onto the floor, to rest practically at August's feet. Holly was momentarily petrified. The Latvian scooped up the tiny trinket in his big paw. He recognized it instantly; it was the one he had given to Elizabeth for a Christmas present. There was no mistaking it because the bracelet had been his own. His heart slowly began to gather speed as he glared at the wretch he had cornered.

'Sit down!' August hissed.

13

I

Elizabeth's fever had abated for a while. Overjoyed with her find, happiness suppressed all else. She hugged fat Colpoesne to her chest; she wanted to laugh, cry and sing all at the same time. For since she had first entered the undercave, and in all the time it had taken for her to reach this spot, the finding of the Misery Door was the first real evidence that her dreams were something more than ordinary.

A long time before (she had forgotten precisely when) in the after-teatime of one Sunday evening, Uncle Tony Lemon had been discussing the virtue of words. He and her father had sat at the table while she had crawled unseen beneath it to draw pictures on pieces of cardboard. Between them they talked of words in books and words in newspapers to which she paid hardly any attention at all. But when they spoke of a word on a door, she stopped sketching so she could listen more intently. That word had been 'Misery'.

It had lingered ever since, emblazoned on doors throughout her dreams and almost always on the same door—the door which hid the Forgotten Room, as it had once been called by her father and henceforth echoed in her imagination.

In the shadows of the cavern, Elizabeth could well imagine her father labouring; she could almost count the cripples and the deformed who had been pushed away, out of sight of shop customers, like a servile race apart, shut away in their cells of brick and iron. She hated for her father, as he must have hated in his time, turning into an island in this dead place, this skeletal place of darkness, now filled with tiny echoes.

Why, she wondered, did they let a despicable, softlegged youth called Youngbeard bring them even greater hardship? She hammered her thoughts long and loud upon the Misery Door and they grew in such speed and heaviness that the resounding din frightened her.

Unbeknown to Elizabeth, a heavy concrete post was precariously balanced against the edge of the door. Her first blows shook free the dust and grit until her more emphatic hammering caused the pillar's whole weight to come tumbling down. Falling sideways at first, the concrete crashed against the door, sliding it open before smiting the ground a few inches from where Elizabeth stood. The shock of the impact shot straight through her legs and spine.

Elizabeth stood petrified and a dark shadow passed over her whole body. She felt cold then hot, then cold again. Sickness revolved in her stomach and turned her limbs to jelly. Feeling herself falling, she stretched a hand forward for support. Only then did she realize, as she struggled to correct her balance, that the door had been moved sideways.

A secluded blackness had opened up in front of her; it seemed to reach out and touch her wavering hand; it seemed to draw her forward. A smell of dust filled her nostrils, a dank smell of soot and disused wardrobes, tumbling out in grateful billows from the unsealed chamber. But the air had a sensuous quality too, as if blessed by earth-magic; and all the powers came into alignment conjuring up a meaning which spoke in whispered words, 'The Forgotten Room—the Forgotten Room.'

Elizabeth was a child of endurance, who, lacking the agility of other children, no more knew how to run to escape her fears than she knew how to leap into a frenzied attack. Her misfortune of being born different was not bound to the region of her lower legs, but imbued her whole spirit. As the world raged about her, she was immobile, an island bred within an island breed. All strengths of waves had crashed against her—yet she had withstood and she had endured.

Her father, too, was an island fastened deeply in her nearest horizon like an iron nail in fabric. There had once been a beautiful bird which had flown between them, who had grown so tired, she had fallen into the sea and been washed away. So the distance between father and child seemed vast and empty and messages were reduced to obscure signals. Yet love was always there; Elizabeth had felt it beneath the beds of sand. It was there, but still austere and remote.

By as little as islands can move, be it less than one fraction of an inch a year, Elizabeth stretched out towards her father to love him better and to cure the misery of his loneliness since his island bird had departed.

The shadow seeped out of the darkness allowing the merest film of thinnest globe-light to outline the chamber before her. The edifice was as forgotten as a room could be, so forgotten that even slothful time, who breathed through every other corner of the undercave, had passed this chamber by. It had been sealed from drifts of air which had coated all else with maps of dust. The floor was naked and pale, without the slightest wart of rock-chip or pebble.

Elizabeth began to notice other things, too, items of furniture whose forms were outlined by the dull glimmer of globe-light. She took a step forward, and almost tripped over the unseen runnels of the iron door. With great deliberation and concentrated effort, the threshold was traversed and she stood on a firm, level floor—the first since entering the undercave earlier that day. She had arrived, triumphant. She was filled by a passion so elementary, her whole body felt weakened in its presence. She had conquered! Elizabeth held the doll, Colpoesne D, straight out in front of her like an emblem of power. Her body shook with uncontrollable emotion and strange, pagan noises escaped from her throat:

'Hit-ur! Zananamma!'

Elizabeth creaked forward on her legs of iron and leather until she reached the furthest wall where she turned in almost total darkness to face the way she had come. The stillness was oppressive. She delved in her bag for the tiny torch again. Though its light was feeble, it helped her to identify some furniture silhouetted against the grey panel of the doorway. She recognized the shape of a small wooden table and the grey bones of a hard-backed chair. There was a dresser or a chest-of-drawers pushed at a peculiar angle against the wall with its back facing outwards. By the side of the dresser in the remotest right-hand corner of the room was a wooden door. Great variegated patches adorned some of the walls. As the weak torchlight trickled over them, they appeared to be plans and diagrams of other rooms while others looked more like coloured pictures. The more the torch-light revealed to her, the more convinced she was that not just any forgotten room had been found—but *the* Forgotten Room.

II

As the battery torch began to fail again, a great feeling of despondency filled Elizabeth's heart. As far as it was possible, her eyes had already grown accustomed to the perpetual twilight of the undercave. They had opened even wider when she had first entered these nether regions. Now near blindness threatened her. Elizabeth's pupils stretched wider than a cat's as they soaked up every tiny dot of grey floating in the inky blackness. The torch beam became lost like smoke in a breeze, yet before it failed altogether, a small, luminescent wax pillar shone briefly, like a fleeting ghost and then fell back into the shadows on the top of the dresser.

'A candle!' breathed Elizabeth.

Her eyes fixed upon the place like fishhooks in riverweed and through the darkness, she drew herself towards the place on in-visible lines. At last, she seized the candle and smelt it in the darkness as if it were food. It was a candle, sure enough, a fat finger of paraffin wax, about four inches in length. Elizabeth put Colpoesne back into the satchel after she had shown him the find. Afterwards, she allowed her fingers to explore the flat surface. The fleshy parts of her palm collected a thin film of black dust. Her finger-tips shuffled like mice underneath loose leaves of paper, but they failed to find that which she searched for: matches.

They searched the edges of the dresser and felt the rough wood of the back panel facing outermost. Elizabeth edged round to the front. The angle between the wall and the furniture was very acute and she had great difficulty in squeezing herself into the space between. Only one small top drawer remained in place, all others she discovered were missing.

Her right hand drifted down and settled onto a tiny plastic handle. She gently pulled. The compartment slid open a few inches then jammed. Before her again was another small journey into darkness, a rectangular pool of stagnant inkiness. She could not actually see or smell it, but it was there, waiting for her.

The chill was coming again. Dampness was seeping into her finger-tips.

As though to help her search, a small book met her fingers. She pulled it straight out as if it were a small fish, plopped on the bank. She pushed her hand deeper inside the drawer to see what else she could catch. Just as the harsh, wooden edges of the drawer were biting through to the bone of her forearm, her finger-tips prodded something fat and slimy lurking in the bituminous blackness. It was something gross and toadlike—something puffed up.

A chill of horror passed down Elizabeth's spine, as she jerked her hand out of the drawer. Retreating sideways a few steps, her eyes cast around the dark area. She stood listening and clutching the satchel like a shield in front of her body.

'Go away!' she yelled to the spectre. 'I won't hurt you. I promise!'

Only the slightest tremble filled the undercave—all else was wrapped in silence. Nothing stirred from the drawer in that silence. As time slipped by and nothing happened, Elizabeth considered that she might have been too rash with her fears. The more she thought about it, the less fearful the 'creature' seemed, and the more balloon-like and cold the sensation became. She rubbed the bruises on her forearm. A much better idea formed almost at once. She would try to remove the drawer—including its contents—and carry it across to the table. The more she thought, the better the idea seemed, except that she was still uncertain about the thing at the back of the drawer.

Elizabeth struck her stick upon the ground. Her courage was summoned. She took up the torch again and shone it in her face. A thin, watery golden light swilled round the tiny reflector. The batteries were almost totally spent, she thought grimly as she turned the beam in the direction of the gaping drawer. The feeble light of the torch also brought to her the colour of the dilapidated dresser. It was the same unnatural green as Mrs Trewly's pea soup. The thought made her smile inside and confidence returned to her again. Bending over slightly, Elizabeth was able to peep nervously into the slit. Her torch fed its failing light into the abysmal darkness. Suddenly, she saw it, a dull glass-like sheen reflecting from the furthermost corner. To her intense delight, the object bore no resemblance to anything animal. As she blew at it, nothing sprang around to meet her on four tiny legs, nothing snarled at her with a toothy grin. For the object turned out to be nothing more harmful than a bulging plastic bag. She breathed an extraordinarily long sigh of relief. She caught the small book in the torchlight, too. It smouldered with a deep glowing red. Thoughtfully, she returned it to the drawer, then squeezed out the light of the fire-fly torch. With a little effort, she was able slowly to edge the compartment from its frame until she had it in her hands.

The drawer was quite heavy and coupled with the encumbrance of both stick and satchel, she had some difficulty in ferrying it to the table in darkness. Like a blind person, Elizabeth felt the separate outlines of table and chair and dragged them apart. One was as sturdy as an iron crate: the bones of the chair had no breaks or fractures, no dislocated joints. Only the table wobbled under the burden of the drawer.

III

Elizabeth's fingers, ever-numbed by the chilled dampness hanging everywhere, strayed into the dusky hold. She picked up the small book and, although its true colour slept, the cover seemed to smoulder in her hands. Next she removed stiff, slender rods from the drawer, which she guessed to be pens or pencils and then a few, mildewed sheets of writing paper. Finally she took out the sealed plastic bag. The bag rolled upon its captive air and as it fell over to one side, rattled out a brief but obvious message.

'At last!' Elizabeth said to the room. 'Matches!' A rubber band had welded itself in sticky coils around the bag's neck and resolutely clung there like the death grip of a snake. The coils snapped and the bag gratefully exhaled, as if it had been holding its breath for a thousand years. Secrets spilled unseen into the black air, too complex in their ciphers for Elizabeth ever to understand, so all that remained, to tease her nostrils, was the scent of age. It was a smell of menthol and eucalyptus which touched her heart like a fire-brand—the smell of her own father. A box of his matches tumbled onto the table together with a small tin and a variety of other objects. After that there was silence.

Elizabeth sat motionless for several minutes, visions burning brightly behind her blank eyes, then sweeping away like sea-foam. Her mind was in a state of confusion. She felt both exuberant and guilty, as if she had stolen something God-given, and then something closer and more awful—as if she had picked her father's pocket.

She opened the cardboard box and match-sticks fell out onto the table. A half-second later, there was a tiny blaze of light which settled into a single tear-drop of fire. Elizabeth laid Colpoesne on the farthest edge of the table-top, so that he half-rested against the side of the drawer, and then quickly, before the flame grew too close to her finger-tips, she picked up the candle and lit it. The room drew back its curtains and became a dancing box of shadows.

Elizabeth's fingers glowed blood-red, cupping and absorbing the warmth from the single flame. How good the sensation! Yet, in this new world of light, all softness had perished. The sights which confronted her now were raggy and haggard, replacing fancy with fact; subtlety with starkness. It saddened Elizabeth a little to see the room looking so drab and unspecial —even though she was certain it was *the* room. The grey walls, floor and ceiling were less inviting to the eyes of a child who had imagined reds, yellows and blues in the darkness. Even the pictures had lost their fascination now she could see what they were—pictures of ladies without clothes, pointing their breasts towards her. They were bad ladies to Elizabeth and she did not like to see them in her room. For a moment or two she fought with her temper.

The candle wobbled on the table and nearly fell right over. Elizabeth played with the hot wax for a while, letting it drip, onto the raw woodwork. Black candle smoke oiled its way to the ceiling as a flame danced over a reflecting pool. Light twitched around the room like a butterfly, while Elizabeth stirred, sighing deeply, thinking what to do next.

First, she opened the small tin. A new aroma immediately sprang into the air, more pungent than menthol, yet strangely related. It was the rich, fruity smell of tobacco. Its perfume was so strong that it reached the girl's stomach where it caused hollow rumblings. Although she did not care much for the smell, she let free the tobacco's spirit to fill the room as if the gesture would bring her more warmth and light. At that time, it was to her like laying a soft, woollen rug over a cold stone floor or putting up floral curtains to remove the bleak stare from windows.

The next object she took from the bag was a complex bundle of rags and thread wound around a cardboard tube. She twizzled it between the fingers of both hands in front of the flame. She gradually recognized it for what it was—a small sewing kit built up of every conceivable colour and thickness of thread, bound tightly round patches of cloth, festooned with buttons and lanced by pins and needles. It was undeniably a man's contraption, made up for a man's use. She found a tiny pair of nail-scissors, too, in the bottom of the drawer. The blades had rusted into a thin, crocodile grin.

Elizabeth treated each find with great respect, placing them side by side to await such time as she could inspect them more thoroughly.

A gleam of metal caught her eye. A smooth, rectangular surface seemed choked by its own shadows. She reached for it, touched it, and plucked it from the bag. It was a worn cigarette-case made of brass with just a trace of chromium clinging to the edges. Elizabeth took it up as if it were an oyster. Her thin, grubby finger-nails bit into its seams and, without warning, the case flew open and clattered onto the table. The cigarette-less wallet rocked uneasily upon its spine and slowly turned to face her. The oyster had a pearl, too, trapped behind a silken band. The pearl shone with blue and white opacity. As the swim of faded tones focused, so another pearl formed and hung quivering in candle-light on the rim of Elizabeth's eye. She sat stunned and motionless.

She took out the tiny, faded photograph of her mother, mumbling her name into the shadows of the undercave. The beautiful island bird smiled quietly back at her only child, as if to comfort her. The woman was young with dark, wavy hair and gentle eyes. She looked purer in this golden frame than in any other picture Elizabeth had ever seen. It wrenched her heart more strongly than she had ever known. She had almost forgotten just how beautiful and loving her mother had been. She had left a long, long time ago. How could the child forget the softness of her eyes and her tender smile so soon? She could not fight the misery welling up inside her any longer and so she gave in, and let the waves crash over her as she collapsed sobbing across the table, taking the light with her.

The smouldering candle-wick had threaded an acrid stench through the air. It made Elizabeth feel sick and, at the same time, brought her to her senses. She raised her head. Her mother's photograph had sprung upon her like a ghost and had brought with it far too many long-forgotten memories and stories half-told. But now she had all she ever needed to prove that in this room, many years before, in the days of the people on Christmas cards, her very own father had breathed the same air which was threatening to smother her now. She called out the strange and pagan words Colpoesne had taught her and new ones, which he whispered in her ear.

The nightmare was over, the mysteries stumbled home dragging their dark, webbed feet behind them.

IV

Elizabeth opened both eyes as wide as she could. She had been adrift too long—too long away from light and air, too long lost in her own labyrinth. And the fear of being so far from life suddenly eclipsed every new achievement, so that even the discovery of the Forgotten Room now shone with no brighter virtue than a mirror playing back the light at dusk.

Elizabeth's numb hands ploughed across the table after the upset candle.

Colpoesne lay on the table top, staring blindly at the water stains on the ceiling. He became silent as the tomb. Before Elizabeth would restore light to the room, she closed her mother's photograph inside the cigarette case and locked it.

A new age of candlelight spluttered into the chamber. Everything now seemed changed to Elizabeth—the position of objects, the faded and mottled hues. She did not pause to mark them all because the thought was only in passing. Then through the slits of her weary eyes, one colour leapt, bounding across the table-top towards her like an acrobat shouting out the urgency of its signal—the red of fire and of living blood.

Elizabeth again took up the little red book. She had completely forgotten that it had been the first thing found. She fed her fingers along its thin, tubular backbone. She knew instantly. It was a fish, in a cage of fingers, cold and damp and trying to wriggle from her grasp. Elizabeth placed her tongue between her teeth in concentration, then quick as a flash, she split the fish's body open with her fingernails and opened its white flesh outwards. She turned it over to inspect.

'Met here today to discuss plans. V. sad. Can trust no one but Ralph. Others too windy or apathetic. We decide to do it alone. Draw up general plan for water, food and other comforts.'

The tidily written phrases meant little to her until the name Ralph—her father's name. But she knew that it was not his writing. She turned to the beginning of the diary, to the page where the owner's personal details are usually recorded. She found nothing more than the word 'Peace' written across the leaf, bordered by squiggles and dots. But on the inside front cover she found two letters faintly pencilled in the top left-hand corner; they were A and L. Elizabeth could not tell whether they were the owner's initials, or even his complete name. But it did not matter. Everyone had to have a name in her world and so the diary's owner was christened simply 'Al'.

The book was placed flat on its back and closer to the source of light. Elizabeth leaned on her forearms, trying not to think too much of the ache in her stomach, in her neck, elbows and fingers or the soreness of her thighs, and settled down to read. She was a good reader—better, perhaps, than most girls of her age. Each diary page was like a tapestry from which a slow re-enactment began—meetings, discussions, arguments and brief passages which described the quality of life in the undercaves. By chance descriptions and her own intuition, Elizabeth slowly began to recognize certain characters.

They never quite matched up to the dramatic roles they played in her dreams but she could see that Zwolinski, Ross, Bates and Dunn were respectively: Patch, Bowback, Blueskin the dwarf and Greybone. The chronicler had made them pale and in his record they hardly seemed to live at all or to do anything remarkable. But he always wrote about Lucy Shoe with certain tenderness as if he were her secret lover. Perhaps she was the constant thought behind every plan which formed itself over the following months. Perhaps, thought Elizabeth, it was for a secret, undying love for Lucy and her kind that Al was about to place himself in great danger. For it had become apparent to the child, as she read through the days between winter and spring, that Al, the chronicler, was a young man and in no way disabled. And with that conclusion, she drew a sudden, shocked breath.

The one character conspicuous by his absence in the account so far had been the hated Youngbeard. Yet, she realized that, the person who did not appear in any of her dreams was Al, the chronicler. Could it be at all possible that they were one and the same person? But how could it be? Elizabeth placed a hand on Colpoesne's body. Youngbeard was hated, she argued—hated for threatening her father and bringing misery to his friends of the undercaves. It had always been so in her dreams. He destroyed their lives by learning all their secrets, then shouting them in the wrong ears! It had been the same story dream after dream after dream! Yet, the chronicler, Al, seemed to be a loving man who felt for the people, who wanted to help them. How could these two men be the same person?

Perhaps she had missed something, thought Elizabeth. She re-read the pages she had already covered, but when she found she had missed nothing, she journeyed through the late spring and on into the summer.

Elizabeth read as if she were gasping the breath of life—as if she would suffocate without learning the truth and, when the written words ended abruptly, it was too much for her mind to cope with. She fell back in the chair, her mind plummeting to new depths of despair.

Colpoesne caught her in his soft arms. He was no longer a doll small enough to be put into her satchel but now stood even taller than her father. He showed her the events which happened and were not recorded in the little red book, dream-spinning his magic so that the story might be completed and that truth would, at last, be hers.

Like Elizabeth, the youth of the diary had once had a dream. His dream was to do something worthwhile for the world; and the cripple, her father, had grievances which he wanted to air. Although the two men were different, they attracted each other like opposite poles of a magnet. Together they would be strong and inseparable.

By chance, the youth had found work in the basements of this huge department store, in the same areas which Elizabeth had come to re-christen the undercave. While he had worked as a porter he came to make friends with the many labourers working there, underground. He couldn't help noticing that a large number of deformed and crippled workers toiled all day long at mindless, thankless jobs and that all (with the exception of one or two with 'discreet' physical abnormalities) were kept well hidden away from the store's customers.

In this he naturally saw great injustice, yet found that only one of all with whom he worked still retained the full vigour of his pride. That man was Elizabeth's father. The others had quietly resigned themselves to fate over the years and were full of apathy.

Together, this youth and her father, they would bring attention to the cause of the forgotten cripples in such a dramatic way, the message could not possibly go by unheeded. Their united cause was to make society see the disgraceful way it turned its back on the needs of cripples. It was to remove the stigma of being a physical reject from the deformed; it was to take the charity out of their lives and restore them with dignity; it was to bring them all the benefits of living in what should be an enlightened age.

The two men decided that they would seal themselves off from the world in protest. They would weld themselves into an underground room, complete with provisions to see them through a few days. The room they would pick would be one which had been neglected and forgotten inside the store. Ralph knew of such a room; he had watched it slowly fall into disuse over the years until even its sliding iron fire door had become hidden behind old crates and the jetsam of the underworld. It would suit their purposes well. When all the preparations had been made and their plan was ready, the two men would sneak into the forgotten room, seal the door and create the biggest sensation the country had ever known.

The youth masterminded everything, wrote letters ready for

posting to all the national newspapers and television explaining what would happen and the reason for doing it; gradually stocked out the room with the provisions they needed, and worked on a chemical mixture which when ignited from the inside would seal the iron door.

He had wanted everything to work smoothly—for the whole incident to be as professional as possible. What was more, he wanted it to appear sensational—so that it would gain the widest spread of publicity ever. Their one protest would cut across years of fruitless political petitioning. They would make the cripples' cause one for national concern and it would at last be pulled out of the mire of diffidence and apathy.

These beliefs alone gave them courage to endure the difficulties in the months which followed. But all problems were met and settled, until the final, fateful day came around.

Both men had arranged to be working on the latest possible Saturday shift which put them among the few left inside the store. Then the youth stealthily clocked himself and his comrade out, and doubled back to the sub-basement; there he met up with the cripple, and they hid themselves away in the Forgotten Room until the last of the workers had left for the weekend and the security man had completed his rounds.

Colpoesne showed Elizabeth how the youth had pushed the chemical mixture into the cracks of the iron fire door as her father unpacked their personal belongings into the only drawer in a broken-down cabinet. Then disaster struck.

A terrific flash filled the room. Her father turned in horror to see the youth ablaze, his shirt flaming around his chest as he screamed out in pain. The mixture he had been preparing had exploded.

It had all happened so fast. Triumph had turned into tragedy in the blinking of an eye and all they had worked for over the months was shattered in that same terrible moment.

While the youth later recovered in a hospital bed, her father attended a police enquiry accompanied by store representatives. The cripple was not the best person to explain their cause or to give concise reasons why protest should have been attempted in that manner. In fact, everything he said only seemed to make matters worse. The two men only just escaped being accused of arson. Besides, the managers could not accept that the store had ever treated crippled or deformed employees any differently from other workers and stressed that everyone, themselves included, must apply themselves to jobs to which they were best suited. In view of the situation and the injury sustained by one of the men, the managers thought it would do no good to press charges of any kind, but they insisted that the cripple and the youth should be dismissed instantly.

So the cripple and the youth gained nothing; public interest and concern had been swept away by one tragic accident. Although the youth gradually recovered from the burns, he never quite recovered in his mind. The memory of failure was to scar him for the rest of his life. Even though he was a young man, his hair turned a premature grey and his eyes sought the impossible horizon forever.

Colpoesne saw all these things in pictures which were as clear as reality. The fire had given out terrific heat. It had moulded three men into one—Youngbeard had become Al, the diarist, and AL had become the initials for Anthony Lemon, the man whom Elizabeth called Uncle Tony.

August stood with a police officer in a small clearing now cooling
in the late afternoon sun. Holly also stood by, as nervous as a cat.
The policeman pointed to a hole in the ground around the
entrance of which were scuffs and scores in the dirt. He looked
at the Latvian.

'What, down there? A crippled girl down there? You must be
joking!' Hair stood on end at the back of August's neck. He
dropped to his knees and peered into the hole. He was amazed
to see a light burning in the gloom.

'Elizabeth! Elizabeth!'

There was no answer. The police officer waved to a colleague
with a dog on the edge of the hollow. Soon after, both man and
beast joined the group. Elizabeth's watch was handed to the
dog to sniff, but it had spent far too long in Holly's filthy keep
to be of any use. The dog sniffed out Holly. She could smell
fear in the man and gave out such a sudden series of barks that
he nearly shot up the policeman's back. The Alsatian was introduced to the opening in the ground. Immediately, she began to
pull and crawl into the darkness but her handler brought her
fretting and whining back from the hole.

'She can smell something—that's for sure,' the officer said.

'Aye, vermin most likely.'

'Well,' sighed the first, 'let's get to it.' With August, he pulled
away at the loose bricks and earth around the opening. When
they had finished there was just enough space for a thin man to
scrape through.

'There! That should do it, Mac. Give us a shout if you need
help. I'm going to call the station.'

Both dog and handler gradually disappeared. On the edge of
the hollow, a flashy, yellow sports car pulled up and out of it
stepped an immoderately dressed young man.

'I wondered how long it would be before they started to turn up,' the policeman muttered to August.

'Who is it?'

'Bloody newspaper reporter—I'll bet you!'

The Alsatian bitch could smell rats. Mac pulled back on her choker. 'Leave it, girl. Leave it!'

The light puzzled him greatly. Surely, somebody must have been down here recently, he thought. But how an old globe-light could still be burning defied all reason.

'Anybody here! Hello?' His voice rebounded emptily from the depths, but the darkness fluttered above him. The dog gave a whine.

'Oh no! Not bloody bats as well!' But then Mac smelt something strong and pungent coming from the deep below the crumbling stairs and he fancied he could see the flickering of a fire in a far corner.

II

When Colpoesne had finished his tale, he seemed saddened. His magic pictures had stopped flickering for they could tell the child no more.

'Elizabeth,' he said, 'I told you from the beginning that it would be a hard truth to learn. I didn't think you would make it, but you have done even better than you yourself ever imagined. I hope you are satisfied with the truth. The truth is not everything; it is not always good to know and is sometimes far better forgotten. But this is all for you to decide, not right now, at this very moment, but as you grow older. Do not expect others to be as interested as yourself in seeking the truth. I do not expect they will understand you even now. But do not worry. You are stronger than you were and you know more than you did. That is enough for one day.

'I can do no more for you now. My work is finished. Goodbye, sweet Elizabeth. You will guide your own dreams from this day forth ...'

Colpoesne D relaxed. At once, he became a fat doll again, with stuffing poking through the tears the little creatures had made.

With his face set in a smile of utter contentment, he faded from her sight for ever through the veils of imagination.

Elizabeth awoke as if from a dream, coughing. Her eyes and nose were filled with smoke while tigers of light prowled all around the room. In the distance she seemed to hear Colpoesne calling her name. But that could not be so. The doll was shrouded in flames. The candle had fallen on its side and the flames had settled on the doll's fabric and consumed him like a torch. Elizabeth no longer wanted to remain in this cold, cold world. She wanted to see the sunlight again, to fling her arms around her father's stubborn old neck and kiss his nose and leave Uncle Tony's fire-burnt mind to heal in the gentle sunshine of the streets.

Colpoesne burned on. The child's cheeks caught the warmth. So this is why he had said goodbye, thought Elizabeth. He knew she would never have allowed him to leave, she would always have found a reason to keep him by her side. With him now gone, she was just an ordinary child again.

When Mac and his dog found her, he thought the child clung to him and cried because she was lost. But it was because she was found, not by him or the dog that barked into the darkness, but by herself. And for that, she cried with great relief. Before they climbed the stairs, Elizabeth chose between two relics of the deep and slipped one of them into her satchel, while the other she kept in her hand. While the humans squeezed through the hole only the dog turned back. She sat silently for a moment, looking out over the darkness and the glassy patch of water like a sea far below. She could smell the rich dampness in the moss and caught the pale yellow light in her eye. Before her master could call her back, she raised her head and let out a long, mournful howl at the moon.

August swept Elizabeth into his arms and hugged her as if she were his own. Tears sparkled in the corners of his eyes. The two policemen drew aside and spoke briefly together. One called the station to arrange for poison to be laid down for the vermin, and for the electricity supply which fed the globe-light to be traced and cut; while the second suggested that the hole should be sealed off with concrete to prevent other kids in the district following Elizabeth's example. Finally, they walked towards the parked car, with Holly between them. August strode behind, carrying Elizabeth on one arm and wondering how he could break the news about Uncle Tony to her.

The young reporter, who had already been told most of the story, had failed to get the girl to tell him anything. She had just played shy. He was about to leave and try to write a news story out of nothing, when he suddenly noticed a brightly coloured object lying in the nettles close to the mouth of the hole. He had seen the object in the girl's hand when she first emerged into daylight—a little red diary. She must have either dropped it, or thrown it away. As he picked up the book he stung himself on the nettles. The reporter flicked through the pages then read one or two entries. He moved back to the hole and sat for a moment, thinking very deeply. Perhaps it was not just simply a 'little girl lost' story, after all. She was a cripple, there was the diary, and then there was this miraculous light shining below.

I

When the blood-ache had disappeared with the last of the light, Rummage and Scratcher were surprised to find themselves in each other's arms with the most stupid of grins on their faces. Geovard, however, remained aside with his back to them and staring upwards. Suddenly, he turned.

'We must go back. We must return—straight away!' With that, Geovard moved away from the area of Starlight and began feeling his way around a large rock.

Rummage looked at Scratcher apologetically. 'It's no good. We'll have to follow him now. He can't make it alone,' he said. 'And besides, he is the only one who can lead us if the light comes again.'

'But we've only just arrived!' Scratcher protested, and would have gone on a lot longer if Rummage had not suddenly disappeared in much the same manner as Geovard. As it was, Scratcher was now forced to follow on, for the light from the Great Star had stirred his heart so deeply he was afraid to be left alone. So, greatly disappointed that he could not linger in that soft, haunting glade on the top of Understar, Scratcher the Rat scurried after his two Jog companions.

Approximately halfway down the road on Understar, Geovard, Rummage and Scratcher paused to catch their breaths. Rummage counted his bruises. What a hasty descent! The wise and sensitive Jog had no doubt that the hurry was in order for them to break the news of having found Paradise to the people below. Even so, being a sensitive creature, he wished his comrade had listened to his pleas as they had bumped and tumbled all the way down the road. Scratcher was positively furious with the whole undignified procedure. It was just not in his nature to run away —even if he had been afraid to be left alone. But long before he ever had time to air his misgivings, Geovard apologized to him in a most profuse manner. He told both Rat and Jog alike that it certainly had not been his intention to flee as if in panic from such a wonderful place as the Paradise which Scratcher had found, but he had been suddenly filled with the compulsion to break the good news as soon as possible to those waiting beneath. And as it was easier to go down the road than it had ever been to come up, he had found it impossible to control the speed of descent until this very point, where the road levelled out into a large plateau.

Scratcher's acceptance of this explanation was overridden by his vanity, as he remembered that it had been he who had first discovered Paradise—with not a Jog in sight. He brushed the dust from his fur. Sitting in the shadows of the plateau with one eye cocked for Swoops, Scratcher also realized that he was now halfway home. How this great discovery would strengthen his position in the Marble Halls of Meltamor—how popular he would become with his own people! Rummage, on the other hand, knew that Geovard was hiding something. It was certainly out of character for Geovard ever to apologize to Scratcher. But it was not until much later that he was able to discover exactly what Geovard had seen, gazing upwards into the face of the Great Star. Although the old soldier was again half blind, the sight-giving Starlight being far behind him, Geovard still looked back with expressions of the greatest dread.

In the second half of their descent, Rummage too looked back along the way they had come in the direction of the diminishing star, but he had the fear of Swoops and other perils on his mind so one extra worry made little difference to him.

Soon the three companions were on the lower slopes. They passed by deserted working lodges and the tools which had been abandoned by the side of the road. A panoramic sight spread out before them—the valleys and hills which led to the outskirts of the Rat township, the dwellings taking their gaze to the harbour and out across the polished blackness of Altos into the mists of darkness beyond. And over all this hung the great luminous globe of the Moon. Adventures and discoveries aside, at least Rummage felt that it was good to be in sight of home.

The three comrades were both surprised and disappointed to discover there were no cheering crowds to greet them on their return. Perhaps they had been expecting too much. After all, they had been away and out of touch for a long time. The streets were empty in the outskirts of the town as if all the inhabitants had closed up their houses and moved to some other quarter. The companions made their way in thoughtful silence. Eventually, when they did come across a few scurrying Town Rats, everyone failed to recognize them. This angered Scratcher a great deal. He was not used to being snubbed by his inferiors. Eventually he took hold of one and dragged him aside so that their conversation could not be overheard.

'What's wrong! What's going on here!' he demanded. 'Something's amiss—I can smell it!'

'Er—nothing, your lordship!' the trapped Merchant Rat stuttered, noting the authority in Scratcher's tone.

'Don't you lordship me!' Scratcher hissed. 'You don't even recognize me—do you?'

'It's not that I don't recognize you, sir. It's just that your disguise is so effective. The bandage obscures your true countenance.'

'What bandage?'

'That bandage, sir.' The Merchant Rat pointed to the blindfold above Scratcher's chewed ears. 'At least—it seems to be a bandage.'

Catching sight of Rummage, Scratcher realized that they had both neglected to remove their blindfolds. He swiftly tore off his own and threw it in the gutter.

'I'm Scratcher—that's who I am! Scratcher! Now do you recognize me? You blind fool!' The Merchant Rat nodded, trembling all over.

'Yes—oh yes, sir. It was the bandage—but even so, you are right. I am blind—a poor blind Merchant, that's all I am, just as your Honour says. And a fool—an utter fool ...' the Merchant Rat simpered.

'All right, all right! Stop dribbling down your vest. Just tell me what's been going on while I've been away.'

Wanting his answers only to please, the Rat began very cautiously. 'Oh, it's the people, your eminence—you know how it is ...'

'No. I certainly do not. So suppose you begin to tell me?'

'Well ... you know how easily led the masses are ... so easily

136

led by rumour ...' At this point the Merchant Rat noticed the other two companions standing in the shadows a short distance away. 'Say, isn't that Rummage and blind Geovard over there?'

'Get on with your story, you old offal-vendor!'

'Ah yes, well ... as I was saying.... You see, your worship, it's the people. They think (not all of them, mind, but a lot of them) ... here and there ... they think that ... His Majesty Emperor Meltamor is ... well ... getting old.' Scratcher began to chew his ear, thoughtfully. The Merchant Rat took this as an encouraging sign. 'And some ... and again by that I mean not all ... some even say that he's getting ... well ... soft—too soft, that is ... for the job ... that is.'

'*Say?*'

'Oh well, perhaps not *say* ... perhaps *think* more. They think that since the New Existence the Rats have lost a lot of the vigour they used to have ...' he lowered his voice to a whisper, '... on account of the laws Meltamor made with the Jogs. They think they have lost a lot of self-respect because of the new rules of working together and that the Emperor doesn't see this because ...'

'He is getting old and soft?'

'Well yes.... That's what some think.'

Scratcher took a deep, satisfied breath. 'Thank you, my friend. You have told me a lot. I shan't forget you.'

'But I haven't told you anything, your worship. It's only gossip. Just gossip, that's all!'

'Really? How interesting. And where are all these gossipers now. The street corner used to be the place for gossip. You can see for yourself—the streets are deserted!'

'That's just it, your eminence. They've all gone.'

'Gone?'

'To a meeting place—so they can gossip in a lump, together. I tell you, it'll be the ruin of a poor Rat like me. I haven't sold a thing for ages.' The Merchant Rat noticed the frown forming on Scratcher's brow. 'Oh don't mind me, your lordship. I exaggerate sometimes. It's only gossip. It's not to be taken seriously.'

'Well, now that I have returned, I'll be the judge of what is and what is not to be taken seriously. Gossip leads to plans and plans lead to organizations. And if the organizing is against the state—that can only lead to one other thing—*revolt*!'

'Oh no, your worship!'
'Oh *yes*—you worshipper!'

That is how it came to pass that before the travellers reached the outer gates of the Marble Halls of Meltamor, Scratcher suddenly took his leave of Geovard and Rummage. His excuse was that he wished to prepare the news of his great find in written form so that it might quickly be registered and added to the records. This seemed so in keeping with the Rat's growing vanity, Rummage volunteered to deliver greetings to the Emperor of All Rats on Scratcher's behalf and added that they would not spoil the surprise by mentioning his discovery of Paradise.

The two Jogs were poorly received at the palace by both the guard and the Minister Rats who kept them waiting in a small, cramped chamber. Finally, they were allowed to be presented to the Emperor. Rummage led blind Geovard through the maze of passages keeping his thoughts to himself, but the old soldier openly and loudly began to curse the Rats for their impudence whenever he smelled a guard, rattling his oaths down the long corridors. There was a strange, uncomfortable feeling in the air which both Jogs could sense.

When they finally arrived at the Great Chamber, poor old Meltamor hardly seemed to recognize either of them. He appeared to have aged terribly since they last met. Doctor Rats were forever rushing round him with foul-smelling potions while the whole procedure was supervised by the keen eyes of Minister Rats. The Jogs gave their greetings but it was only when Rummage apologized for Scratcher's absence and gave the reasons for him not being there that Meltamor responded to their words. Slowly, then, he began to recognize his old friends and gave them a warmer welcome. He was clearly disturbed that Scratcher was missing. Rummage began enthusiastically to relate their adventures on Understar and probably would have gone on to describe every inch of the journey to Paradise and back had not Geovard tugged firmly at his spines. The blind soldier whispered to Rummage that he was probably tiring the Emperor. It was obvious to him that Meltamor was ill. Speaking for them both, Geovard told the Emperor that they were very tired after their long journey and would return to give him their full report just as soon as they had rested.

After they had left Meltamor at the mercy of his Doctor Rats, Geovard urged Rummage to lead him straight from the Marble Halls to rid his snout of the wicked stench of bad-ooze potion.

As they made their way to Geovard's cottage, the two Jogs again noted how deserted the streets were, the one by sight and the other by sound. They were glad indeed to close the cottage door behind them, light candles and start a fire to warm their aching limbs. Rummage sat Geovard by the friendly glow from the fire-rock in the soldier's favourite chair and afterwards prepared a small supper. For the first time in a long while they could relax, at least that is what Rummage had first thought. He drew himself up to the fire the moment supper was over, and gazed out of the tiny window. In the distant sky he could see the Great Star twinkling like a point of blue fire. Immediately his heart filled with the memory of the warm blood-ache he had experienced in Paradise. It had been so mysterious, clearly the most powerful passion he had ever experienced and because of that very reason he desperately needed to discuss it with someone. He made an awkward start.

'Did we really behave like children?' he eventually asked, remembering his own and Scratcher's behaviour in the Starlight and the way in which Geovard had briefly described it.

'Like complete babes—innocent, and free!'

'And you—did you not join in—even once?'

'I ...' remarked Geovard, laying great emphasis on the pronoun, 'I was too busy—watching!'

'What, watching us?'

'Certainly not!' Geovard answered in disgust. Then he controlled himself, for he knew that if he did not he would never be able to reveal—even to his closest friend—just what he had witnessed, and keep calm and collected. Settling himself deeper into his old soft chair he took a draught of the mossbrew Rummage had poured for him and began again.

'Rummage, my young friend, although we are a long way from that mountain, really it is right here in this room with us.' Rummage knew exactly what Geovard meant and began to feel a little uncomfortable, instinctively looking all about him and particularly at Courage, his handy stick for Swoops which had been placed by the door. 'It's with us in our minds. We both have pictures of

Paradise, yet both of our pictures are incomplete because I am blind in the light of the Moon and you're blind by Starlight. In other words, my friend, while your eyes saw everything right up to the top of Understar, only my eyes could see the real Paradise and the Great Star itself. Well, now we are alone in the privacy of our own dwelling, I can tell you *exactly* what I saw while you were dancing over the grass and moss. I saw a monster. Through the Great Star I saw it. A monster of hideous proportions and the horriblest face I have ever beheld. I tell you, my friend, I am no coward, but when I saw how I stood like a crumb in its enormous shadow and it gazed on me with its terrible eyes all my strength left me. As it moved its great mouth not far above my head, my worthless hide shrank back on its bones and my spines drooped. And all this happened while you and Scratcher romped and played by my side like children. When eventually the monster turned away, only then did my strength return. That is why we had to leave so quickly—to escape its terrible gaze, not so that we could rush and tell the people about Paradise. Because there is no Paradise. Oh, my friend, we have uncovered something of far darker foreboding. I can feel it in my bones. Now the creature has seen, it will return. It will climb out of the Great Star and use our own road to descend Understar. And what it will do then I dread to think for we are powerless to stop it—and what is worse, we are unprepared.

'Whatever happens, the people must not panic. We must control the situation even though we do not yet know how. But we must try. That is all we can do.'

Rummage's head was spinning as if he were in the middle of a sleep-fear. He was struck dumb for several moments, then gradually Geovard's words seemed to make some abominable sense. So that was why Geovard had fled from Understar's mysterious tip, Rummage realized, and why he had preoccupied Scratcher with his own vanity and why he had himself been hushed by the old soldier when they visited Meltamor's court! As all the reasons became clear to him, a cold, dark shadow passed over his soul.

Of course, Rummage could in no way tell what this latest monster looked like and it was simply beyond his courage to ask Geovard to describe it in greater detail. It was clearly in a category of its own, for no other dreaded creature had ever troubled Geovard to the extent of making him tremble whenever he thought about it—until now. Rummage even became afraid to look out of the window again and deliberately moved his chair round so the Starlight was hidden from his sight.

'Somehow,' Geovard began again, 'somebody has got to get back to the old country to warn the Jogs of this monster. The person to carry the message must be a young and fleet-footed soul while, at the same time, a respected and popular Jog with the people.' Ironically, he stared directly at Rummage with such accuracy the young Jog almost believed Geovard could see again. Rummage's thoughts had been far from him going anywhere. In fact he had been considering digging a hole right there in the centre of the room so they could both hide in it. But now it seemed, particularly by the awkward lapse in Geovard's conversation, that he was about to offer his services as a courier.

'Er—I . . .'

'You will? Splendid—then that's settled. And might I say that not for one moment did I think you would let me down. I'm proud to be the best friend you've ever had—positively proud! Now, let us waste no more time. I want you to meet an old Ferry Rat I know of who lives down by the far shore. He's retired now—but like any Rat, he's not above being bribed.'

'Bribed?' Rummage cried aloud. He had hoped that he had made it perfectly clear many times before that he was against such things.

'Well . . . *paid* then. The Rat has got to be paid for his services, hasn't he—or do you expect him to ferry you across Altos for nothing? Anyway, I happen to know that he has a particular weakness for mossbrew and I'm prepared to let him have three of my best jars of Mushgrove V. All he has to do in return is take you across Altos and keep his mouth shut. He'll have to keep quiet anyway. Rats of his order are not allowed anything stronger than Grade VIII. But that's by their law not ours.'

'But, what about you? Won't you come—or better still, take the news yourself. Then I could stay here and . . .'

'And?'

'Well, I could tidy up the cottage—or dig you a cellar. Wouldn't you like a nice deep cellar right here in the middle of your room—for your mossbrew?'

'After we've paid the Ferry Rat, there won't be any more mossbrew this side of Altos. Those three jars are the last. Rummage, you're not afraid to go, are you?'

'What me?'

'Are you?'

'Well ...'

'Afraid?'

'Not so much afraid—as scared.' Rummage was embarrassed that he should be made to confess his deepest feelings.

'And so you should be!' Geovard boomed. 'Especially when we're being threatened by the horriblest thing ever.'

'Horry what?' asked Rummage, cautiously.

'Horriblest!'

'Horribillis? Is that what it's called—Horribillis?' implored Rummage. Geovard thought quickly. The monster would mean more to the people if it had a name. And as Geovard had been the only one to see it so far, it seemed only right that he should be the one to name it. But he had not quite caught Rummage's pronunciation. 'Say it again. I want to see if you have it right,' demanded Geovard.

'Horribillis?'

'That's it, my boy! You have it now—Horribillis!'

'Oh no!' Rummage moaned with the deepest dread.

'Oh *yes*!' affirmed Geovard. 'Why, the Horribillis is so horrible it makes Swoops and other nasty creatures seem like your best friends.'

'Oh no!' muttered Rummage, chewing his knuckles. 'You're my best friend.'

'Yes, you're right. Of course I am,' said Geovard after a thought. 'In that case—second best! Remember, whoever stays behind—closest to Horribillis, I mean—has the task of breaking the news to the Rats. That job is going to need a lot of patience and tact. By now, Scratcher will have told everyone that he has found Paradise and, of all Rats, he is going to be the most annoyed when a Jog tells him that he has not. You know how he thinks that Jogs interfere in everything. You know, that being the case, perhaps it would be wiser for you to remain here while I break the news to our own people and organize things so they won't be caught with their spines down.'

Rummage certainly did not relish the idea of breaking the bad news to the Rats or being the only Jog in the land when it happened. He thought he had better say something quickly, otherwise Geovard might make the decision to return to the Land of the Jogs leaving him behind and all alone.

'Er—well, Geovard, you do seem to get on better with Meltamor than I do, if you remember.'

'Really? But I also seem to remember that you get on better with Scratcher than I ...'

'Yes, but that is only *one* whereas *all* the Rats will listen to what you have to say.'

'Rummage,' Geovard said at last, 'you are not only an incorrigible flatterer—but you are *right*, too!'

II

So that was how Rummage not only came accidentally to give a name to the monster, but also to talk himself into sneaking away from the cottage shortly afterwards with three heavy jars of Mushgrove bumping against his back and carrying only Courage, his handy stick for Swoops, for comfort. He crept along the deserted back-streets of the Rat town until he came to the coast. On Geovard's instructions, he kept himself well hidden from view as he followed the path along in the direction of the far shore—a barren and desolate place on the edge of the Moonlight. After quietly chanting several of his favourite walking poems to the rhythm of the lapping tide in order to keep his spirits up, Rummage eventually came across the tumbled-down residence of the Ferry Rat.

Quite the filthiest Rat he had ever seen opened the door to him and invited him inside with a yellow-toothed smile. Rummage introduced himself to the character as a Jog mossbrew merchant who, having missed his boat connection, now desperately needed to return to his own country to supervise a harvest. Seamoon, as the Rat called himself, seemed well content with this explanation. Rummage was about to put his proposition to the old Ferry Rat when, quite spontaneously, Seamoon sprang to his feet from a mound of earth on which he had temporarily squatted and took his prospective customer on a tour of the humble dwelling. It soon became clear that Seamoon lived, slept and worked in only one of his many rooms, for it was in fact impossible for him to occupy any of the others. They were all so crammed with wealth Rummage's eyes nearly fell out of his head as he was led from one doorway to the next. Far from being the poor, bedraggled Ferry Rat he had first appeared to be, Seamoon was in fact exceedingly rich and Rummage wondered how he could possibly be in need of anything. Unlike Rummage's own prized collection of samples from the mines, Seamoon's treasures were of far greater commercial value. It took Rummage quite a while to discover that the whole purpose of the collection was not to see it piece by piece as the occasion demanded, but simply to impress visitors such as himself, in the fond hope of raising the value for any job the Ferry Rat might be asked to undertake.

After the tour, Rummage was invited to sit at the one table available. As he sat, wondering how to begin bargaining with such an eccentric character, Rummage's eyes wandered around the room. It was then that he noticed for the first time that everything in the room—the door, the walls, the floor, the fireplace, tables and chairs—had great pieces missing. A moment later he knew why, for without warning or any apparent reason, Seamoon suddenly fastened his enormous yellow front teeth on the corner of the table at which Rummage was sitting and began to gnaw. Rummage jumped up, alarmed. Then just as suddenly as he had started, Seamoon stopped his assault on the table and looked up, surprised to see his guest making for the door. Seamoon, apparently, was completely unaware of his fit, and again cordially invited Rummage to be seated so they could continue with the business in hand. The Ferry Rat was pleased to hear the nature of the job and even more pleased when Rummage produced one of the jars. Apart from his other disgusting habits, Seamoon apparently had a great weakness for drink. As he had been instructed, Rummage presented two jars of Mushgrove V only. Seamoon grabbed them both enthusiastically.

'Mushgrove V—eh?'

'The very best!'

'Well, you should know, with being in the trade and all ...'

Rummage cleared his throat. 'Yes, of course—the very best!'

'You'll forgive me for saying so, but with me not being such an expert as yourself who can judge the contents by looking at the outside of a jar, I would be obliged if you would let me sample the quality of the brew before we go much further.'

There was little Rummage could do but to agree, even though he knew that the contents would not keep for very long after the seal had been broken. He quickly opened a jar and then immediately looked around for a mug in which to pour a drop, but there was not one to be found anywhere. This in no way deterred Seamoon. In a flash, he took up the jar and began to guzzle the contents, pausing only for occasional breaths in which he managed to say:

'I'm ... beginning (wheeze) ... to think (sniff) ... that you might (cough) ... be telling (pant) ... the truth (gasp)...! But just ... to make (slurp) ... absolutely ... sure (glug) ... I think (splutter) ... I'll just (groan) ... have one (gulp) ... more ... tiny (rumble) ... sip (burp)!

'Oh dear,' moaned Seamoon, when he had found his voice again. 'The jar seems to be completely empty!' His eyes had grown enormous and bulged from his head as if they would pop. The potency of the brew was already having its effects on the greedy Rat and Rummage found it difficult to hide his own self-satisfaction. Before Seamoon could come to his senses, the Jog grabbed the second jar from the table.

'Now,' he said, 'perhaps you will listen to me. If you ferry me across Altos straight away, I will give you an extra jar—to replace the one you've just emptied.'

'Another?' Seamoon could hardly believe his ears.

'Yes, another—one which I was going to keep for myself.' For a moment Seamoon's whole face lit up, then he turned very pale and staggered from the room. It soon became apparent to Rummage that there would be no journey for a little while yet to come.

Seamoon's raft turned out to be the most dilapidated and un-seaworthy vessel Rummage had ever seen. It was no more than a jumble of all things floatable, stuck together with clay. As Rummage suspected, the whole contraption had been hastily flung together for the sole purpose of transporting him across the sea so the deal could be concluded and Seamoon could get his hands on his jars of mossbrew. The drunkard's eyes still rolled wildly in his head while he wore a stupid grin of self-admiration. Occasionally, Seamoon staggered off into the darkness, only to be heard thrashing about in the shallows in search of another piece of driftwood. Then he would stumble and fall flat on his face in the cold water, the shock of which would bring him temporarily to his senses.

Rummage was for abandoning his journey completely when suddenly, he caught sight of the Great Star's dim, blue light. All at once the fear of being trapped by Horribillis returned and he scrambled on board the half-submerged craft. It was all right for Rats, Rummage moaned to himself as he felt the platform sway under his weight—at least they could swim for it if the worst came to the worst. And to his great amazement, this is precisely what Seamoon did. There was a more professional sort of dive into the Sea than those the Rat had previously undertaken, so that his head emerged next to the raft's transom onto which he clamped his ugly teeth while kicking out merrily with his back legs.

'This is it—here we go!' Seamoon called out to his terrified passenger. 'I'll push while you steer!'

And so, gradually, the little craft began to leave the far shore behind as it zig-zagged a course into the mainstream of Altos. The zig-zagging was not a result of Rummage's inexperience as a helmsman, for he soon grasped the idea of tugging the Rat's left or right ear, depending on whether they needed to go to the moonboard or starboard side, but because Seamoon, being far from sober, had a great tendency to swim in a circle, a fault which had to be corrected on every other stroke.

Halfway out to sea, the journey was seeming to pass off without further incident. Rummage crouched lower beneath an old piece of awning (to keep himself well-hidden from Swoops) and was at the point of wishing himself to sleep when a strong vibration shook the whole vessel beneath him. He immediately opened his eyes and was horrified to see a great pair of yellow teeth gnawing into the woodwork a short distance away.

'What do you think you are doing, you mad Rat! You'll drown us both. You're tearing the boat to pieces. Stop! Stop!' But Seamoon could not hear him. He was having one of his gnawing fits again, this time brought on by excessive consumption of potent mossbrew. Terrified that the raft would disintegrate in the middle of Altos, Rummage desperately searched the horizon for a glimpse of his homeland. The faint twinkling of miners' lamps could just be seen on some distant hillside. They offered a faint ray of hope to the wayward Jog. Rummage held Courage tightly in his hand for comfort as the gnawing grew more and more severe. Then all at once, a brilliant idea came to him, just as the black sea-water began to wash over his ankles.

For the moment, Seamoon's fit had passed over after having destroyed the transom completely and dislodging more than one large piece of wood.

'How are we doing?' he asked Rummage, completely oblivious of the damage he had just caused. Rummage realized that it would be pointless telling the Rat about the fits.

'Oh, nicely,' he replied weakly. 'We're doing very nicely.'

'That's good,' the Ferry Rat remarked, 'because I'm feeling a bit pooped myself.'

'Oh, don't feel that—for goodness sake!'

'How's that again?' Seamoon enquired, this time draining some of the water from his ears.

'Don't give up—*please*!'

'I wasn't thinking of giving up. I was simply considering having a short rest. I seem to be quite tired, for some reason. Anyway, what's the hurry? Surely it doesn't matter if you're a bit later, considering you are late already, in your arrival?'

'But I wasn't thinking of myself so much as I was thinking of you—or rather, your property.'

'What property?' enquired the Rat.

'The two remaining jars of Mushgrove V. I fear that unless we arrive at the shore soon, they will go bad. Mossbrew of this potency is such a poor traveller—especially through the cold and damp climate of the sea. And I would gladly replace them but these are the last two jars in the whole Existence, which is why I am rushing home for the harvest, so a new brew can begin straight away.'

Without further ado, Seamoon began to kick out again so vigorously, Rummage felt sure that he would soon be on dry land. Still, he could not rid himself of his great fear of the sea and the old saying sprang into his mind—'A Jog in Altos is a Jog lost!'

Three-quarters of the way across Altos, Seamoon suffered another gnawing attack and this time began systematically to demolish the very platform on which Rummage was trembling.

The Jog was beside himself with anxiety and, in an effort to bring the Ferry Rat to his senses, struck out with Courage. But he missed Seamoon's nose by a fraction and somehow managed to get the stick caught between two pieces of the splintered deck. Before he could do anything to stop it, Rummage saw two great teeth begin to chisel away at his favourite weapon. Seamoon set about this new, unspoilt piece avidly, and to his senseless delight found Courage afforded far better gnawing properties than the water-logged wood of the raft. Now up to his tummy in foul sea-water, Rummage cringed beneath his soaked awning in horror as he watched his favourite handy stick for Swoops gradually being whittled away to nothing.

'This is it,' thought Jog Rummage. 'The end has finally come for me!' and waited, trembling, for the black waters to fold over his head.

'Er—excuse me, sir,' whispered an exhausted voice. 'But I think we've arrived.'

Rummage looked slowly about him. Seamoon was lying flat on his back in the sand, puffing and blowing with the exertion of having pushed the raft halfway up the beach quite unwittingly. A short distance from his snout, among many chips of wood, was a half-chewed knobble—all that remained of Courage. Seamoon staggered to his feet somewhat amazed at his own strength as he looked back down the furrows in the sand towards the sea. Eventually he turned and helped Rummage out of the wreckage, saying, 'There's a job well done—wouldn't you say?' But the Jog would not say anything—he could not. Rummage simply flung himself onto the sand and embraced it lovingly like a long-lost relative. Seamoon was a little puzzled by the ceremony, but he did not pretend, as some did, to know anything about the Jogs' strange ways so quickly helped himself to the two Mush-grove jars. After he had dispensed with the contents of the first and was struggling to unseal the second he looked back over his shoulder at the prostrate Jog.

'Er—excuse me interrupting you again,' he whispered, 'but I was wondering ... will you be needing my services for a return journey?'

148

Walking along the lanes he loved so well, Rummage soon forgot about his terrible experience at sea. Were it not for the fact that he felt so exposed to Swoops he might have forgotten about losing Courage. He was grateful, therefore, when he came to the first Jog household, to find a light in the window. Knocking gently on the door, it was eventually opened by an elderly Mother Jog who welcomed him home as if he were her own son. A good nourishing meal was made for him while he relaxed in the comfort of a mustard bath and told her of his adventures since he had been away. The old Mother listened intently and afterwards, as he set about the wholesome food, told him a few tales of her own.

Apparently, old Snug had become something of a popular figure since Rummage and Geovard had left with Scratcher to climb the road. The story of how he had beaten Meltamor at several games of Pebblepocket had earned him considerable fame in the land of the Jogs and, of course, the game too became extremely popular among the young. Snug had spent less and less time in the Rummage mines and devoted more and more to the holding of public meetings. There was a considerable amount of unrest in the land and the meetings gave the people an opportunity to air their grievances. Rumour had it, the Mother said, that things were not so very different in the land of the Rats.

After hearing this, Rummage was very soon on his way again with a determination to speak to Snug and to seek his advice about the best way to break the news to the Jog nation. He did not have to wait long. As he came to the centre of the town he noticed how deserted the Streets were of workers—a situation very similar to that which he had experienced in the land of the Rats. Rummage wished, not for the first time, that Geovard had come with him. Rounding the next corner, he saw before him the glowing outlines of a doorway which led to one of the largest warehouses in the land. It took the form of a deep cavern let into the roadside to make it all the more convenient for the workers to deposit their produce. From deep inside he could hear the sound of many voices in earnest discussion. Rummage quietly turned the door handle and entered the chamber.

Hiding in the shadows behind the gathering, he could just

make out the candle-lit figure of the speaker appealing to the crowd. By the shape of the long sensitive snout, twitching with concern, Rummage was at once able to recognize the speaker as Snug.

'Friends, friends, listen ... not that what I say will make much difference to you, seeing how you've all made up your minds. Let me ask you one question—do you really want a leader? There has never been one before, not called as such anyway, so why must it be so now?'

'That's two questions, Snug,' someone called out from the middle of the gathering. 'Anyone who can ask two questions in place of one is the Jog for us!'

'It's a natural choice,' yelled another.

'You've always been our speaker,' called out a young front-ranker.

'No, not always, my friend. That was a job you offered me only a short while ago. But since you called me here in the first place to speak for you, I suppose the sooner I get it over with, so we go away from this place all of the same mind, the better it will be for the nation. Now, in view of what we have been subjected to through the despicable activities of the Rats, it is clear that something just has to be done. They seem to have totally disregarded the terms of the New Existence and have reverted to their old ways of—piracy and robbery! In consequence (as has always been the case, I seem to recollect) the Jogs have come off the worst. But it's no good us expecting miracles —marble will never be mustard, that's what I've always said. Perhaps we should not have expected the Rats to behave like decent and honest Jogs when the terms for the New Existence were being drawn up.'

'We didn't!' interrupted a young and angry Jog in the front row. 'It wasn't the people who drew up the terms—it was Geovard!' The young Jog's name was Cudgel.

'Yes!' cried another. 'And Rummage!'

'Now, now.... They were only acting for the best. It was a complex and awkward situation. The whole nation was depressed after the Light created by the Smelly Sticky Black Wet Stuff and then the foul-smelling ghost which engulfed us afterwards. Only Rummage and Geovard offered any guidance or help—and we were all grateful to receive it.'

'And where are they now—these two heroes?' asked Cudgel, who seemed to have a persistent and personal interest in the matter. 'Gone in pursuit of their own dreams, that's where! Living with the Rats—preferring their ways to ours!' He answered his own question firmly and loudly enough for all to hear. In response, a deep murmur spread through the whole chamber like a dark liquid.

'My friends ... my friends, how can you think these things? These are two of the most courageous and far-seeing Jogs of Our Times. Just think for a moment. Who taught you your skills— Rummage! Who showed you how to defend what those skills produced—Geovard! Who has brought wisdom and respect to the people—Rummage! And who has made the Rats sit up and take notice—Geovard! Who has always tried to solve the mysteries and rid us of our fears—Rummage! Who is absolutely fearless—Geovard!

'Now, how can you deny them the loyalty they so justly deserve —how—how—how?'

Snug's speech moved the crowd enough to raise a weak cheer, but the majority had heard the same line used many times before. They really did not expect him to desert his two closest friends easily. But young Jogs like Cudgel, who could barely remember Rummage or Geovard, thought the matter grossly irrelevant to the main issue.

Every moment seemed to bring fresh news of bands of marauding Rats attacking warehouses along the shore. It was an insult to the hard labours of the Jogs who were far better working folk than they were fighters, and an insult, too, to the pride of the nation. They did not work so hard in order for the Rats to steal whatever they produced. Perhaps that had been the way of life long ago, but the young had been brought up in a time of peace where the lazy Rats had been forced to buy what they needed from the Jogs.

Since their two ambassadors, Rummage and Geovard, had apparently deserted them, Jogs were left to fend for themselves against the entire Rat nation across Altos. Communication had almost totally broken down between the two lands and the Marble Halls of Meltamor seemed only to have a place in the tales belonging to the Old Existence. All their pleas to that great noble Rat, Meltamor, seemed to fall on deaf ears, and, as the attacks from Pirate Rats increased, it was the young in particular who called for action.

Snug had fallen foul of his own popularity, for the same crowd which had listened enthusiastically to his instructions in the art of playing Pebblepocket, now turned to him again for instruction and leadership in politics. And there was really very little he could do other than to accept the challenge. Either he stepped into the vacancy and became leader of the Jogs or the whole nation would fall into disorder. In his own, straightforward way, Snug had made up his mind. He turned to the milling crowd beneath him.

'Reparation is what we want!' he called out, suddenly.

Eyes and ears slowly turned in his direction.

'Reparation, friends, for the ills waged against us by those cowardly Rats—those who have dared to break the code of the New Existence. And if the Rats will not hear us and will not see us when we come to them with our demands—then they will *feel* us!'

'Reparation!' Cudgel yelled from where he stood in the crowd. *'Reparation!'*

Then the throng took up the cry repeating it over and over, until the noise was deafening and everyone became wild with excitement. But just as the din seemed to reach its peak, it just as rapidly began to fall away again. The crowd turned its attention towards the back of the chamber and, slowly, the numbers divided to allow one solitary figure to make his way towards Snug. Even though the figure walked at a solemn pace with his face downcast, he was recognized almost instantly and a name was whispered from face to face—'Rummage!'

When Rummage reached the raised bank on which his loyal friend stood he looked up and smiled briefly. For a moment he stood among the gathering like a spirit, saying nothing. Snug stared down at him in utter amazement. Eventually he helped his friend climb onto the crude platform. Another murmur swept the gathering. As Snug shook Rummage joyfully by both hands a spell seemed to break. 'Rummage!' Snug breathed. 'I thought you were ...' But then he quickly changed his choice of words. 'Why didn't you tell me you were back ... why didn't you write! What's happened—where's Geovard? Is he with you?'

'No, I am alone,' Rummage said quietly.

'Oh, Rummage—it's so good to see you again!' exclaimed Snug, as he shook his friend again until he rattled.

'I came back urgently—on Geovard's instructions,' Rummage was at last able to say. 'Snug, I was hiding at the back—I heard everything!' Snug's joyful expression seemed to slide from his face. He thought for a moment then took a deep, authoritative breath.

'You've been away a long time, my friend,' he said. 'Times have changed.'

'So I can see.'

'But how can you? It would take more than a few moments listening at the back of the crowd to catch up fully with all the events ...'

'Snug, there is something very important that has happened which you ought to know about—that all the Jogs ought to know about. That is why I have come—to tell you.' Snug's face beamed with a smile. He turned to the crowd.

'Quiet! Quiet everybody. Look who has returned—it's Rummage. He has returned from his perilous journey to the Great Star especially to be here at this meeting. Because he brings us all an urgent message sent by Geovard. There—I told you our old friends had not deserted us. Now, even I do not know what this news is about yet, so let him tell us all, with no further delay! Go ahead, Rummage. We are eager to hear your words!'

Rummage could see that he had no other choice than to do just that, even though he had hoped to speak privately with Snug before delivering the message. After having heard the general trend of the meeting, he was no longer confident the news would be taken seriously. Both he and Geovard seemed to have been totally out of touch and most certainly they no longer could claim to have the ear of the people, as Snug could. Rummage now saw himself as a simple messenger—but delivering a terrifying message.

'My dear comrades, the message I bring you from Geovard is this: a new peril is about to strike us coming not from the sea, nor from the Shadow, nor from the Rats. This peril is like nothing we have ever experienced before. It comes from beyond the Great Star taking the shape of a most hideous monster. Its name is Horribillis; it is uglier than ugly and as high as a High Mountain. It moves with the speed of breath and crushes all in its path to dust. I have returned to help you prepare for its coming—if you need my help. Geovard has stayed behind to tell the Rats and to lead the first attack against the monster, should he be called to do so.

'That is my message. Thank you for listening.'

Every Jog in the chamber fell silent with their mouths agape.

'But why?' asked Snug when he finally found his voice. 'Why should it attack our land? What have we ever done to deserve such a thing?'

'I don't know,' Rummage replied simply.

'And when?' asked Cudgel from the front row. 'When is it coming—how long have we got?'

'I don't know that, either.'

'Well, what do you know?' cried another in the crowd.

'Very little—and that's a fact.'

'Well, can you describe this monster—Horribillis—or whatever its name is?' Snug asked again. 'I mean, what does it look like—have you actually seen it, yourself?'

'No. I haven't, but Geovard has—he told me so himself.'

Snug suddenly looked at him, both amazed and concerned, and the crowd broke out in whispers.

'But Rummage, my dear friend, Geovard is *blind*—isn't he?'

'Yes, unfortunately. He is still blind.'

'And now the blind can see monsters!' Cudgel laughed out aloud. He turned to the crowd. 'Did you hear what Rummage said? Blind old Geovard has started seeing monsters—so we'd better watch out!' The crowd soon responded and laughed in turn with great relief. It was far easier too for them to believe that Rummage had brought them the message of a mad Jog than the truth.

At that moment an old Jog was led forward so that he could have a turn to address the crowd. He came to the place where Rummage and Snug stood and cocked his head at a funny angle.

'Remember me, Rummage? Remember me?' he asked. 'I have called out to you from a crowd before. I met you in the lane not long after I had been blinded by the Light.'

Rummage thought back to when the lands had been in turmoil when he had prevented a crowd from disturbing Geovard.

'Yes, Rummage, I am still blind—just like your friend Geovard. In fact, it was he who made me blind and filled my head

154

with terror when he lit the Smelly Sticky Black Wet Stuff at sea.' The old Jog then turned in the rough direction of the crowd and addressed them. 'Do you know what he said to me then when I complained of my suffering? He said that Geovard suffered ten times more than me because he had ten times the imagination! Do you remember saying that, eh, Rummage? Well, my friends, I just want you to know that I agree with him. Oh yes I do—I agree that a noble and distinguished Jog such as Geovard has ten times my imagination. So perhaps when I tell you all that I too see monsters and other terrible things in my blindness, you will not find it too difficult to believe that poor old Geovard's are ten times more horrific and ten times uglier in every respect than anyone else's. Why shouldn't they be—answer me that?' The crowd, quite naturally, answered with shouts of uproarious laughter and there was little Rummage could do but wait for the noise to subside.

'If you remember,' he began when he had the chance, 'I said other things, too. When you asked me to lead you because you were blind I answered that if you needed me, it was only because you saw yourselves in me, therefore I could not lead you. And if you followed me, it would not really be me you were following, but yourselves. Now I can see that this is no longer the case. You have lost your way completely. Now you just follow each other!'

'Of one thing you can be sure,' Cudgel shouted back in anger. 'We will never ever follow you again!'

A tense silence spread out over the chamber and no Jog moved or dared to draw breath for several moments. Anger flooded into Rummage's heart when he saw how futile both his own and Geovard's words had been. In an instant, he jumped into the crowd and pushed his way towards the back, jostled and laughed at all the way.

'Here comes the thinker!' they laughed. 'Tell us what you think about this, then!'

'Goodbye, dreamer! Farewell, poet!'

'Good riddance—Rat-lover!'

By the time Rummage had reached the exit the crowd had already forgotten him. He turned to see Snug bravely trying to control the mob amid a rising chant whose rhythm was measured by dozens of Swoop-sticks striking the ground ... 'Reparation ... reparation!'

16

I

Rummage returned as swiftly as possible to the sanctuary of his own neglected little cottage, his head and heart filled with humiliation. Never before had he been so badly treated by his own people or so sickened by the sight of mob rule. What a terrible homecoming it had turned out to be. Everything had gone so wrong. The people had laughed at him when his only intention had been to help them. They had laughed at Geovard, too.

'Oh, how miserable I am to be alone at a time like this!' he cried, crawling into his favourite fireside chair. But the hearth was cold and threw back nothing but his empty echo. 'Oh, what a miserable, miserable Jog I am!' he sobbed heavily, and the tears trickled down to his toes. In an effort to console himself, he pulled from under his seat a dusty jar of ancient mossbrew and in a manner after Seamoon, steadily began to drain its contents with hardly a gasp for breath. Soon, the room that was once cold began to glow with a dark, secretive warmth and Rummage actually believed that he had somehow managed to put himself to bed. Secure in that thought, his eyes at last closed to envelop him in a deep and perfectly dreamless sleep.

When Rummage opened his eyes again it was to a room of dancing light. Shadows pitched and reeled above his head while his hearth was a blaze of fire-rock. As his eyes adjusted to the dazzling brightness, he tried to remember who and where he was. His memory slowly came back to him as he stared at the empty jar by the chair, but he just could not recollect lighting the fire or actually getting into bed.

'I don't remember any of this,' he said to himself, carefully getting to his feet. 'I just don't remember this at all.' But he did eventually remember everything else with absolute and saddening clarity. He became suspicious of his own room and sniffed the air. It looked as if someone had been very, very busy while he had slept. He began to make a most thorough investigation of the matter, even though his head throbbed mercilessly with every step he took. With meticulous attention, he examined every object that he had ever collected—the wax, weapons, fluffs and stuffs—spending a great deal of time and energy wiping a layer of dust from each object and giving an extra polish to the mysterious invaluable shapes.

When he had finished his tour and assured himself that nothing had been touched, let alone removed, he sat down again with a great sigh of relief. But his relaxation was short-lived. A sudden noise behind nearly made him jump out of his skin. He reeled his head round and saw—not a robber Rat—but Snug, looking extremely apprehensive of taking another step.

'Er—good morning, Rummage. Sleep well?' Snug asked him awkwardly. 'Er, I was just passing and I thought, er—well, just to see how you were getting along and, er—have you had anything to eat yet?'

'I don't want anything to eat,' growled Rummage, moodily.

Snug took a step closer. 'Not even beetle-broth and mushrooms? Er, I have some here which—just in case your larder is empty—I brought on the off chance that I might pass this way.'

'Oh, for goodness sake. Don't stand there dithering, half in my house and half in the street—come inside!' Rummage had raised his voice so much by the time he had finished, Snug tumbled into the cottage and quickly closed the door for fear of them attracting a Swoop. Rummage put his head between his hands and groaned. Snug looked at him in a most concerned manner.

'Oh, Rummage—you're as pale as softrock. Sit down. Go on —sit down and I'll get you something to eat.'

'I don't want anything. I told you before!'

'But you *must*!'

Rummage gave him a severe look. 'Please don't shout!'

'Oh yes, I forgot—I'm sorry,' Snug whispered. 'You've had quite a rough time, you know. You really should not have drunk so much—particularly when you are not used to it.'

Rummage looked at him closely then noticed the jar placed neatly by the chair. 'So it was you who broke into my home and interfered with me while I took a little nap, was it?'

'That was no nap. Do you know that you have slept through a whole Pause? And what is worse—you left your door wide open to the whole of the Shadow. I was surprised to find that you had not been carried off—you and all your precious belongings!'

Rummage looked at Snug, horrified. Had he really got himself into such a senseless state? Even though he knew it was the truth, for his head was spinning with the proof, he still could not imagined why he had behaved in such a reckless manner. He began to shake, both inside and out.

'Here, take it easy,' said Snug. 'It's all over now. That's it, you rest back there while I get something for your head. What you need is a cold slab of marble. That will soon draw all the aches out.'

'On second thoughts,' said Rummage, feeling that the last thing he wanted right then was one of Snug's rock remedies, 'I think I will have just a little something to steady my insides—perhaps the beetle-broth will do the trick.'

'As you please,' sighed the rock expert, remembering his quarrying days. 'But I still think you need a little something for your head. Then I would advise you to take a bath. You are beginning to smell like a pot of bad-ooze, if you don't mind me saying so.' Snug then emptied the contents of the bag he had been carrying as noiselessly as possible onto the table. 'You know, I wish you hadn't run off so quickly from the meeting.'

'I didn't run off—I left.'

'I know. But it looked as if you ran away from them—the noisy ones I mean.'

'As far as I remember, they all seemed to be noisy.'

'Ah, you shouldn't be so hard. Your message really frightened them, especially with your sudden appearance. The younger ones have not had your experience of affairs outside the land.'

'Where are the older ones then? There were plenty of faces missing from that rabble.'

Snug stopped mixing the broth for a moment. He did not like hearing his people being referred to as 'rabble' even by a fellow Jog and a friend. In the end he said, 'You have been away a long time.'

'And the people forget all too soon, it seems.'

'We have had many things on our minds. Surely you must know by now that the Rats have revived the Old Existence and have taken to raiding our warehouses again. Yes—well you can guess what is at the bottom of it all. They are after the Smelly Sticky Black Wet Stuff. And what's more, under the rules of the New Existence, which we, at least, still abide by, no nation is allowed to have either a guard or an army. We are supposed to be at peace with our neighbours, the Rats, yet they are attacking us with increasing hostility.'

'But tell me, Snug, if they are so desperate for the Smelly Sticky Black Wet Stuff, why don't you destroy it by fire?'

'But don't you recall, when Geovard devised his plan and when it was put into operation, it did not take just a drop of the filthy black liquid—it took all.'

'Then why don't you tell them?'

'Because so long as they think we still have it we can use it as a deterrent and we might be able to hold them at bay. The unfortunate thing is, though, the Rats believe that with the Smelly Sticky Black Wet Stuff they will be able to restore themselves to their former power and glory of which they claim the New Existence robbed them. Personally, I never have trusted Rats and if I was one myself, I think I would trust them less. They have no respect for their own kind—look what has happened to Meltamor.'

'What?' gasped Rummage. 'Nothing has happened to him. I saw him myself not so very long ago.'

'Well, I don't know about that. All I know is what I have been told by some of the last Jogs to have travelled that side of the sea. They say that Meltamor has lost all his authority—the Rats themselves think that he has grown mad in his old age. But the truth of the matter is, they say, that the Emperor is drifting into a world of make-believe, aided by weakening potions served to him on the instructions of his very own Minister Rats. They have reduced him to such a state so that he even doubts the soundness of his own mind. I fear the days of nobility are dead, my friend, and soon so will all those be who ever believed in them—unless strong action is taken.'

When he had finished, Snug handed the broth over to Rummage who did not yet feel like starting it, and seated himself in the other fireside chair. It was the one Geovard had occupied so many times in the past. 'I'm a practical Jog, you know that,' Snug began again. 'You can see how unprepared—how badly organized we have become as a nation. The old Jogs, which you mentioned earlier, can only think of one thing—work. They busy themselves in the fields, mines and warehouses, much the same way they used to in the Old Existence, faithful as ever to their old beliefs. The young, too, can think of only one thing—reparation. They do not like to see their futures falling foul of Rat-raiders. They also think—and this is probably the most important thing to them—that the Jogs were never paid back sufficiently for all the ills waged against us by the Rats in the Old Existence.'

'And where do you stand?'

Snug gave one of his characteristic sighs which usually indicated he was about to say something disagreeable. 'When I came back from the road after leaving you, Geovard and Scratcher to do what you liked with it I came back to a land without leaders. I brought back with me all sorts of tales and bits of news and very soon I became something of a popular Jog. Even though I was made out to be more than I am, there was little I could do about it—in fact, I quite enjoyed the lectures and the meetings which were held so I could tell of my experiences. I brought back the game of Pebblepocket which was quickly adopted by the young and that made me very popular among them. I did return to the Rummage mines and tried to settle down to the old job again, but the people wouldn't let me. Besides—not that I ever thought I'd live to admit it—life seemed to be so dull there for me! So where I stand, Rummage my friend, is with one foot in the past and the other in the present. That is where I stand —straddled between the two. I believe that work is still the best way of life, but I also believe in looking after that which the work produces and being paid in full for the comforts it provides. I have resigned myself to lead the Jogs' fight for reparations at the request of the people. Without a leader the land would be in turmoil and I have no doubt that the Rats would soon take keen advantage of that.'

Rummage drained the very last drop of the broth. Already, and with no help from marble slabs, his head was beginning to clear. He thought of all the time which had been wasted because of his stupidity. Seeing Snug reclining in the opposite fireside chair in much the same manner as Geovard reminded him suddenly of his errand.

'I had a very rough reception when I first arrived,' he said eventually.

'It would not have happened that way if you could have warned me of your return. It would have given me a chance to prepare you, at least,' Snug remarked.

'Snug, I really do need your help because what I said in the message....' But Rummage had no more time to explain. The sound of a distant rumble froze the words in his throat. Both Jogs sprang up and cautiously moved to the door where they opened it a tiny crack. Never before had they heard so terrifying a sound. It was like rock being torn from rock. The street outside was deserted and now the noise had ceased, deathly quiet.

'It's just as Geovard warned. It is coming,' breathed Rummage.

'Save my snout—*what is?*'

'Horribillis, the monster! Look—look at the Great Star. It's opening. Oh, Geovard—poor Geovard!' Rummage suddenly flung open the door, scampered over his friend and ran into the street like a thing possessed.

'Rummage—stop! Beware of the Swoops. *Rummage!*'

II

Rummage did not stop until he reached the harbour. As he shivered with fear on the edge of the quay the sight of the dark and uninviting waters beneath brought him swiftly to his senses. What on earth had possessed him to go dashing out, unarmed, unprotected in any way, into the openness of the harbour without a thought for his own safety? Quickly, Rummage scuttled underneath a sheet of old awning to escape the naked light of the Moon, and stared steadfastly across the expanse of water before him. In the very very far distance he could just make out the shape of a hideous shadow emerged from the Great Star— just as Geovard had predicted it would. Soon it would have left the place they had foolishly called Paradise and begun its descent through the wild grass and moss-beds on the top of Understar, down the road into the land of the Rats. And there he knew his best friend would attempt to stop the beast. Somehow, Rummage told himself, he must cross the black and foul sea which separated the lands and rejoin blind Geovard while there was still time.

Not long afterwards a cautious and equally nervous Jog crept along the shadows with an old blanket over his head and a hefty stick in his hand. It was Snug.

'Rummage—where are you! Are you mad?'

'I'm over here, beneath this cover. Snug, I must find a boat as soon as possible and get back to Geovard.'

Snug crept up to his side. 'Oh, Rummage, what's happening—is the world falling apart?'

'Can't you see? It's just as Geovard said in the message I brought to you. Horribillis is coming. Quickly, go and find your followers and prepare. Hide the food, hide the produce—hide yourselves in the deepest tunnels of the mines. There is no time to lose. Oh, I wish you had listened in the first place!'

'But what about you—where are you going?'

'I've told you. I'm going back to Geovard. He's sworn to lead the first attack against Horribillis along the road on Understar. I must get back to him. He needs me.'

'Aren't you afraid?'

'I don't know. I don't know anything any more.'

Soon, Rummage was alone again after saying farewell to Snug and embracing him, perhaps for the last time. All fears, other than not being able to reach his friend in time, evaporated from his heart. It gave him extra strength—extra will—to the extent of his doing things he would not have the courage to do at other times.

Scampering along the harbour wall, he came to a small raft moored to one of the large barges. He could see that it was intended for carrying a small cargo only, but the sight of such a small and personal craft filled his heart with hope. He then did something he had never done before. He jumped onto the vessel, ignoring the terrible swaying and sinking sensations beneath his feet, and emptied the entire cargo into the sea. His idea had been to paddle his way out and over Altos, once the load had been lightened. But as he held the awning aloft in one hand, a very strange thing happened—the fabric filled with a light breeze and began to blow the raft out of the harbour. As the vessel became lighter still and clear of the sheltered foreshore, it began to move forward with such amazing speed that Rummage could hardly believe what was happening. The Moon passed by, high above him, and the sands of his homeland became distant and obscured by shadows. Again, the tip of Understar seemed to call him forth by unnatural powers, as it had done once before ...

'You have found me,
You have found me,
In your dreams I'll always be.
Whether in sleep-fear
Or in sleep-smile
You'll always hold the sight of me ...'

And by the time the chant was over, the far shore stretched before him once again, just as if he had never left.

Even before Rummage had a chance to pull the raft onto the beach and scramble through the damp patches, he could hear the sound of a land in great turmoil. Rats were running everywhere, each carrying as much as could be carried in haste. Nobody took the slightest notice of the Jog, or if they did, simply chose to ignore him, even though he was fighting against a stream fleeing from the centre of the town. When he eventually reached the Rat harbour, he saw a strong body of soldiers guarding all that remained of the fleet.

'No one can board a vessel until our leader has given the order!' he heard a captain say to an old noble Rat with his family.

'But that's *my* vessel down there—I own it!' the dignitary protested.

'Not under the new decree, you don't. Our leader has ordered that *all* vessels must be handed over to the Army—even the merchant vessels.'

'Pah! Our leader is an old Rat—he's losing his wits!'

The guard caught him by the ear. 'Careful, friend. I'm not speaking about the Old Emperor—whom your generation chose to lead the entire Rat nation. I'm talking about our leader, Lord Scratcher, Roadbuilder and Champion of Jogs. So, if you know what's good for you, you'll make him your Leader, too. Now, clear the way, or you'll be placed under arrest for obstructing his Lordship's word!'

Quite naturally, the news that Scratcher had taken full advantage of the situation and had set himself up as leader distressed Rummage somewhat. Apart from anything else, it must have made Geovard's job almost impossible, Rummage thought as he drifted into the shadows to escape being recognized. Neither was he keen to hear of Scratcher's new title, 'Champion of Jogs' and wondered to what particular event it referred. Rummage made up his mind to challenge Scratcher on this point when they next met.

Geovard's cottage was found to be in chaos when Rummage arrived and there was definitely no sign of the blind soldier. It looked as if he had left in a great hurry and in great temper —tables and chairs were upturned and many cherished belongings were carelessly strewn over the floor. It was a very depressing sight to one who loved neatness and orderliness, but the picture of destruction seemed to go with the Times. Outside in the street again, the very air seemed to be hostile to the keen senses of a thinking Jog and despair tugged him back at every step.

The middle of the town was filled with numb quietness at the centre of which the deserted Marble Halls of Meltamor formed a mound of ghostly Moonlight. There was no guard at the gate to challenge the Jog, no petty official within to prevent him walking along a corridor—yet there was a sound. It was not until Rummage had entered the Great Chamber that he heard it, at first a faint whisper hardly perceptible above the sound of his own breathing and then, as he drew nearer to a small and insignificant chamber, he knew it to be the sound of a Rat weeping. Rummage entered the room quietly and carefully.

Meltamor was sitting on a small carved throne staring into his lap. He was dressed in his most regal colours. Scattered around his feet were all the orders, decrees, laws, rules, memos and notes he had ever made during his long and difficult life. They were torn in half and soaked through by his own tears.

Rummage approached him gently, whispering, 'Your Majesty.'

At first Meltamor did not hear him so Rummage tried again. 'What have they done to you, Your Majesty?' Slowly, the old Rat lifted his head and stared at his visitor through watery, pink eyes. 'Who—who are you? You're not a Rat—are you?'

'I'm Rummage, Your Majesty.... Jog Rummage, friend of Geovard and a good friend of yours.'

'I have no friends,' sobbed Meltamor, 'not any more. They have all left me now.' A large teardrop slid to the end of his snout and splashed onto the papers beneath. 'Look—look what they've done! They've torn all my rules—my own rules which I made for them. My Ministers won't serve me any more. They say I am mad. They are right, you know. Just look at me weeping. I am weak, I have no power left to either help myself or my people. They are right ... death is the only thing left for me now. They are kind ... look, they've left me a bad-ooze potion for me to drink so I can end it all.' He held up a small black cup which Rummage had not at first seen. 'It's the only thing left, they say, because my Doctors can do no more for me ... you see, I'm insane ... I must remove myself from office to make way for a younger Rat.' He moved the cup closer to his lips. 'I know they are only doing it for my own good ... I'm finished!'

Before the Rat could swallow the death-potion, Rummage knocked it angrily from his hand. 'Don't! You've been tricked!'

Meltamor was both startled and offended by the action. 'How dare you!' he shouted with just a trace of the old dignity in his voice.

'You've been tricked, Your Majesty—can't you see? You are no more insane than I am!' Rummage insisted.

'Tricked?'

'By your very own Ministers. I don't quite know how—perhaps by potions—but they have slowly taken advantage of your trust.'

'But—but they said that I had lost my reason and the laws which I have issued have caused the people to flee from the town. You must have seen that for yourself ... isn't the town deserted? I have looked and searched, but I cannot find a soul!' moaned Meltamor.

'Oh sir, please listen ... you're not mad. Your laws were always true, wise and just. The people have not fled their homes because of you but because a terrible monster is descending into your land from the Great Star and the whole nation is afraid of what it might do.'

'Monster? What monster?'

'The most horrific, ugliest monster ever known to Rat or Jog,

165

Your Majesty. But haven't you been told—didn't Geovard come to bring you the awful news so that you could prepare?'

'Geovard? Oh ... Geovard ... yes, I remember him. Wait a moment, aren't you his friend? Rummage ... that's it ... I remember now. You both came to see me a short while ago ... or was it a long while ago? I should be able to remember—I have had so few visitors in recent times. My Ministers would not allow it ... said it would tire me. But, you see, they did not realize how much I needed to see friends after Sulk, my cross-eyed companion, died. I missed him very much and no one realized. He was such a good friend ... humorous and wise, too. And then a Swoop attacked him on the road and pushed him over a cliff ... and I tried to go on, as if nothing had happened. Do you remember my cross-eyed companion, Sulk? ...'

Meltamor seemed to drift off into a reverie as Rummage said that he did remember, but eventually the Rat returned to him with a puzzled look. 'But wait ... you were asking about Geovard, weren't you? Yes, I seem to remember he did come to see me ... somebody told me, after he had gone away again ....
Scratcher, I believe. My doctor said I was unwell and must not have any visitors ... so Scratcher saw him for me. Scratcher is a fine Soldier Rat, don't you agree? He is the best we have, you know. He will replace me as Emperor, I think, when I am gone.'

'What about Geovard, Your Majesty?'

'Geovard? Oh yes ... he's a good soldier, too. I've always thought so. But you could never have a Jog as an Emperor for the Rats, no matter how good he was ... It's just not right ... it goes against the custom.'

'But I didn't mean that, Your Majesty. I meant, what has happened to him—are you sure he came here?'

'Oh yes. Yes, he came to see me ... just before my people fled from the town. But I was ill ... that's it ... I was ill and Scratcher took the message.'

'But did Scratcher give you the message?'

'I think so ... yes, I believe he did, now you mention it.'

'Oh please, Your Majesty ... please tell me what the message was. It is most important.'

'Is it? But it didn't seem very important ... something about going back up Understar ... and also bid me farewell, as he didn't think he would ever see me again ... but everyone was

166

saying that shortly afterwards.'

'Oh no!'

'What is it—are you ill, too?'

'Your Majesty, we are in great peril. A monster is descending upon us at this very moment!'

Meltamor looked at him curiously, dried his eyes then frowned. 'You have said that before, I recollect. What kind of monster could this be—has it a name?'

'Oh sire, it is like nothing we have seen before—worse than all the monsters of the myths and legends. It comes from beyond the Great Star without cause or reason and it has been named Horribillis. Haven't you heard the terrible rumbles coming from the top of Understar?'

'But my doctors told me that those noises were a sign of my insanity and that they were in my head alone.'

'Well, they are not. They are in everyone's and they are real! Forgive me now, Your Majesty, though I may be too late I must go to Geovard's side so that he may not be alone when he faces Horribillis on the mountainside.'

'No—wait. Don't go. Please stay here with me so I have some-one to talk to.'

'But I can't stay ... Geovard's life may be in danger. I must go straight away or I may be too late.'

'Then—take me with you. But don't leave me all alone in my empty palace. If you believe me not to be insane, won't you take me with you?'

III

Rummage had no other choice than to take old Emperor Mel-tamor with him, even though he knew it meant the journey would be much slower. He simply could not, under any circum-stances, leave the Rat at the mercy of his enforced solitude for he would only fall back into the stupor of his own imagined insanity. So the two set off for the heights of the road, carrying with them blindfolds to protect their eyes against the light, tackle for the difficult terrain and a grim determination to find the lone soldier, Geovard.

They passed through the deserted streets and through those

167

territories which eventually led up to the first cliffs of Understar. It was a terrifying journey for both. The ground very often trembled beneath their feet and the powerful, destructive noise of the monster resounded in the air about them.

The Great Star had grown to twice its original diameter so that its powerful rays of light picked out the shapes of jagged rocks all along the road. Rummage and Meltamor climbed slowly upwards not knowing what they would meet on the next ledge. Occasionally, they came across some of Geovard's tracks, especially when he had missed his way and was forced to grovel in the dust before he could overcome some obstacle. They were welcoming signs to the two followers.

They had climbed just over a quarter of the mountain's height when they first caught sight of the blind Jog. He was standing upon the edge of the large plateau, high above them. Rummage's heart skipped with joy as he pointed the figure out to Meltamor who had finally caught up with him. But then, both their hearts almost stopped beating entirely. A short distance in front of the blind warrior stood Horribillis, towering upwards and disappearing into the Shadow.

'A Shadow creature!' Meltamor gasped. 'So all the legends are true!'

Rummage tried to call out to his friend, but his voice would not leave his throat. He could only stare helplessly upwards.

Geovard had been waiting. He had chosen his spot carefully. He knew the plateau better than any other part of the road because of the number of camps which had been made there. The extra light from the Great Star had improved his vision tremendously, but after he had taken his bearings Geovard had hung back in the shadows. Upon this quiet and simple spot he would do or die with Horribillis, the first thing he had ever feared in his whole life. But all fear had left him now. He was like the cold stone of the mines. His spines were fixed in the darkness and he was ready.

At first there had been the terrible sounds of Horribillis destroying Paradise, tearing rock from rock and tearing up the earth. Then the rocks were sent tumbling down the mountainside, some of which nearly hit him. But Geovard stood firm. Slowly, cautiously, the monster approached on three legs—two fat, lumbering ones, and a much thinner support which swung over and tested the ground all round. Downwards came the three legs, descending cliff-faces in one step and sending up choking dust clouds. The accompanying noise was deafening and echoed into the Shadow so that even the Swoops held back in fear. But Geovard, who was above all things of darkness, was without fear of any kind.

Horribillis finally reached the edge of the plateau where it paused. Its slow, voluminous breaths filled the air as if the journey downwards had been exhausting. At last, Geovard caught the first sniff of its foul odour. Through his half-blindness, he could see two mountainous legs reaching ever upwards and the thinner probe testing the ground all about. Every other feature of the monster was lost in the Shadow—body, neck and head beyond his imagination.

Geovard had a simple plan. He would first challenge and assault Horribillis and then attempt to lead it to the sheer cliff at the edge of the plateau—the same place from which Sulk had been pushed to his death by the Swoops. There were steep, sharp rocks at the foot of the cliff and, beneath that, the sea. As the monster approached, Geovard moved from his hiding place.

'Advance no further, Horribillis! I am Geovard the Warrior— the fearless Jog. I will not let you pass so you can ravage the lands beneath Understar!'

With that, Geovard moved towards the beast. But Horribillis failed to acknowledge him. The Jog did not know that his voice could not be heard above the sound of the monster's heavy breathing and the grinding of earth and rock beneath its heavy feet. Neither did Geovard realize that he was still obscured by shadow.

The monster moved forward with unnerving speed. Geovard suddenly found that he was trapped between Horribillis and the steep edge of the plateau. He backed away trying to escape the sweep of the thin leg, crying out defiantly, 'It's death to those who wantonly destroy that which was made in peace. Come no further—Beast of the Light—but do battle with Geovard the fearless, here on Understar!' But Geovard's challenges were useless and could not lure Horribillis from the path of the road.

'You cowardly and senseless beast. Fight me—fight me!' Geovard's temper rose in his blood. 'Do you think that you are too good for a blind Jog? Fight me then! I can see all there is to see of you—you're a coward!' And with that, Geovard made a desperate rush forward for one of the enormous legs but as he did, the limb rushed to meet him, struck him heavily in the side and knocked him from the plateau to the ledge beneath. Geovard lay stunned and helpless as he caught sight of the Moon reeling above him. Then all his life senses came to an end with a small cry.

From a ledge far below, Rummage heard the cry and it pierced his heart. He had seen Geovard knocked from the plateau and then a huge mountain descend and crush him underfoot as if he had never existed. He had seen it all, with Meltamor, and much, much later, after they had fled from the path of Horribillis and sought sanctuary in the Marble Halls, he still could not believe that his best and lifelong friend was now dead. But Meltamor knew it.

The cry had reached him also and somehow had shattered a spell his own kind had cast about him. Meltamor suddenly saw with far-reaching clarity how his trust had been abused by the Minister Rats and how they had weakened his spirit. It horrified him to think of the terrible disgrace he had almost incurred on the whole of his family line—that he should fall from office by taking his own life—and thought himself greatly indebted to Jog Rummage for saving him. Meltamor now realized that there was only one thing left for him to do. He served Rummage a special sleeping draught so that he might get some rest after his long ordeal and, afterwards, retired to his own room to think out a plan.

In the chamber Meltamor gradually pieced together all that had happened and saw the lies and ploys that had been used to undermine his confidence in his ability to rule. Working with the Minister Rats, experts in bad-ooze potion had devised methods of concealing the essence of their brews in the Emperor's drinks and food. This had weakened Meltamor's health and when he knew himself that there was no reason for his falling ill so often, it was then that his doctors admitted that they had been treating him with sweet-rock medicine knowing that there was nothing wrong with him at all. The weaker the Emperor became, the more it was suggested to him—by first one courtier then another—that he was imagining the illness.

They then began to show signs of doubting his ability to draft new laws and to govern the people. And from that time forth, as he grew weaker still, he began to doubt his own sanity until he relied completely on the Minister Rats for guidance and the Doctor Rats to keep him alive.

Those who had plotted against him knew that the only way he could be removed from the throne was to get him to end his own life. In that way, the people would not be suspicious if it was coupled with the Emperor demonstrating the unsoundness of his own mind. To effect this, they issued phoney laws which they later got him to sign. These laws were designed to annoy and enrage the people—good examples of which were the Jog Superior Laws declaring that Jog intellect was superior to the Rats' and that their philosophies often afforded a better way of life.

The Ministers hoped to achieve two things by this, repealing the terms of the New Existence so that the land of the Rats might once again profit by the labour of the Jogs, and bringing to an end the Meltamor line of imperial rule. After the road had been abandoned by the majority, they also believed that Scratcher—the only other possible contender for the power of the land—had perished on the road, so once Meltamor had been put out of the way, the spoils could be divided between the conspirators.

But now Scratcher had returned it was almost inevitable that he would become the leader of the people. Meltamor knew himself to be too weak and too old to hope that his power might ever be restored. But his dignity remained and he could do something to save the name of his family. He began to devise his own plan to bring about the downfall of Horribillis, taking his examples from the way in which he had been systematically attacked at his weakest point, and from Geovard's courage.

17

I

Rummage awoke after a fitful rest. Food had been placed by his bed, but on recalling the tragedy of Geovard's death he found he could not eat a thing. The end, he knew, was an inevitable fact of life, but that did little to ease the pain of lost comradeship. Yet, there was a little comfort to be gained in knowing the circumstances of his best friend's death and that Geovard had not given himself easily to Horribillis.

Eventually, Rummage arose and went to find the estranged Emperor Rat. He found instead an uninhabited chamber strewn with garments of war. To Rummage, it looked as if Meltamor had been in a great hurry to leave the palace and also had been in confusion about what he should wear for the occasion. As he stood there wondering, he began to feel tremors shaking the earth beneath his feet. They were hardly noticeable at first, but they gradually increased in intensity until the walls, ceilings and floors all began to shake at regular, rhythmic intervals. The furniture began moving along the floor in a series of jumps—pursued in much the same manner by a very frightened Jog—until the roof above began to crack, shedding dust and rubble over everything beneath. Rummage knew exactly what it was. It was a giant approaching with crushing feet; it was Horribillis walking through the land of the Rats, pulverizing everything in its path. And it was exactly when Rummage realized this, that he sped from the chamber, along the crumbling corridors and out towards the main door in a desperate attempt to get out of the hideous creature's path.

When he eventually reached the main door, already in a state of panic, the sight which then confronted him drained him of all his remaining energy so that he sank, prostrate, upon the cold marble floor. For just a short distance from where he lay shivering, he could see a most incredible figure defying the monster of the darkness beyond. It was Meltamor—brave and terrible;

a silver-grey naked ghost of the Moonlight. Not so much as one whisker quivered in fear of Horribillis. The Rat stood perfectly still, like a stone, and seemed transformed by the light glistening on his unclothed fur into the youth he must have once been. To Rummage's eyes, Meltamor was both beautiful and unreal, like something out of a sleep-smile. And the Jog's heart was at once in awe of the spectacle on the edge of the parapet. There seemed no one left in the whole land except for the naked, silver Rat and the colossal Horribillis, shaking the ground underfoot as it approached. And still the Rat did not move. Rummage wanted to turn away, for he felt sure nothing could stop the monster from crushing both the Emperor and the Marble Halls of Mel-tamor. But he could not move, so he closed his eyes tightly as the footsteps shook everything about him, and waited for it all to end.

To the Jog's amazement in his secluded darkness, the end did not come so swiftly—in fact it did not come at all. The footfalls gradually faded away rather than increased and the rubble stopped falling. Rummage slowly opened his eyes. But there was nothing to see apart from the Moonlight and the shadows beyond. The spectre had fled from the edge of the parapet—the Emperor had vanished. Rummage crawled out as quietly as he could. The tremors were still pulsing through the ground beneath his belly but they were definitely moving away, in the direction of the harbour it seemed. What had happened to Meltamor, the Jog wondered as he reached the edge of the parapet. Perhaps he had fallen over the edge—perhaps Horribillis had scooped him up ... Rummage stood up in the Moonlight as he began to grow more anxious, and peered intensely into the shadows around him. Then to his horror, one of the shadows spoke.

'Rummage—get back out of sight!' The voice was distinc-tively that of a Rat, yet it was not the voice of Meltamor. 'Get back, I say, before the Shadow creature sees you!' Rummage withdrew from the patch of light into the nearest shadow.

'Is that you, Scratcher?'

'This way—over here, quickly, while you still have a chance!' Rummage turned on his heels and fled to the nearest rock where he was very surprised to find three Rats piled on top of each other, the topmost of which was Scratcher. They all shook from nose to tail and were as pale as stone.

'What's the matter with you all? Are you ill?' asked Rummage, startled. Scratcher looked at him with fear still in his eyes.

'But—didn't you see the great beast pass by?'

'Or hear him?' asked the Rat beneath.

'Or feel him?' asked the Rat beneath him, who was closest to the ground.

'*Silence!*' ordered Scratcher in an effort to bring himself back to normal. 'Get out from underneath me and find another rock to hide behind!' And with that, he kicked them both out into the darkness before they could utter one word of protest. A weak smile slid over the new lord's face.

'Of course I saw the beast,' Rummage said at last, as he drew closer. 'But didn't you see Meltamor, as well?' Rummage added.

Scratcher looked shocked all over again. 'Meltamor? But isn't he ... ?'

'Brave?' interceded the Jog. 'Yes, he is brave—just like Geovard was. The Emperor of *All* Rats is taking on Horribillis single-handed, while the humbler creatures, like you and me, shiver in fear behind rocks.' In case some of the Rats hiding close by should have heard Rummage's remarks, Scratcher was about to announce that he was not in the least afraid of the monster, but he was very fortunate for, at that moment, a look-out suddenly called from the ledge above.

'Look, sire. The monster has reached the harbour and demolished the fleet!' As Rummage's eyes grew accustomed to the shadows he could make out more and more of the Rat shapes. It seemed Scratcher had the whole army with him. 'What are we to do, Your Lordship—we are *doomed*!' The word rang out like the note of a bell and was heard by all.

'Hold your tongue, look-out!' hissed Scratcher. 'I will tell you when you are doomed!' The anxious cries and moans began to subside. Scratcher wondered what on earth he was going to say and do next. Rummage's presence made him feel uneasy. 'Anyway,' he finally said to the Jog, 'what are you doing here? I thought you were back among your own kind.'

'I suppose you know that Geovard is dead?' replied Rummage, bleakly. Scratcher felt even more awkward. In the distance, the sound of Horribillis brought news of destruction to the ears of every horrified listener. The monster moved without reason. Never before had such a disaster befallen their land. Horribillis towered above everything; its very shape and size was beyond their understanding and it cast aside roads and dwellings as if they were no more than grains of sand. One moment Scratcher thought he had found Paradise and then, the next thing he knew, the Warden of the Land of Shadows pitched its wrath in full fury against him.

'Horribillis killed Geovard on Understar,' Rummage muttered.

'Who did?'

'The monster. It is called Horribillis.'

'By whose decree?' Scratcher demanded, alarmed that he had not been informed or even consulted on the matter.

'Geovard's!' A coil of anger unwound within the Jog. 'Since he was the first to perish in attempting to save our skins, I think the least we can do is use the name he chose for the monster— don't you?'

Scratcher nodded, reluctantly.

'Now that we've agreed on that, let us try to prevent another tragedy.'

The Rat looked at him closely. 'What are you talking about?'

'Meltamor—your Emperor. At least, he was. But he tells me you do not think that he is good enough for the job.'

'Rummage, you do not understand. Meltamor is no longer fit to lead. He has gone quite mad.'

'Perhaps he is mad—or perhaps he is surrounded by madness.'

'Rummage! I ask you to remember that you are on foreign soil. This is not your land; this is mine. And these are not your affairs, these are mine—so don't meddle!'

'But what about your soldiers? They saw Meltamor facing the monster alone. Who will they follow now—a hero like Meltamor, or an opportunist like you?'

Scratcher's pride suffered a heavy blow with those words, but he was able to hold back his feelings. His soldiers had closed in, attracted by the raised voices. 'Who gave you the order to leave your posts? Get back to them at once and wait for my command.' As the Rats faded back into the shadows, Scratcher turned to Rummage and gave him a sickly smile. 'You are tired, my friend, and your heart is full of grief. You do not see things as they really are. To them,' he whispered, pointing vaguely in the direction of the army, 'Meltamor is already dead. He died a mad Rat's death. What we all saw in the moonlight was not Meltamor standing in defiance of this—Horribillis—but Meltamor's ghost. That is what they believe. And they will not follow a ghost no matter how brave he appears to be. So you see my friend, I no longer have to prove myself better than he is any way —for to do that I would have to prove myself madder than he is.'

As Scratcher finished what he thought was a perfect speech, a terrible noise filled the air. It was the sound of the sea being torn from its bed and pulled apart by mighty limbs. The soldiers moaned and the Sea Rats called out. Horribillis waded through the depths of Altos as if it were no more than a pool of Shadow-fall. The image of the Moon was sliced by a thousand dark-edged waves. It brought dread to everyone's heart to see their world so haphazardly profaned. Rummage gazed at the Moon above them and then back to the colossus from the Great Star. In the wake of the mindless Creature he saw a small white form following close behind, bobbing in the boil of black water. Scratcher and the other Rats, too, saw Meltamor's ghost in single-minded pursuit of his own destiny.

Rummage and the Rats soon parted company. The Jog was sickened by what had come to pass and wanted to be alone. Scratcher watched him go down towards the harbour along the path of destruction. Rummage was trapped and helpless in the Land of the Rats. If he wanted to get back to his home land, soon he would have to strike a bargain with Scratcher, and then the Lord Rat would have him.

Rummage stared out after the monster and watched its every move from a safe distance. It seemed to wander aimlessly, without purpose or reason, crushing things underfoot, oblivious to everything sacred in their lives. The Jog followed on, as far as he could, hardly aware of his own purpose. His own fear now seemed to be in ruins like the town around him, crushed from his body like the juice of a mushroom. He was so light and empty of feeling he seemed to tumble along in the gutters. But as he reached the harbour wall he paused and held his breath as the gigantic form of Horribillis touched the farthermost shores of Altos and then plunged into the sands of his own land. Awkwardly, the monster's great body turned in the full light of the Moon and at once Rummage caught his first sight of Horribillis' face. It was the most frightening of all sights he had ever seen. After Rummage found that he had survived this shock, there seemed little point in his ever being frightened by anything again.

II

In his madness, Meltamor followed the great Horribillis over land and water. His pink eyes were fixed on one point of the monster's anatomy, his teeth gritted and sharpened especially for the task. If his thoughts strayed at all from his one objective, it was to the memory of his noble family and his ancestral line—all of whom had met some noble end. Nobility was as much a part of the Meltamor's family character as his silver-grey fur and aristocratic snout.

When Horribillis turned to face the path of destruction and pay homage to the Great Star, it took so long in its manoeuvres, that Meltamor had ample time to take cover and observe. His wet fur clung sleekly to his body. He felt like a youth again in the prime of life—seeking out a quarry to administer justice with his fore-teeth. The terrain was unfamiliar to the Rat. Meltamor did not quite realize where he was. But it did not matter; he used his senses to their fullest capacity in orientating himself. His one task was to get in front of Horribillis without being seen. He took his chance when the monster was preoccupied and sprang up towards the hills, melting into every shadow along the way. Higher and higher climbed the heroic Rat, effortlessly, and exhilarated by a magic running through him from whiskers to tail. Up above the mines he scaled, above the groves and the plateau that Rummage knew so well until he reached the place of the Jogs' High Mountains, where they stretched endlessly upwards into the Land of Shadows. Meltamor had no fear now to look into that once dreaded canopy, or to cower from the menace of Swoops. The mountainside would be a final throne from which he would issue his last decree.

Horribillis rebuked the world into which it had come, in deafening tones. One thin leg swung high above the hills in which the Jogs hid and trembled. It moved closer to where Meltamor crouched in silence, baring his finest weapons—long white teeth. He saw the second leg lift to make a step forward. Only one leg now remained to support the beast. Meltamor sprang for the

177

knee with all the strength in his body. He seemed to fly through the air—the finest leap he had ever made—and struck his target as easily as if it had been a whisker away. The long teeth sank home. But the flesh would not tear. Horribillis filled the air with a terrible cry. Yet the monster did not topple and its other legs soon corrected its balance. The noble Rat bit again and again into the flesh of the monster's knee, even as the first blows rained down upon his back. Meltamor stood little chance now of escaping with his life. He did not seem to care. He was full to the brim with fury as the last of his energy blazed like a torch in his blood. Soon, his whole body burned in a final spasm before being dowsed forever in a total and inky blackness.

The heroic battle did not pass unwitnessed. Several young-blooded Jogs had followed the Rat who followed the monster. They had never seen a Rat alone before and they were very suspicious of its silent and secretive actions, fearing that already the first looter had entered their lands. They did not know they were watching the Emperor of All Rats until Snug recognized him slipping through a pool of Moonlight and whispered his name.

Snug was suspicious too. He had led the small and brave troop of Jogs through the fields and groves beneath the foothills. They had observed everything as it had happened—the silent, magnificent leap of Meltamor, his attempt to bring his quarry down and finally, Horribillis' brutal reprisal as the Rat buried his teeth into the obnoxious flesh in a death-grip. They watched in awe as, during the struggle, the monster's spawn tumbled from the sky and rolled into a shadow.

Now there were two monsters in the land.

After Meltamor's body had been thrown down onto the bare cold rocks, Horribillis moved away, bellowing into the Shadow the loss of its only child. The watchers saw a dazzling, orange star-eye stare out across their land and then close. Little Horribillis, the fat spawn of the monster, lay motionless in the darkness of a small valley. Perhaps, hoped the Jogs, it had been stunned by the fall. After a great deal of time had passed and Little Horribillis still did not stir, Snug found enough courage to lead his army up the slope of the valley so that they might observe the new monster from a ledge.

When they reached a suitable spot, Snug crept out to the edge to survey the scene. Beneath him, Little Horribillis gave out no signs of life, and a short distance from the new creature's stubby legs lay the pathetic, broken body of Meltamor the Noble. An icy hand gripped Snug's heart. Under normal conditions he was a Jog of little emotion, but something reached him that moment. For there, wasted and bleeding on the rocks, lay the body of the finest exponent of Pebblepocket he had ever known. Then, the heat of revenge entered the Jog's blood.

Unbeknown to Snug, the bravest of the young Jogs, Cudgel, had crept out from the shadow to get his first glimpse of Little Horribillis. On reaching the ledge, Cudgel was so over-awed by the sight of the vast, round body beneath, he lost his balance. Before Snug had time to catch him, Cudgel plummeted into the valley below and landed on the monster's chest. The Jogs all caught their breaths and fully expected to witness another wretched slaughter. Feeling that his end had truly arrived, Cudgel put up a desperate, though somewhat one-sided fight with the monster under his feet. But the creature did not stir, even as the Jog tore frantically into his chest. Cudgel was both delighted and suspicious about not being eaten alive. He tasted Little Horribillis' fabric, then listened to the great body, then smelt it. Having convinced himself there was absolutely nothing to be afraid of, he gave a sudden shout of joy and leapt into the air.

'This is no beast!' he yelled to those staring wide-eyed down at him. 'This has no life! Come, jump, my friends—jump onto this bloated rag!'

Snug looked from one Jog to another 'Are you sure? Are you absolutely sure?'

'Of course! Of course I am!' Cudgel yelled back, indignantly. 'If you don't believe me—watch!' The young Jog first took a deep breath, gathered his courage, then danced all over the Creature's chest and upturned face. Finally he kicked its nose, and swung to the ground by its ear into which he screamed '*Wake up!*' Still, the monster did not move and that was enough to convince everyone present that, unlike its parent, Little Horribillis was as lifeless as the rocks on which it lay. They all cheered Cudgel for his bravery and then let out individual sighs of relief.

Horribillis had moved far away. The monster's rumblings could still be both heard and felt, but the Jogs were much safer now it had passed beyond the land of the High Mountains. No one, as far as they knew, lived there, for it was far too distant from the light of the Moon and was a dark, damp and dismal place. Out of respect, Snug carried Meltamor's body to a high, open area where the Moon shone full and brightly, so that, piece by piece, his good spirit would turn into Moonlight and that which was bad would be carried off by the Swoops back to the Land of Shadows. That was the custom. When the Jog returned, he found that the young Jogs had already begun to tear at the fabric of Little Horribillis in tests of strength and mock courage. He was in the middle of this spectacle when, to his utter surprise, Rummage found him.

The two Jogs drew aside, leaving the others at their play. Rummage quickly told Snug of all the events in the order of their happening. Snug was very grieved to hear of Geovard's death, as Rummage was to hear of Meltamor's when it was Snug's turn to tell the news. The Jog leader was alarmed to hear that Scratcher had brought Rummage across Altos in the last boat of the fleet, and even more alarmed when it was revealed that Scratcher and a small army were anchored at the harbour. Rummage assured his friend that the Rats had come in peace and sought counsel with the Jogs.

Soon afterwards, Snug took his own army to the harbour once they had made the necessary preparations, leaving Rummage all alone with Little Horribillis. He was dismayed to see how the young Jogs had abused the carcass. The Jog nation, it seemed, was becoming unruly and losing the simple and dignified respect it once had for things not fully understood.

Rummage felt bewildered by the tumultuous events which had come to pass and grew melancholy for companions who, but a short while before, had upheld his spirit in troublesome times. He left the valley and Little Horribillis to the shadows, and wandered through the mushroom groves to his favourite plateau overlooking Altos. He took from a small pouch a piece of parchment and a writing stick which he normally used for poetry, and wrote down all the fears occupying his mind. The list was long and detailed, but when the task was completed, Rummage carefully folded the paper and returned it with numerous heavy stones to the pouch. In a series of slow arcs, he swung the heavy bag by its draw-string around his head three times saying, 'Troubles—be gone!' with every turn. On the last swing he let go of the string and the pouch flew out over the edge of the cliff and plummeted into the depths of Altos.

As he watched his troubles sink without a trace, Rummage immediately began to feel better. It was as if a great weight had been taken from his back, but more importantly, he had begun to think clearly once again. The phenomenon of Little Horribillis, the speechless, lifeless effigy, filled him with fresh wonder. There was nothing like it in either the Land of the Jogs or the Land of the Rats. Why should such a powerful monster such as Horribillis need to carry such a thing; what was its purpose and how had it been manufactured, in the Shadow or the land beyond the Great Star? Rummage wondered how he would ever manage to find answers to his questions and still keep a sane mind.

He was thinking in depth about the matter when, at the same time, he noted an irregular shape on the shore beneath. In all the times he had sat in that same spot on the high plateau over-looking the fields, shore and sea, he had never noticed anything different before. It was as if he had been waiting all of his life for such a sign to appear.

As he stared at the mysterious marks which were pressed into the soft sands, something stirred in the back of his mind, and then his imagination began to spring from one realization to the next. He could not get back to the shore quickly enough, dashing through the groves and fields past the mines and dwellings and out onto the open sands. There, he paused, breathless before a gigantic impression, crushed into the soft and moist grains. He followed the Shape around and viewed it from every possible angle and, struggling to get everything into perspective, he drew a much smaller version of what he saw in the sand. Then all at once—he knew. He remembered where he had seen the shape before—in his own cottage, amongst his own collection. Rummage's heart almost burst with the joy of this discovery. He cried out aloud, but there was nobody about to hear him. But then he stopped and thought again. What a challenge to their knowledge this new discovery would make, more disturbing than the effects of the light, the road, the Great Star or Horribillis itself, but the challenge was there and just had to be taken, sooner or later.

Before Rummage could reveal his new discovery to anyone, he knew there was one mistake which had to be put right im-mediately. Perhaps the task could not be undertaken alone—he did not know—but, in any case, Rummage thought it very unlikely he would be able to persuade other Jogs to help him with the task at such short notice, so he made his way, just as quickly as he could, back to his own cottage. There, he made up a pack of tackle, hooks and ropes. Then, from out of his most precious collection he took a large, flat piece of stiff white fabric on which was illuminated a black Shape. This, he placed by the door so that it could be picked up when he returned.

III

Snug had never really taken to Scratcher—or Scratcher to Snug, for that matter—which made the discussions they were now engaged in very tedious indeed. Affecting a grandiose pose, Scratcher insisted that his Minister Rats were consulted on every matter and that his Scribe Rats should note down every full-point and comma of the difficult conversation. Snug, on the other hand, was quite content to lean on Cudgel for advice, although it soon became obvious that the young Jog had more enthusiasm for talking than he had common sense.

Scratcher maintained the story that the Rats had come in peace, searching for the lost Emperor; a story which Snug might well have believed had not Rummage got to him first. The Lord Rat also suggested that an alliance might be formed by the two armies so that, together, they might effectively do battle with Horribillis. The idea appealed to Snug, but whispering in his ear, Cudgel reminded him of the reparation policy. He also reminded the leader of the Jogs of the motives behind the many recent raids on their lands by the Rats—to locate and to steal the Smelly Sticky Black Wet Stuff, so, by and large, Snug was warned off any permanent notion of Jogs joining forces with the Rats, regardless of the extra power it would give them against the might of Horribillis. But the real truth concerning the Smelly Sticky Black Wet Stuff was a closely guarded secret now known only to Rummage and Snug, who had discovered it in the first place.

It seemed that the largest warehouse in the land now had a new use. Even the sign on the door had been altered to read, 'The Great Meeting Hall'. Inside, the atmosphere was tense. The discussions so far had taken up a great deal of time, yet no decisions had been reached or firm conclusions drawn and the two sides were growing extremely tetchy and restless. The verbal contest so far had consisted of first one idea being suggested by one party and then another, issued from the other side, to negate the first. Having had very little experience of this sort of banter, Snug firmly believed that he was doing the right thing, even though it was giving him a frightful headache.

The two sides had reached a point where both thought it was the other's turn to speak and so a very rare silence settled throughout the Hall while the Rats and the Jogs stared blankly at each other, astonished. But the silence was brief indeed, shattered by a great commotion around the main door. Snug sent Cudgel to see what it was all about. He returned after a short while and informed the Jog Leader that Rummage was seeking an audience. Scratcher overheard the message. 'So,' he said, looking warily at Snug, 'the meddler returns.'

'I would be grateful if you wouldn't use that sort of expression when referring to my colleague. He used to be known as Rummage the Sensitive—Rummage the Wise to you, even in the New Existence.'

'I think you forget, Your Excellency, that I have spent a good deal of time in his company recently. I know him well—even better than yourself, perhaps. I can say this for him, he is not the Jog he once was. Oh, but he is still clever and knows a great deal. We have all benefited from his knowledge in the past, but I wonder how long it will remain sound? You have a saying for it I believe: "A cracked pot is best forgot".'

Snug did not appreciate this kind of talk from a Rat he had no particular affection for. But he realized there was an element of truth in what Scratcher had said. In many ways, Rummage seemed to be out of touch with the realities of their existence, and without bothering to think any further, Snug assumed it was because he had been so disturbed by the recent deaths. He told Cudgel to ask his old friend in. Cudgel returned to the door where, in a tone of great indifference, he told the older Jog that they had decided to see him. Rummage was far too elated by his recent discovery for the rudeness to affect him. He virtually burst into the Hall, struggling with the board bearing the Shape, which he eventually propped against a pillar for all to see. Rummage looked extremely dirty and bedraggled, and there was a wild fire in his eyes.

Snug felt very uneasy.

'Snug, Scratcher—thank goodness I've found you both at last ... Something has happened—something so marvellous, I hardly know how and where to start.'

Scratcher gave a short laugh. 'Why not try the beginning?'

'But that's the whole point—it's the beginning I'm talking about. Our beginning!'

'Rummage, what are you talking about? We know all there is to know about our beginning,' Snug reminded him. 'We were created from Moonlight and Shadow at the time of the First Pause. And there have always been Jogs and Rats from the beginning.'

'Yes, I know that is what we believe. But remember, we always thought the Shadow was endless until the Light ... and we always thought Swoops were our greatest fear, until Horribillis came along.'

'And Little Horribillis,' Cudgel reminded him.

'Don't tell me you've found something even worse!' mocked Scratcher.

'Please listen, all of you. This is no joking matter.'

'Go on,' said the Rat, 'tell us what you have discovered this time.' Rummage moved across to the Shape and picked it up for all to see.

'Do you remember this, Snug?' he asked.

Snug thought hard, back to the days of the mines. 'I don't remember that one in particular, but I guess I must have seen it—sometime.' He rubbed the end of his snout and turned to Scratcher. 'Rummage's ancestors began the mines and my family has always supervised the running of them. From time to time, while digging for sweetrock or mustard we came across certain objects which the Rummage family always collected as part of their tradition. On the whole, the objects turn out to be things which can be put to some good use—but the Shapes have always been the most mysterious. Rummage has collected so many it soon became impossible to remember them all. I have not his head for such matters.'

'But this Shape of all Shapes will go down in history. And do you know why? No, I can see that you don't, so I will have to tell you. This is the Shape of Horribillis' spoor—a print of the monster's foot.'

The room grew so silent it almost hurt the ears.

'Impossible!' Snug said stubbornly, breaking the spell at last. 'That Shape is a symbol of the ground in which it was found. I took it from the mines myself, long before anyone had ever heard of Horribillis. How can you say such a thing? Where's the sense in it—where's the proof?'

'The proof is out there on the shore, where the monster stepped into the soft sand. It is so big, the Shape can only be compared properly from the high plateau above the bay. As for the sense ...'

'There is no sense!' shouted Scratcher, angrily. 'How can our past have anything to do with that senseless, mindless wrecker of civilization?'

'If you please, let me offer my suggestion. I suggest that long ago, even before our beginning, the world was made by Horribillis, or its fellow creatures, who came down from the Great Star and scattered ...' The Hall quickly began to fill with laughter, beginning first with the Rats and then spreading infectiously to the Jogs. Rummage gritted his teeth and continued, for he had known from the start the task would be difficult. '... Who came down from the Star and scattered the ground with all the various rocks and stuffs and Shapes, then sowed the first seeds of moss and mushroom and then those of Rat and Jog and formed the Moon and the Shadow and Altos beneath to make our lands and give us a peaceful place to live so that we might look at what they had provided—and learn by it!' By the time he had finished, he was having to shout to make himself heard above the din. Scratcher and the Minister Rats were hysterical with laughter. The young Jogs gripped each other for support, with tears in their eyes. No one had ever heard anything more ludicrous than Rummage's suggestion.

There was only one among the listeners who did not mock him and that was Snug, because he considered the matter to be a very serious one indeed. For, to Snug, what Rummage had just committed was a public, verbal act of profanity against the all-sacred custom, around which the whole of civilization had revolved for both Rat and Jog since the world began. And Rummage had dared to question the custom.

It was a difficult thing for Rummage to believe that he had not made sense to anyone who was present in that room. For he had spoken in the golden light of new knowledge and could not understand his audience's reaction at all. He had been prepared to defend his argument, to tackle the doubts and questions that were bound to come his way, but he had not been prepared to face ridicule by the same people who had accepted his table of lunar occlusions, his theories about time and the stellar variations.

Snug gave him a severe look. 'Rummage, I think you are in great need of rest. You have worked hard for so long now, and so many things have troubled you recently. This meeting hall is no place for you. Why don't you go back to your own little cottage and lie down? I will come to call on you in a while and we can discuss things.'

Rummage looked at him incredulously. 'You don't believe me —you won't accept a word I have said!'

'You're tired, my friend.'

'I'm not tired!' Rummage protested. 'And I'm not in need of rest. I've come here especially to place this discovery at your feet, to open your eyes a little to things as they really could be— not as you want them to be for the sake of the custom. I tell you it's a mistake to make an outlaw of Horribillis just as it was a mistake for us ever to think we could dictate its motions or control its power—when it could be the founder of Our Times!'

'Is he serious?' Scratcher asked Snug.

'Rummage, enough is enough. You are making a fool of yourself.'

'I'm not ... I'm not! Why won't anyone listen to me?'

'Because you are talking utter nonsense. Oh, Rummage, I never thought I'd have to remind you of your duty as a Jog to the custom. You must always and at all times honour its principles.'

'Why should I when the custom itself could be dishonourable?' A compounded gasp of horror passed through the hall. 'I can see it all now,' he went on, 'by the looks on your faces. You have lost the will to challenge. We used to say, "Once you discover a threshold, it just has to be crossed." Now you no longer even want to acknowledge a threshold when it is the biggest thing ever to have happened in our entire existence. You are facing the wall with your eyes closed—all of you!'

'Oh, please don't be too hard on us, Rummage,' sneered

Scratcher. 'We don't have your marvellous vision to enable us to see round corners. But surely, even you must agree that you cannot be cleverer than the rest of us in this room put together. If there was a grain of sense in what you have suggested, wouldn't one of us see it and speak up on your behalf? Alas, my friend, even your closest companions will not be converted so easily. It hurts me to see you going the way of all base creatures. I implore you—throw out your ideas before they turn your mind completely!'

'My mind, Scratcher, cannot so easily be turned. The pattern has been with me since my birth. So for those of you who are unsure where my beliefs now lie, I will say again: do not harm Horribillis, Shape-maker. Its ancestors were the founders of Our Times. Our beginning was by their decree as is our destiny. I have already laboured to return Little Horribillis while its owner was sleeping on a cliff. We should not abuse anything which belongs to the monster or try to punish it for any wrongs which we think it has carried out against us.'

'It's a murderer—or have you forgotten already the death-blows dealt to Meltamor and Geovard!' said Snug.

'Scratcher was right!' Cudgel called out suddenly with rage. 'You are a meddler! Who gave you the right to touch, let alone move, Little Horribillis? That bag of rags belongs to me—not you!' But Rummage ignored him. It would have been impossible to explain anything sensibly to that hot-blooded youth.

'The best thing,' Snug said at last, 'would be for you to leave this meeting now. It has become clear that your mind is disturbed. Perhaps you will take my advice and get as much rest as possible. Things will look so very different then, I'm sure—especially if Horribillis returns.'

All at once, everyone was looking at him. He had become an embarrassment—even to his closest friends. Rummage then knew that he would never get them to change their minds. The custom would be continued in the same habitual way and everything associated with it—the Pause, the myths and legends, the beginning, the end—everything would continue in exactly the same way no matter how many suggestions he were to make. The Rat and Jog nations were far too busy with their own affairs to ever seriously challenge the nature of things about them. Rummage seemed to be a Jog alone. Perhaps it had all been inevitable that

187

he should out-grow the land into which he was born.

As he stood at the focal-point of a thousand gazes, with a great and heavy sadness in his heart, a voice called to him from within in a deep rhythmic song:

> 'You have found me, you have found me,
> In your dreams I'll always be,
> Whether in sleep-fear,
> Or in sleep-smile,
> You'll always hold the sight of me ...'

Then suddenly he knew perfectly well what he must do—he must challenge his own destiny, cast off the shackles which bound him by the habits and rituals of fear and find out what lay beyond that place they had called Paradise and through the Great Star.

These were the things he told the people in the great meeting hall. As far as the majority were concerned, his plans confirmed his own madness. Snug, he knew, would do his best to persuade him against undertaking such a perilous journey, but in the end, everyone would have to let him do what he wished—for that, too, was part of the custom. Cudgel and many of his friends were openly pleased when they heard that Rummage was planning to visit the Great Star. Naturally, they wished him no real harm, being a brother Jog, but their plans for the future of the Jog nation had no place for wild dreams—particularly from one born in the Old Existence.

Scratcher leaned over backwards to help Rummage remove himself from society. The Lord Rat even went so far as to write out a special decree to ensure Rummage's safe passage across Altos, through the Lands of the Rats and up where the road began on Understar. He also arranged for a small escort led by a captain Rat to accompany the Jog as far as the foothills. So, with the exception of Snug, everyone in the meeting hall was very relieved when Rummage bade them all farewell and left them to the all-important task of squabbling over tactics to trap Horribillis. And it was true to say that the Jog himself was not unhappy at the prospect of leaving them behind. He had reached a turning point. When one felt as sure as he did about something, carrying it out personally was only the next natural step. He was no longer prepared to argue about it.

After returning to his cottage, Rummage tried collecting to-

188

gether the barest essentials to take with him on the journey. But each time he collected a small heap of belongings, he found other things he did not want to leave behind. It was as if every item in his room was a life-long friend and having to decide those who could go with him and those who could not soon became a heart-breaking task. In the end, the only fair thing to do was to take nothing with him at all, so he said goodbye to everything in the room, individually, and then to the room itself, then the cottage and then the door, which he closed firmly behind him and walked out boldly into the Moonlight.

If he passed any of the Jog people on his way to the harbour, he was certainly unaware of it. Perhaps some had even said good-bye to him—he did not know. His heart was so vacant of feeling, time and distance meant nothing to him.

The Sea Rats were ready to leave when he arrived at their boat and moaned about being kept waiting by a Jog, although it was all talk, for none had the courage to come anywhere near him. Rummage sat quietly alone in the stern and slept dreamlessly for most of the sea journey.

Life had gradually returned to the Rat town. Merchants, Noble Rats and sightseers grouped on the harbour wall. As the crew made ready to disembark after the sea-crossing the crowd's attention was immediately drawn to the Jog.

'Is he a prisoner?' someone asked.

'You could say that. He's condemned himself,' said the captain of the vessel. 'This is Jog Rummage. He thinks we should all be paying homage to the monster who has destroyed your town. But even his own people now agree that he is mad, so now he has decided that he is too good to live with either Rat or Jog.'

The crowd began to mill around the lone passenger. 'What are we going to do with him?' they asked.

'Nothing!' shouted the captain, angrily, and he got a few of his sailors (who were in fact re-trained soldiers) to push the crowd away. 'Stand back everyone—stand back! I have a decree from Lord Scratcher here which guarantees the Jog a safe journey through our lands. Anyone who interferes will be dealt with severely. Do you understand?'

'Yes, we understand—but where are you sending him?'

'We are sending him nowhere. He is journeying of his own accord. He wants to climb the road again—don't you, Rummage? He wants to leave us all behind so he can communicate with the monsters beyond the Great Star—isn't that so?'

'But that's preposterous!' remarked a Noble Rat. 'The Shadow creature which has wrecked our lands and torn up the bed of the sea came from beyond the Great Star. The fool will be blinded by the light and killed the moment he enters their territories—if the Swoops don't get him first.'

'Be that as it may,' said the captain. 'If that's what a mad Jog wants to do—who are we to stand in his way?'

'Sir,' implored the Noble Rat, taking Rummage by the arm, 'I beg you to think again. What you are attempting is sheer suicide!' The captain grew angry and pushed the Noble Rat aside.

'By the decree!' he hissed, showing his foul teeth. 'Do you want me to bite your tail? Now stand aside and don't interfere!'

Rummage was escorted like a prisoner from the boat. As he passed through the harbour he chanced to look behind him. There he saw more soldiers getting into the boat for the return journey to the Land of the Jogs and the first real pang of concern tugged at his heart since his dismissal. But then he realized that his views meant nothing to anyone any more and in any case the politics of Rat and Jog all seemed so futile in the light of his new discovery. He was very glad, therefore, to get right away from the Rat town and gladder still when the escort left him alone to scale the road on Understar.

Rummage took one break only in the entire journey up the road and that was to enable him to take care of Geovard's body according to the custom, in the manner his dear dead friend would have most appreciated. He paid the great, heroic soldier a final unspoken tribute, then laid his body on a soft bed of fresh moss. From his own snout Rummage plucked a whisker and placed it in the hand of his comrade and there, in the privacy and quiet of the mountainside, wept openly in the Moonlight.

The road seemed so familiar to him now. He knew of all the best places to erect a camp but never used one of them. Something filled him with boundless energy—it was the will to explore.

It helped him to stay his fears and measure his step; it helped him to reassure himself that he still had a purpose for living and to overcome all obstacles in his path. Up and up he climbed until he lost sight of the lands in the mists of shadow below. The Moonlight was finally left behind and a bright white Starlight lit the way ahead. And then, all at once the face of the Great Star itself shone before him like a huge blinding doorway.

In a manner of which Geovard would have been proud, Rummage gathered all his strength and courage together. He then sped forward, hands over his eyes to shut out the light ... out through the Great Star just as fast as he could, until at last he fell amid a tangle of roots. Protected from the dazzle by a canopy of leaves, all enthusiasm to begin the adventure was soon overcome by a feeling of great drowsiness. Before he knew it, Rummage sank into a rich deep sleep.

18

I

The ancient blood-ache returned as he awoke and sniffed the gentle breeze. For a moment he wondered where he was. Then he remembered and tingled with excitement. Round about him the earth had been ruptured and the fragrance released. He wanted to stay forever just in that one spot and bathe in this giddy tranquillity. But there were smells and far cries calling him on and he knew he could no longer stay. He ran forwards. He ran and ran and ran ... it seemed to be forever.

All was far behind him now. He had risen magnificently above the dark clouds of the Shadows, through the eye of the Great Star and out into a new world which was fresh, free, alive and beautiful. He was so beguiled by what he found that he had no way to describe it—even to himself. The wonder and splendour of it all filled his eyes with tears of joy. He danced! Oh, how he danced, freely and effortless, rolling across the soils, bumping into tall, swaying plants. The deep dark blue above him seemed to stretch indefinitely, while around him a crisp, exciting green territory swept up towards the horizon. He was intoxicated by the air which brought to him the sweet smells of earth and vegetation. The perfumes mingled with his blood. He felt free, so free— and something else which he could not quite explain: he felt as if he belonged.

But nothing really surprised him on his first few steps into Starland, as he was to call it; nothing encouraged him to be cautious or discreet. His only true sensation was that of feeling so small and insignificant as he crept out across the soil plain and beneath the giant plants. He was a child again, full of pristine wonder, and he felt as if he wanted to investigate everything below above and around him at once, in case he never had the chance again.

On the edge of the forest of plants, he listened to the sounds in the wind. It was full of the voices of insect life and creatures deep in the green surrounding him. They were strange and hypnotic and beckoned him onwards. Rummage was suffused by a strange emotion. Never, in the most pleasant of his sleep-smiles, had he ever dreamed of such a wonderful place as Starland, yet it seemed to know him well enough and opened up paths for him to follow. To go forward without fear here seemed the most natural thing for him to do.

The excitement made his head spin and in spite of his sleep he was tired, after having climbed the road with hardly a break and nothing to eat. This at least had the effect of reassuring him that he was not dreaming because at times he began to wonder. Coming suddenly into this new world had been like being born again; it was a second chance to begin, to learn from the start and be aware of that learning all the time. It became clear to him then that he had outgrown his purpose in the world beneath. Soon, when others found the need to expand beyond the Lands of the Rats and the Jogs, they would want to join him. It would be for these people and these alone that he would return after he had carried out his journey of exploration.

Growing pangs of hunger brought on by the excitement compelled him to stop his dreaming and to move off into the forest in search of food. The forest was full of game and he discovered a very nourishing plant root which went down well with his first catch—a task made easier by the fact that most things seemed to be asleep. So with very little trouble at all he prepared and dispensed with a delicious meal. Afterwards, he ventured deeper into the swaying vegetation, puffing and panting at times as he struggled up mounds and down hollows filled with thick under-growth. Rummage felt happy and content. Starland at least presented no greater dangers than he had encountered in the Lands of Rats and the Jogs and there were many things to favour the new world. Beauty and richness here were so complete. He could see much further in the dark blue light than he had ever managed before in Moonlight where everything disappears into a shadow. Distant objects became more distinct and the colours all around were so vivid. The oppression of the Shadow had dis-appeared from above his head. For that reason alone, his heart felt a thousand times lighter.

Rummage saw many marvellous things as he journeyed—

bright new insects sleeping beneath overhanging leaves, finely spun threads which had collected specks of dust and pollen between their weaves. He saw the power behind the roots of enormous plants and how they had split the ground around him. How wonderful it would be, he thought, to harness that power and make it work for him, or to use the great plants themselves to suck up the water from the ground deep beneath. It was with this thought he became thirsty and tested the wind for the smell of water. The breeze gave him a faint clue, all that was needed to send him off again, fearlessly into the unknown.

The scent of water became stronger but there were other messages too. He could smell living things and the first shadow of caution crept into his heart. But the scents were confused: one was very strong and utterly unknown to him, the other was very faint and reminiscent of something. Then, a terrible scream ripped through the air. Rummage moved slowly forward, his sharp spines raised in their deadliest position, until he reached the edge of the cover, and there, a confusion of sights and sounds met him all at once.

There was a clearing in the forest out of which a small hill arose. The hill itself was made of so many pieces, most of which were beyond Rummage's understanding that it made the Jog's head spin to look at it. But that was by no means all, for also on the hill were two creatures; one was trapped in a cave of some kind and the other, which was much the larger of the two, crouched menacingly at the entrance where it spat and hissed.

Rummage made a move towards the side to enable him to get a better view. The crouching beast heard him. He cocked his pointed ears and drew a little way back from the cave looking about him, almost in fear. At that moment the whole heavens seemed suddenly to grow much brighter and a golden round disc appeared over the edge of one of the dark horizons. Rummage knew it was the Moon of the new world; the moment he saw it he felt a great deal happier. Though it was smaller than the Moon he had left behind it was much the prettier. He gave it a name straight away—High Moon—by which he referred to it for ever more.

The High Moonlight showed more clearly the beast upon the hill, whose attention he had momentarily distracted. It had a fearful, squashed face, like a monster from a tale of old, eyes which shone like the Moon and long, sharp teeth. Behind the beast twitched a long furry tail. Rummage was not afraid of the animal. He named it Screamer (after the noise it was making) even as it stared him in the face without actually seeing him. The creature in the cave now took its chance to attempt an escape. As it moved out into the High Moonlight, Rummage saw the most incredible sight he had ever seen. For the creature trembling in fear at the mouth of the cave resembled the Jog exactly, except that it was smaller and of a much darker hue. Rummage's heart raced with expectation. He did not quite know what to make of it all. He wanted to call out to the fellow creature, but then Screamer would have known exactly where he was. So he thought of a much better plan of how both to rescue and make contact with his strange fellow-creature.

Screamer suddenly lashed out with a long, hooked arm which sent the Jogling rushing back into hiding. Rummage wasted no more time. He moved around to the edge of the hill which was bathed in shadow and then climbed the slope until he reached its very pinnacle. Underneath the ledge on which he crouched was the entrance of the cave in front of which Screamer still spat and hissed. For good luck, Rummage tugged one of his spines and then jumped for all he was worth, yelling a cry of battle as he did. The unfortunate Screamer chose to look up just as Rummage came tumbling down and received a faceful of Jog weaponry. Screamer let out a most diabolical noise and somersaulted backwards in agony. Rummage got unsteadily to his feet then rushed at the beast again, tumbling down the slope, but Screamer had had enough and dashed off into the forest howling.

Rummage himself was not without injury. Although the beast's face had broken his fall, the Jog had ultimately landed on his left leg. However, now he limped back to the cave just in time to see the Jogling and three little ones disappear into the forest of plants. Rummage tried to run after them but he was quite exhausted. Slowly, he climbed back to the cave where he lay down in the entrance. Two beady eyes stared out at him from the cover of the forest.

'Hey! Hey, you there!' Rummage called out. 'Don't be afraid ... Can't you see I am a Jog just like you?'

The eyes stared at him for a while longer, but not one word was uttered in response. Then the black, shiny eyes, quivering in the light of the High Moon, suddenly disappeared and Rummage knew that the Jogling had left him alone to his fate.

The injuries were not severe. He could easily have moved on after a while, but the hill had already proved to be such an interesting place that Rummage felt that it was fitting that he should set up upon this spot his first camp in Starland. The cave could be used as a temporary shelter in which he could rest and study some of the objects found right under his feet, and there was always the chance that the shy Jogling might return to make contact. For Rummage, that would be the most exciting thrill of all.

II

Rummage soon settled into his camp on the hill. After very little time had passed at all, he noticed some things which at first disturbed him and later fascinated him completely. It all started when he went to get a drink of water from a pool not far down the slope. It was this pool which had first attracted him to the hill and the water was trapped in a large vessel which was half-buried into the hillside. To drink from this pool he was required to bend his head right over it before he could get a decent mouthful. He had taken his first dip into the water and, without having moved his position was going down again for his second, when something caught his eye. It was the reflection of the High Moon, the edge of which had just made contact with the edge of the pool. That alone was not too strange, even though on the first drink there had been no reflection at all. But when Rummage lowered his head to take another mouthful after thinking about this, although he had still not moved so much as a whisker from his spot, the full reflection of the High Moon could now be seen in the pool.

He was left to draw one conclusion, but even that he did with the greatest difficulty. For it seemed the ground on which he was sitting was in some way passing beneath the High Moon. To test whether or not this was in fact the case, Rummage placed two sticks in the ground which he aligned with some distant point on the horizon. From time to time he sighted along these sticks while noting the apparent position of the Moon's reflection in the pool of water. In the end, he found that although the reflection had moved completely across the surface of the pool, the sticks were still in alignment with the distant point on the horizon. His findings were too much for his weary head to cope with, so he abandoned questioning the matter until some later time. After all, he argued to himself, there were plenty of other, simpler and more immediate mysteries to be solved on that very same hill.

He came across a great many new shapes made out of materials which were unknown to him. These he found either buried, or simply lying around on the hillside. His findings added a great deal of evidence to substantiate the belief that the world he had left behind him was in some way connected with this new world. It was around this time of discovering the new Shapes that he realized that he must take the evidence back to the Lands of the Rats and the Jogs. Though, before he could do that, there was still much to be explored.

Delving among the half-buried objects in the hill brought Rummage greater fatigue. He then realized that the last time he had slept properly was in the Marble Halls of Meltamor, after Geovard had been killed. He could hardly believe how it was possible for him to have gone on for so long. Thinking this, his attention was drawn once again to the High Moon. He then received his biggest shock of all, for while he had been busy with other things, the whole ground had somehow slipped beneath the silvery shine. Now the High Moon was on the far horizon and falling out of sight.

Rummage panicked. Forgetting everything else, he rushed after the High Moon, dashing down the hill and away into the forest. On the opposite side a new and blinding light was already coming, as powerful as the light he had met on the top of Understar when they thought they had found Paradise. Rummage staggered on and on. Exhausted, he crashed first into one thing and then another in a desperate effort to catch up with the High Moonlight. Then he came to a sudden halt. Right in front of him and stretching into the far distance either side was the highest and steepest cliff he had ever seen. He then heard a stealthy noise behind him. The Jog swung around and there he saw Screamer.

The hissing beast crouched a short distance away, just as it had done before the cave on the hill and then, with great agility, moved slightly to the side. Screamer peered at the Jog through eyes which shone like candle flames; it opened a thin slit of a mouth and showed him its rows of sharp fangs. Rummage could see the bloodstains on the beast's squashed face from their first encounter. It was obvious that he would have to fight again. Rummage was not afraid, but his energy had almost vanished from his body. His head was heavy with sleep and his limbs would barely keep him upright—so what chance would he have against this vengeful creature? He had been taught by Geovard that the best kind of defence in a situation like this was to attack. He moved away from the cliff towards Screamer who sprang towards him at the same time and almost bowled him over. Many of Rummage's spines, however, were successful in finding a soft target in the beast's paws and Screamer withdrew, spitting, to reconsider the situation.

Rummage would give him no such chance. He rushed towards Screamer again with the last of his energy. Screamer cried out in fresh pain long before Rummage ever had a chance to reach him then, to the Jog's delight and astonishment, he saw why. For all at once Screamer seemed to be surrounded by a sea of dark and needle-sharp spines. Joglings closed in on all sides although they paid Rummage no attention at all.

Screamer was trapped. He tried to attack the new force but each and every time, the Jogling concerned rolled tightly into a ball and presented his armoury in the most effective way. Screamer soon realized that he was hopelessly surrounded and defeated. Uttering a final scream of anger, he gathered himself up on his haunches and sprang over the heads of the Joglings to escape once again through the vegetation.

The blaze on the opposite horizon, which Rummage called the New Light, was coming very quickly. Already the heavens in that quarter were changing colour from dark into a dazzling blue and it was having a bad effect on Rummage's sight. For the moment, he could not move. The Joglings had surrounded him and stared at him, expressionlessly.

'Thank you for saving me. I'm very grateful to you all.'

The Joglings just continued to stare.

'My name is Rummage. I belong to the nation of Jogs.' They did not seem to understand him. Rummage noted that they were all extremely dirty—some even had running snouts. A few

approached and sniffed him, cautiously. 'It's all right. You have
nothing to fear from me. I come in the name of peace, from the
world beneath the Great Star. You seem to be the same as myself,
only smaller and darker. What are you called? Have you a leader
you could take me to?' Still he drew no response from the crowd,
except their expressionless stares. Rummage began to grow
anxious. His sight was beginning to dim because of the New
Light.

Suddenly, one of the Joglings turned and started to move off.
The rest soon followed and Rummage found himself being jostled
along with them. The journey was very short and ended when
they came to a very large flap under which was a narrow space.
One by one the Joglings squeezed themselves underneath this
covering, carrying Rummage with them. How he did not die
from suffocation, Rummage never knew. After they had ensured
that he was well and truly housed, the majority left and Rummage found himself in the company of four adult Joglings and five
of their young. In the short time before Rummage fell into a
deep sleep through his exhaustion he was able to observe some
of the habits of his curious fellow-creatures.

He had called them Joglings from the start only because they
were smaller in stature than the average Jog. He discovered, in
fact, that there was only the barest superficial resemblance between these people and his own. They could not communicate
with each other above a sniff or a grunt, they did not seem to
wash, they were infested with fleas, they knew nothing of fire
and ate everything raw—in fact, Rummage was left to conclude
that the Joglings were little more than animals. These findings
left him with a very sad and heavy feeling in his heart and he
was fortunate that sleep overtook him before depression got the
better of him.

III

When Rummage awoke, he found that he was alone and shivering with cold. He was still beneath the flap, but outside, the New
Light had gone and the High Moonlight pervaded the cool
breezes. Peace and tranquillity were around him once again and
he began to wonder whether he had dreamt his domicility with the

Jogling family until he discovered, to his horror, that he was infested with their fleas. He itched from head to foot and felt most miserable about it. He also reeked of the odour of the Jogling den.

Rummage pushed himself out into the open air. A deliciously fragrant aroma met him almost immediately and restored his sense of values. He searched the heavens above for the High Moon and was naturally delighted to find that the ground was moving back underneath it again. All the same, he shivered visibly, half through feeling chilled, and half through thinking about the phenomenon of the two lights. The fleas began to bother him again and this, more than anything else, decided what he should do next. First, he would try to find the hill with the water and having found it, take a good bath. After that, he would see what he could find to eat for breakfast.

Finding the hill again was not easy. He could not smell the slightest scent of water—the breeze was in the wrong direction—so he was left to retrace his step. Eventually he found his way back to the cliff where he had met with Screamer. From there, he picked up his own scent from the many paths running into the forest and retraced his steps to the hill. Rummage was fortunate to find the water vessel half-full, so after he had taken a long drink, he climbed right into the pool for a good soak. Although he had no idea why it should, the water made him feel quite warm again and refreshed him in body and spirit. It also seemed to do the trick as far as the fleas were concerned. He must have drowned every last one because the itching ceased to bother him, shortly afterwards.

After the dip, Rummage gathered a few young and tender shoots which he had to eat raw, having brought no fire with him and having discovered none since he had first entered Starland. While he ate the short meal, he thought more and more about returning to his own world. It was becoming obvious to him there were many things he would need, not necessarily for survival, but for comfort here—things which the natives did not seem to know about, let alone possess. He also realized that in time he might need the companionship of someone who could understand him, who could share the triumphs and failures with him in this strange and beautiful land. To go on, utterly alone, would destroy him in the same way it had destroyed Meltamor. So Rummage decided, after he had gathered together a few specimens, that he would return through the Great Star to the lands beneath the Moon where he would try to convince them about the beauty of Starland.

He collected together a few Shapes, brightly-coloured insects and various samples of vegetation, then gradually made his way back through the forest to the flat, soil plain which spread before the Great Star. Almost as soon as he reached the spot where the cover gave out to the soil, he knew instinctively that something was wrong. The ground itself carried the same message. All around the earth had been torn up in a terrible fashion and over on the far side of the clearing, a channel had been flattened through the forest. Rummage dropped his specimens. Something had happened to the Great Star; he rushed over the plain to see what it was. When he arrived, he just could not believe his eyes —for there was no longer a Great Star there at all. He frantically searched and re-searched the whole area but the more he surveyed, the more it became obvious that the door by which he had passed from one world into the next had now been closed. Huge blocks of stone had been used to shut out the Light of the Great Star and prevent him from ever returning to the Lands of the Rats and the Jogs.

He called out the names of those whom he had been separated from, until his voice ran dry, but even as he wept and beat his fists against the solid rock, the barrier kept the real truth from him. He, Jog Rummage, was the lucky one. He knew nothing of the terrors of the four-legged howling monsters, or of the poison which had been put down which tasted like the best food, or of having the Moonlight snuffed out as if it were a candle, so those remaining were left to perish in total darkness. Neither did he know just how alone he had really become.

IV

After a great deal of time had passed, Rummage became almost a native of Starland and the detail of his former existence often faded from his mind. Now and again, when he was out grubbing in the forest for food with the Joglings whose way of life he had eventually adopted, he came across the flat, soil plain and the memories would come flooding back. He had ceased to feel bitter about being shut out and always imagined the nations of the Rats and the Jogs were far better off without him. But he was ever a wise and sensitive Jog, so when the heart-ache became too strong he would wander into the middle of the plain, smile wistfully at the High Moon moving slowly overhead, circle three times beneath it and set off for the nearest green horizon. He had learned from the natives that this was undoubtedly the best cure for feeling lost.

About the Author

GRAHAME WRIGHT was born in 1947 in Leicester, England. He started working in a garage at the age of fifteen, and then became an apprentice as a precision engineer and scientific instrument-maker. Besides attending college, Mr. Wright has worked at a number of jobs in London, including a department-store porter, an insurance clerk, a music shop assistant, an assistant stage manager, and an editor of a laboratory trade newspaper. He is married now and lives in Surrey, where he is at work on another novel.